Zac Hammett

INTERNATIONAL RELATIONS

International Relations is Zac Hammett's second novel. His previous novel, *See You At The Finish Line*, is currently being adapted for television. Zac has had an eclectic writing career which includes co-writing the Gold-Certified Clean Bandit single 'Baby', participating in the writers room for the Disney Plus series *Rivals*, and writing the acclaimed memoir *A Class of Their Own: Adventures in Tutoring the Super-Rich*. He grew up on the south coast of England, the second of four children to two teachers, and now lives in London with his partner and their dog Snufkin.

Also by Zac Hammett

See You at the Finish Line

Zac Hammett

INTERNATIONAL RELATIONS

ZAFFRE

First published in the UK in 2026 by
ZAFFRE
An imprint of Bonnier Books UK
5th Floor, HYLO, 105 Bunhill Row,
London, EC1Y 8LZ

A CIP catalogue record for this book is available from the British Library.

Paperback ISBN: 978-1-80418-995-5

Also available as an ebook and an audiobook

1 3 5 7 9 10 8 6 4 2

Design and Typeset by IDSUK (Data Connection) Ltd
Printed and bound in Great Britain by CPI (UK) Ltd, Croydon CR0 4YY

The authorised representative in the EEA is
Bonnier Books UK (Ireland) Limited.
Registered office address:
Block B, The Crescent Building
Northwood, Santry
Dublin 9, D09 C6X8
Ireland
compliance@bonnierbooks.ie
www.bonnierbooks.co.uk

*For anyone who has ever listened to, learned from
or loved someone different from themselves – and
discovered something beautiful in the process.*

My darling Max,

I hope you never have to read this letter. But your dad gets so worried every time I go abroad that I promised to leave you a note in the event that I don't return.

So, if you're reading this, sorry for dying. I definitely didn't plan on doing that, at least not yet, but as I've come to learn in my line of work, sometimes these things can't be avoided.

Promise me you'll look after your dad. I imagine he'll only worry about you more now that I'm not around, but don't forget that he needs looking after too. Listen to his advice, but ignore him if he tells you not to eat deep-fried doughnuts. That is never a mistake.

The only other thing I ask is that you enjoy your life. Don't let living on an island blind you to the fact that there's a whole world out there full of people, every one of them with hopes and dreams and a story to tell. Other people are the only thing that can bring you true happiness. Never forget that.

Apart from that, there's nothing I can tell you. None of your problems are that serious, trust me.

You've got this.

I love you,

Mum

1

Max

It was very nice of my mum to write me a letter from beyond the grave. Can't say it makes up for the whole dying part, but I've tried to take her advice to heart. It really does help to remind myself that none of my problems are that serious. Not even the one I'm facing right now. I'm standing at the gates of Buckingham Palace, dressed in black tie, and wondering what to do about the fact that my date hasn't shown.

'Would you like me to eliminate him?' asks the woman on the door.

'Sorry, what?'

'It's a security issue. If he's not coming, we'll need to eliminate him from the system.'

Eliminate. That's a strong word. Maybe my date has a perfectly good excuse. I start to suggest some – he's been mugged; he's stuck in a tunnel; he's got the wrong address.

'This is Buckingham Palace,' says the woman. 'Hard to miss.'

When you put it like that.

The woman gives me a pitying look. 'I think you've been ghosted, love.'

My stomach drops and my cheeks flush red. Is there anything more humiliating than being ghosted? The last time it happened to me, I sent about forty-three follow-up messages of increasing desperation before finally accepting that the guy wasn't going to reply. I mustn't do that again. It's really not that serious.

'Go ahead,' I say. 'Eliminate him.'

She presses a button on her iPad. 'There you go. His loss.'

I don't think it is, but I appreciate the support. The woman looks like she wants me to either burst into tears or commission a contract killing, but neither option feels very me. After all, it's my fault. We'd only been on three dates when I asked him if he wanted to attend a work thing with me. He said sure, as long as it wasn't too fancy. I promised it wasn't, because I was worried he'd say no if he knew where it was. He stopped replying to my texts after I sent him the address. Like I said, totally my fault.

'Am I good to go?' I ask.

'Absolutely,' she says. 'Just head over to my colleague. He'll check you're not carrying any explosives.'

For one deranged second, blowing up Buckingham Palace sounds cathartic. But no. Mustn't dwell. Time to straighten my bow tie, walk in with dignity, and appreciate how far I've come.

Look, Mum! I'm in Buckingham Palace.

I grip the signet ring that my mum gave me for my eighteenth birthday. She would have loved that I'm here tonight, even if she wasn't really a fan of the royals apart from Diana. It's a shame she only got to witness the start of my career as a diplomat, when things were never this glamorous. In the early days, my tasks included drafting an apology when a British politician described his Australian counterpart as 'a dingo in a wig' and trying to clarify what the Latvian Ambassador meant when he listed his dietary requirements as 'only meat'. Since then, I've been promoted several times, and I'm now no stranger to high-level meetings and swanky invitations. But tonight beats them all.

A footman in a bright red waistcoat offers me a glass of champagne, then shows me along a corridor into a ballroom. The sheer scale of it takes my breath away. It must be forty feet high, the walls lined with enormous gilt-framed portraits of past monarchs, from sturdy old Henry VIII to an impressionist painting of the late Queen Elizabeth II that makes her look like she has chickenpox. Half the guests tonight are the kind of crusty old toffs who make a career out of snagging invites to the palace. But it's the other half, who are mostly dark haired and olive skinned, who are the real guests of honour.

It's been more than fifty years since Greece was invited for a state visit, Britain's highest diplomatic honour, but our two countries recently struck a trade deal to boost Britain's standing in international shipping. To mark the culmination of more than a year of negotiations, Britain is rolling out the red carpet, which is one of the few things we still do well. I can see the King and Queen standing in the middle of the room, swarmed by excited guests. I'm not talking about the actual king and queen. Who's excited to meet them? I'm talking about David and Victoria Beckham. Presumably David's here to show off his knighthood, or maybe I'm being mean, and he's always had a passion for bilateral trade deals.

I stand taking in the scene with satisfaction. The fact that two countries have been able to come together for mutual benefit despite all the conflict in the world is precisely why I got into this line of work. Tonight's agreement allows for the creation of hundreds of jobs – including one I've got my eye on. They're looking to hire a trade deal ambassador at the British Embassy in Athens, or to give it its technical term, *in the field*. What I'm doing at the moment is called *desk*. And yes, desk might have its glamorous moments, and field work can involve sitting at a desk, but we're talking about Athens, the birthplace of democracy. Across the room, I spot the British ambassador to Greece, who would be my boss if I got the Athens position. Tonight is the perfect opportunity to put myself on his radar. I finish my champagne and head towards him.

'Where is he?' says a familiar voice.

I turn to see my colleague Quentin accompanied by his girlfriend Flora. As usual, they are both looking immaculate, Quentin in a tuxedo that Flora no doubt picked out for him, she in a striking but understated blue dress. Flora is a hotshot lawyer who was once described as 'the brilliant Flora Forbes' by one of her clients in a *BBC News* article. It's a phrase that so perfectly captures her formidable head girl energy that I now think of it as her full name.

The brilliant Flora Forbes works very long hours, yet is somehow always available to accompany Quentin to events like this. She handles conversations on his behalf, organises his diary, and presumably wipes his bottom for him.

'Who?' I say to Quentin, even though I know exactly who he's talking about.

'Edwin. The orthodontist.'

I made the mistake of telling a few of my colleagues I was bringing a date. Trust Quentin to remember the details.

'He couldn't make it,' I say regretfully.

Quentin and Flora share a look. I can't have them thinking I've been ghosted.

'Yeah,' I say. 'He got stuck in surgery. Broken jaw.'

Quentin frowns. 'Orthodontists don't perform surgery.'

Shit. I didn't actually know that.

'He's the patient,' I say hurriedly.

'Gosh,' says Flora. 'He broke his jaw?'

I nod sadly.

'How ironic,' says Quentin.

'These things happen,' says Flora, ever the diplomat.

'It's fine,' I say. 'I think I'll enjoy myself more without him.'

I'm not sure how much I believe that, but I hate the idea of Quentin and Flora pitying me. Quentin and I both joined the civil service straight out of uni, which means I've known him and Flora for years. Throughout that time, they've been solid as a rock, while I've never found a guy who wants to stick around.

'Can you believe we've made it to tonight?' I say. 'I never thought we'd get this deal over the line.'

'Yes,' says Flora. 'Much to celebrate.'

Quentin eyes me coolly. Since he and I took the lead on the team that implemented this deal, we're the two front runners for this job in Athens.

'Have you seen the seating plan?' asks Quentin.

'No,' I say. 'Why?'

Before Quentin can answer, a man with a neat side parting and an iPad comes hurrying up to us. This is either Henry Herbert or Herbert Henry – I can never remember which way round it is. Henry or Herbert works in the Cabinet Office, who are in charge of logistics for this evening.

'Sorry to interrupt,' he says. 'Are you Max?'

'I am.'

Henry or Herbert glances at his iPad. 'There's an issue with your guest. He's been eliminated.'

'Yes, I know. What's the issue?'

'Broken jaw,' says Quentin.

'Much worse,' says Henry or Herbert. 'He's created a gap in the seating plan.'

We all share an ominous look. It might not sound like much, but seating plans at diplomatic functions are incredibly delicate. I still remember the dignitary who refused to sit where we'd put him because he claimed it would look like he was taking sides over the Battle of Trafalgar. Yes, the one that took place in 1805.

'We can't have no one opposite the Greek Finance Minister,' says Henry or Herbert. 'He'll interpret it as a snub.'

'Can we move up someone from a lower table?' I ask.

'No,' scoffs Henry or Herbert. 'It's not that simple. The whole plan was devised based on who was bringing guests. You were asked to confirm several times.'

That's true. I didn't check with Edwin the orthodontist because I didn't want to give him a chance to say no.

'We don't mind swapping with Max,' says Quentin quickly.

'Really?' asks Henry or Herbert.

'Not at all,' says Quentin. 'Happy to help.'

'Super,' says Henry or Herbert.

'Wait,' I say, 'that doesn't solve anything. Who's going to take Flora's place?'

Henry or Herbert is swishing around on his iPad like he's David Hockney.

'Don't worry,' he says. 'I'll bump up a couple from a lower table.'

'But who will take *their* place?'

'No one. But we can live with a gap on an outer table.'

'Great,' says Quentin. 'Problem solved.'

This is what I love about diplomacy – the way that potential disasters can be avoided when everyone shows up with the right attitude. Henry or Herbert scuttles off towards the official seating chart to rearrange the names.

A short while later, a man blows a bugle and everyone starts making their way towards their places for dinner. I cross over to the seating chart to see where I've been repositioned. Henry or Herbert wasn't joking when he said I was on an outer table. It's right at the back of the hall.

I glance over at Quentin, who catches my eye with a look of smug satisfaction. I check the seating chart to see where Quentin's name is – the seat that should have been mine. He's on the top table, right next to the ambassador; the man who could be our future boss.

And that's when I realise that I've been played.

2

Max

'You'll get a chance to meet him at some point,' says Mariam.

'I know,' I say. 'I'm not worried.'

I shovel down a prawn. We're seated for dinner, and I've ended up next to Mariam, our department director. Mariam doesn't do glamour, dressed in the same brown pantsuit she wore to our Christmas party at a bowling alley. She probably chose to be at this table so she could sit here and check her emails in peace. Joining us are a retired civil servant, a minor baroness, the British Eurovision contestant from the time it was hosted in Greece, and a man who introduces himself to everyone as *the* Giles Wibberley, as if the name speaks for itself, which it absolutely doesn't.

'It's not a big deal,' I say to Mariam. 'I just . . .'

I pause. It's not very professional of me to criticise a colleague, but I want her to know what Quentin did, plus I'm on my second glass of champagne.

'Quentin took my place so he could sit next to the ambassador.'

Mariam is well aware that Quentin and I have both applied for this promotion and there's a good chance she will lose one of her top team. But she simply shrugs.

'Sometimes you have to be ruthless in this job.'

I feel a rush of indignation that she's defending him. 'Are you saying I'm not?'

Mariam chooses her words carefully. 'You have a lot of skills that Quentin doesn't.'

She looks over at him. 'The problem is . . . Quentin has Flora. She balances him out.'

I look at Quentin and see precisely what Mariam is saying. Even from here, you can see the brilliant Flora Forbes at work, carefully monitoring Quentin as he talks, in case she needs to leap in to clarify his point or smooth over his edges.

'Has it never occurred to you that you're at a disadvantage?' asks Mariam.

I frown at her. 'What do you mean?'

'Max, you're applying to work for an embassy. It's not like other jobs. It involves a lot of hosting. When Quentin has someone as charming and accomplished as Flora to accompany him to functions, that's a huge advantage. Haven't you heard how Nancy Reagan prevented nuclear war in the ladies' bathroom at the Geneva Summit?'

I stare at Mariam. 'That is so . . . old-fashioned!'

'This is the world that we're part of,' says Mariam nonchalantly. 'How many heads of state can you name who are single?'

I pause to think. 'The Pope?'

Mariam opens her hands as if I've just proven her point. Watching Flora and Quentin, I can't believe I didn't see it sooner. They fit the traditional mould that

Mariam is talking about. It's so easy to imagine them installed in some far-flung outpost serving cucumber sandwiches and working the room together.

'So if you're a single gay man, you might as well not bother?'

'I wouldn't say that. They would never openly discriminate, but that doesn't mean these factors are irrelevant. Why do you think I always stuck to desk jobs?'

Though it always surprises me to recall it, Mariam is married to a member of the briefly famous anarchist rock band Chumbawamba. By all accounts, her partner is the last person who would want to accompany her to a function like this, but it never occurred to me that Mariam has actively avoided a career as an ambassador.

'What about this Edwin chap?' Mariam asks. 'Is there any future there?'

I glance down at my phone. Still no reply.

'Orthodontics is very time-consuming,' I say forlornly.

Mariam's eyes soften. 'I just don't want you to be disappointed.'

Just then, peals of laughter ripple across the room. I look up to see Quentin, Flora, the ambassador and his wife chuckling at something that is no doubt extremely unfunny. It fills me with resolve. This isn't fair. And just because Mariam opted out of a career as an ambassador doesn't mean I have to. I turn to her decisively.

'I appreciate the advice, but I don't need a partner to help me do my job. Watch me.'

The second that dinner is over, I get up from the table. There's still plenty of time left. I can talk to the ambassador about the crucial role I played in the trade deal.

Surely that matters more than whether or not I have a boyfriend. As everyone moves towards the ballroom for drinks, I seize my moment and race up to him.

'Ambassador Gibbons,' I say, out of breath. 'I'm Max. From the Foreign Office.'

'Nice to meet you,' says the ambassador, clearly having no clue who I am. 'Please, call me Wrettham.'

Yes, the British ambassador to Greece is called Wrettham. Wrettham Gibbons, to give him his full name. The *w* and the *h* are silent, and it's a shame the other letters aren't. Britain's reduced influence on the world stage is hardly a surprise when our institutions are still being led by men with names like Wrettham Gibbons. He's an exceptionally sturdy man who looks more suited to playing full-back in an amateur rugby league than leading a foreign embassy. Wrettham's wife is just as sturdy as him and perhaps stars in a rugby team of her own. She seems like she can be relied upon to be called something sensible like Susan.

'This is my wife Jane,' says Wrettham.

Jane smiles at me. 'But everyone calls me—'

'Topsy!' shouts Quentin.

Of course they do, Topsy, of course they do. I'm not sure why I thought the wife of a man called Wrettham would be called anything other than Topsy. I certainly don't know why I thought Quentin would leave me alone with them for more than two seconds.

'Ah,' I say, gritting my teeth. 'You've met my colleague Quentin.'

'Met?' says Quentin. 'We're best friends.'

'*Kalyteroi filoi gia panta*,' says the brilliant Flora Forbes, sliding in beside us.

I frown at her in confusion.

'Flora speaks Greek,' says Topsy.

'I did Classics at Oxford,' says Flora. 'Bit rusty.'

'Nonsense,' says Wrettham. 'Over dinner, Flora was able to reassure one of the shipping magnates in fluent Greek over some of his concerns about the port regulations.'

Oh for god's sake. Everything Mariam said was right. No matter how good I am at my job, how can my non-existent plus one compete with what Flora brings to the table?

'Thank you for taking the hit tonight, Max,' says Wrettham. 'Quentin let us know about your no-show. Very noble of you.'

I force a smile. Thanks for that, Quentin.

'Max doesn't have the best luck with men,' says Quentin.

'Yes I do,' I say impulsively. 'He just couldn't make it.'

'Broke his jaw,' says Flora. 'He's an orthodontist.'

'Gosh,' says Wrettham. 'How ironic.'

'Do you want the number of my friend's surgeon?' asks Topsy with concern. 'She had to have her jaw rebuilt after she was attacked by a baboon. They did a fantastic job. She was featured on *The Jeremy Kyle Show*.'

'I think he's already sorted,' I say politely.

'Yes, no, he would be,' says Topsy. 'Well, do send our best. It would have been lovely to meet him.'

'You will.'

Quentin raises an eyebrow. 'We will?'

It's one thing to lie to yourself when reality is against you. But sometimes, when the situation is really drastic, you have to lie to a few more people.

'Yes,' I say. 'At tomorrow's event. I can't wait for you all to meet him.'

3

Hunter

This is why I don't date British men. I'm sitting opposite a middle-aged guy on the tube who is dressed in a suit, sweating profusely, and eating a Scotch egg out of a grocery bag. I have several issues with that. First, the concept of a Scotch egg. You're going to wrap a boiled egg in sausage meat, then dip it in breadcrumbs? No. Just no. Second, when are you supposed to eat those things? They're not substantial enough for a meal, but they're too much for a snack. I'm pretty sure the correct time to eat them is not 8 a.m. on a packed London Underground train. As he stands up to get off, he sprays crumbs all over the floor. A woman getting off at the same stop looks up at him.

'Morning, Bernard,' she says. 'Congratulations on your engagement.'

Maybe I should be more open-minded. All my current problems would be solved if it was me who was getting married to Bernard. My visa runs out in exactly two weeks. And no, I'm not being serious, but there are times when I've thought that finding a husband would be easier than my current plan of trying to land a job in my chosen discipline. I'm an actor – that famously over-subscribed, under-paid profession. I'm not sure why I thought I could just arrive in a foreign city and launch a career here. I'm not even supposed to be auditioning. Technically, my visa doesn't permit it, but I figured I'd move here and try anyway. I've been auditioning for five and a half months, and I haven't had any luck.

But maybe that's about to change.

As I arrive at my tube stop, I try to manifest a successful audition. Positive thinking, right? Not my forte, but I've prepared for this audition meticulously. I've thought about the character from every angle, left no stone unturned. By all logic, I should be walking in with the quiet confidence of a man who knows what he's doing.

But then my brain starts offering counterpoints. What if the director doesn't like my face? What if the producer once got dumped by someone who wears the same after-shave as me? What if the casting director decides that my posture is too stiff, too jaunty, too proud? Unfortunately for the optimists, casting directors are always looking for a reason to say no.

Walking through the doors of the casting rooms in Soho, I feel sick to my stomach. Every actor I know has had some sort of traumatic experience on these premises. Auditions are typically preceded in the worst way possible: you sit in a corridor with a load of other actors who look almost exactly like you only slightly more handsome. The role I'm going for today is gender-blind, which means I will avoid my usual doppelgäng-ers, but also means that anyone with a pulse might be my competition.

After I've been sitting for a few minutes, an assistant calls my name and shows me through to the audition room. The casting director is a woman in her fifties with a pair of sunglasses on her head even though it's been raining solidly for the past two days. She doesn't look up as I enter, just systematically swipes on her phone. I frown – is she on a dating app? Then I hear the familiar swishing sounds and realise she's deleting emails.

Her assistant coughs to get her attention. The casting director looks up and takes me in from head to toe. She doesn't seem very impressed.

'Shall I do it from the top?' I ask.

'Do what?'

'The scene.'

'What scene?'

'I've prepared all my scenes.'

The woman frowns. 'Prepared what? You don't have any lines.'

Fair point. I'm auditioning to play the cow in *Into the Woods* – a part so minor that it's sometimes played by a puppet. Not quite my dream job, but beggars can't be choosers.

'I've prepared my reactions,' I say defiantly.

'Right, well that's not much good, because I don't have a script.'

'What? Why did you call me in?'

She shrugs. 'To get you in the room and see if you have a sort of bovine quality.'

I can't believe what I'm hearing. My shoulders tense. 'And?'

The woman peers at me. 'Not really, no.'

I feel heat crawling up my neck. 'Could you not tell that from my photo?'

'No actually. You'd be surprised.'

An email pings into her inbox. She looks down and swipes immediately. This is humiliating. I prepared for this audition using the Stanislavski technique, and the casting director is more concerned with deleting spam emails.

'I'd like to run the scene I prepared, if that's OK,' I say, my voice cracking.

The woman rolls her eyes but waves for me to proceed. It's pretty hard to continue in these circumstances, but I've done the work. I close my eyes, take a deep breath, then go somewhere else in my mind. I tap into the emotional devastation of being sold by my owner for a handful of beans, my silent knowledge of Jack's folly. I communicate all this with the most subtle of facial expressions. Once I've finished, I glance up hopefully.

The woman is looking at her phone. Her assistant nudges her.

'Can you moo?' the casting director asks.

'What?'

'Moo.'

She moos to demonstrate, as if I wasn't aware of the concept.

'The cow is silent!' I protest. 'It's a famously silent role. That's the beauty of Sondheim's creation.'

'Yeah, well our director wants the cow to moo.'

If I'd known, I would have spent days perfecting my moo. But I can hardly refuse. After a few false starts, I offer a plaintive moo that I feel speaks to the cow's state of mind. They don't look convinced. The assistant shields her mouth with her hand.

'What about the back end?' I hear her mutter to the casting director.

'I'm not sure he has the gravitas,' the casting director whispers back.

Great. Now I don't have the gravitas to play the back end of a cow.

'Thanks,' says the casting director. 'We'll be in touch.'

I step toward the door, my hand on the door knob, ready to slam it behind me and never look back. Rationally, I know I should walk away. Save myself the humiliation.

But my mouth has a mind of its own.

'No you won't,' I snap, spinning on my heel so my glare meets hers.

She gives me an astonished look. I could still walk away. I don't have to do this.

'You never are,' I continue. 'I obviously haven't got the role, and when that happens, I don't hear back. It's so disrespectful.'

I'm not sure what I'm doing. I'm burning my bridges, but this was my last shot to stay in the country. Plus, speaking my mind always feels good. The woman is clearly not used to being spoken to like this.

'Talk about disrespectful!' she scoffs. 'Looks like we've dodged a bullet. You'd obviously be a nightmare to work with.'

The words land like a blow to my chest. Her comment cuts to a place I never let anyone see. My lip trembles before I can stop it. I swallow hard, but the sting lingers.

Desperate to escape this feeling, I turn and walk out. As I leave, I hear her swipe.

'Bingo!' she cries. 'Inbox zero.'

Being an actor was never the plan. Growing up in a small town in Rhode Island, I had nothing in common with the theater kids, who in turn had no interest in a black-hearted loner like me. Then one day, my mom took me to see a production of *Into the Woods*, presumably thinking it would be a load of innocent fairy tales. That show was a revelation. I was only eleven, but the way the Baker's Wife stood on stage and bared her soul hit me deep within. I realised that day that theater didn't have to be about escapism. It could be a vehicle to express hard emotional truths.

I became determined to speak those truths myself. It didn't always work. My high-school drama teacher refused to cast me in *Beauty and the Beast* because he said my candlestick was too emotionally devastating. Instead, I started posting my performances on TikTok, where I was in complete control of what roles I played and how I played them. It was more out of a need to express myself than any kind of career strategy, but after years of posting into the void, I had one of those experiences that people dream about. My performance of 'There Are Worse Things I Could Do' from *Grease* went viral. A young director called Rafferty got in touch and said he'd been working on the idea of a gender-flipped production of *Grease*. I found out much later that it was my performance that had given him the idea.

He invited me to audition, but the production was off-Broadway and wouldn't have paid enough for me to live in New York. Rafferty said I could live with him if I got cast. The day I moved into the East Village apartment bought for him by his parents, I felt like Barbra Streisand in *Funny Girl*. I was so young and naive and Rafferty so in command that when he made a move on me less than a week after I moved in, I just sort of went along with it. Before I knew it, we were dating.

Rizzo was the perfect role for me, a character famous for speaking her mind. I was good – too good. Every review said I was the best thing about the production. Rafferty got jealous. He couldn't handle the attention I was getting. He convinced me I was ruining the show. I was young and in love and desperate to please him. So when the show transferred to Broadway, I did the one thing I thought would save the relationship. I turned down the role.

Rafferty wasn't grateful. The Broadway transfer still took over both our lives. I became his personal assistant, with no time to audition for other parts. We started to resent each other. When the transfer finally opened, reviews were scathing. The *New York Times* even said that the new Rizzo was no match for me. Rafferty was furious. He blamed me for everything. That was the night I finally got the courage to leave him.

But the ordeal didn't end there. Rafferty was mad that I would dare to break up with him, and terrified that my career would eclipse his. He was also a nepo baby with a lot of powerful friends. He told the entire Broadway community I was a nightmare to work with. I have no doubt he was spinning the story to make me look like the villain. But ever since then, a small part of me has wondered if he was right.

With my reputation ruined in New York, London became my next best option to launch a theater career, a place where I could be myself without having to negotiate someone else's insecurities – at least, that was the idea. Even though I didn't know anyone here, I figured that since I'd had a hit role in America, it wouldn't be that hard to find an agent.

I was wrong. All the reputable agents lost interest the second they found out I didn't have the right to work here. I ended up signing with one who did things a little more unconventionally. But being with her has its perks. She works from home, and when she found out about my situation, she didn't just agree to take me on as a client, she invited me to live with her. For free.

I get off the tube and walk to the square that I still can't believe I get to call home. There are bicycles with wicker baskets leaning against iron railings, window boxes spilling with herbs, cherry trees in full blossom, and on one corner, a café with a hand-lettered chalkboard and counters crammed with artichokes and olives.

I let myself in and peek my head into the office. It can't have been properly tidied in years, stacked high with old scripts, Post-It notes, and theatrical props that include, for some reason, a stuffed kestrel. At her desk, talking on the phone, is my agent, dressed in a camel jacket with a silk scarf, her silver hair in a sleek bun. I signal that I'll come back later, but she motions for me to wait.

'It's not my problem,' she says down the phone. 'She started it.'

She pauses and listens in distaste.

'Can't you finish the scene with CGI?' she yells. 'We don't have time for mediation.'

She hangs up and smiles at me.

'Is everything OK?' I ask.

'Not exactly,' she says. 'One of my clients got into a fist fight with Helena Bonham Carter on the set of *The Gummy Bears Movie*.'

This woman isn't real, I swear. Doily – yes, my agent's name is Doily – came into my life like a whirlwind of vintage silk and Chanel No. 5. She's the founder, owner, and sole employee of London's most singular acting agency. She knows seemingly everyone in the business, but has fallen out with all of them, leaving her client list a little more curated. The last five months have been nothing if not entertaining.

'How did the audition go?' Doily asks.

I give her the thumbs down.

'Oh, Hunter. I'm sorry.'

As I see her expression, I'm hit with a fresh wave of sadness about how today turned out. I put everything into that audition. I always do. And Doily has tried her best. The problem is that only the big productions are willing to sponsor visas. If I didn't need a visa, Doily could have got me cast in a regional pantomime without lifting a finger.

'Shall I make you an eggnog?' asks Doily.

'No thanks.'

'How about an episode of *Murder, She Wrote*?'

'I'm OK.'

Doily drums her fingers on her desk. 'Do you want to help me find an entertainment lawyer who is willing to be paid in gummy bears?'

I really don't deserve this woman. She has always gone the extra mile for me, even if her approach is, shall we say, unique. But ever since what happened with Rafferty, when someone shows up for me, my first instinct is to put a wall up. I give Doily a grateful smile.

'Thanks. But I want to be on my own.'

I have no desire to go and sit in my room, so I wander back out into the square. The Victorian terraces curve around a communal garden, a tangled mess of wisteria and banana plants. I've developed a habit of coming out here and sitting on the swing. I sink into it, letting the ropes creak under my weight. I'm aware that I live in a beautiful part of London, but even if I wandered to the parts of the city that I like to moan about – the garish candy stores on Oxford Street, the endless chain supermarkets that pop up like a rash, the lines outside random bubble tea shops that have gone viral – it wouldn't make a difference. This city has a rhythm that fits me, scrappy and loud and often pessimistic, but stubbornly alive. I feel at home here. I don't want to leave.

But I don't have a choice. It's not up to me. My acting career has failed to take flight. What I need now is a miracle.

4

Max

He's out there somewhere. Just because he's ghosted me doesn't mean he's vanished into thin air. He can't have, because I promised the ambassador he would be meeting him tonight. That was a wild one, even by my standards. That's going to take some figuring out. So allow me to do what I tend to do when faced with a problem: pretend it's not an issue for as long as possible. After all, I'm curled up in bed right now with the love of my life. He just so happens to be a five-year-old cavapoo called Mr Peanut.

I've been told by more than one person that you shouldn't let your dog sleep in your bed or they'll become too attached. It's a bit late for that. Faced with the choice between lying here alone or cuddling up with a creature that looks like the offspring of a teddy bear and a luxury bath mat, there was never any question. If it was up to me, I'd stay in bed all morning, but Mr Peanut needs walking.

I get up to open my curtains before remembering that my room doesn't have a window and the curtains were installed as a decorative feature. Amazing how the half-awake mind will play tricks on you, such as convincing you that you're not paying £1,200 a month to live in a prison cell. I push my bedroom door but it stays firmly shut. After some forceful shoving, I make it out onto the landing to find it occupied by a partially reupholstered fainting couch. I live with a pair of polyamorous furniture restorers who are always abandoning their work to embark on their latest tryst. I can hear some light whimpering coming from their bedroom even at this early hour. You have to admire their stamina. It's not the ideal living situation, but on the plus side, polyamorous furniture restorers make really good dog sitters.

There's no better way to lift your spirits than going on an early morning walk with a dog. Unfortunately, to get to the nearest park I have to walk right through the middle of a cheap and cheerful market where the pavement is strewn with rotting fruit and the stalls stacked with suspicious-smelling fish. Mr Peanut has never found a cut-price haddock he won't risk it all to lunge at. To add to the chaos, this is the best time of day to speak to my dad. I call him and he picks up instantly.

'Max, glad you're safe. Did you get that article I sent you?'

'Hi Dad, no, I don't think so. What do you mean, safe?'

I'm barely awake and my dad is already in fifth gear.

'I sent you a news article about the recent Buckingham Palace renovation. Between you and me, I have some concerns about the light fittings.'

Classic Dad. I go to my first event at Buckingham Palace, and he spends the whole evening worrying that a chandelier is going to fall on me.

'Don't worry, I made it out of there alive.'

'This time,' he says, totally serious.

Mr Peanut has pounced on a fallen guava. I should probably stop him, but I don't like to get mad at him, plus he looks so happy.

'Apologies if the sound cuts out, by the way,' says my dad. 'I'm on a live feed with a simulator group.'

'Right. So if the sound cuts out, you're—'

'Averting a major aviation disaster.'

'A simulated disaster.'

'Imagine the lives we could have saved.'

My dad recently retired after thirty years as an air traffic controller. There are certainly worse things he could be doing with his time than simulating major air crashes and figuring out how they could have been averted. Still, I'm not convinced it's the best way for him to spend his retirement.

My dad was always the cautious one in his marriage. My mum was a nurse, a stable enough job, if she hadn't regularly volunteered abroad, sometimes for months at a time. I found it daring and admirable how she flew off to these faraway continents to help people in need, but even as a kid, I was aware how much people judged her for abandoning her child, as they saw it. In fact, she was always careful to avoid going anywhere truly dangerous. Then five years ago, a conflict erupted while she was on the ground, and she got caught in the crossfire.

'Dad, can you log off for a minute?'

'They might need me.'

'How many people are on the feed?'

'Twenty-three.'

'I think they'll be all right.'

My dad asks me about last night, but all he really wants to know is what was on the menu and whether any of those ingredients are known carcinogens. I answer dutifully, but it does get a bit exhausting, especially when I'm the type of person who will put a positive spin on almost anything.

'I'd better go, Dad. I've got a lot on.'

'Oh,' he says. 'All under control?'

I hesitate. It's not that I've never spoken to him about my love life, more that he's so anxious about everything that I don't like to burden him with my worries.

'Yes. It will be.'

'Good. Well, you stay safe. And make sure Mr Peanut doesn't step on any broken glass. That could cost you hundreds of pounds in vet bills.'

I feel a duty to look after my dad, but talking to him always puts me in a weird mood. I've tried to convince him to travel, actually see the world, but he isn't interested. As far as he's concerned, simply leaving the house means exposing yourself to danger, and what happened to my mum closed the argument decisively.

Not for me. My mum taught me that there are people all over the world in need of help, but my dad would never forgive me if I plunged myself right into the heart of the action like she did. Instead, I chose a career in diplomacy, where I could work to prevent those conflicts from even occurring. Becoming an ambassador is the next step on the path to that goal. And I'm so close. At least, I was until last night.

What the hell was I thinking, telling the ambassador he was going to meet my boyfriend? It's not like I can't get out of it. I told everyone he'd broken his jaw. He could easily be out of action for the remainder of the state visit. But where will that leave me? If I don't find a Flora to my Quentin, I'm at a serious disadvantage. It's pretty clear that I'm never going to hear back from Edwin. If not him, who?

I trawl through my recent romantic history, which turns out to be a terrible idea. There's no one in the past few years who it doesn't sting to recall. There was the one-night stand who I made the mistake of telling he was husband material because I thought that might cure his erectile dysfunction. There was the friend with benefits who wouldn't look me in the eye when we had sex, but I kidded myself it was because he was falling in love with me. There was the situationship who literally walked out of the door when I tried to have a chat about our future. I kept seeing him for two more months after that.

Now that I think about it, I have a problem. Why can't I accept the evidence in front of me? That's too big a question for today. For now, all I need is someone who can take the place of Edwin the orthodontist at short notice. But where the hell am I going to find him?

* * *

'Morning, Max,' trills Nessie as I arrive at the office. 'What do you think?'

It's barely 9 a.m., so forgive me while I stop and process this. Nessie was part of the contingent who joined the civil service at the same time as me and Quentin. We've been work buddies for years, although we rarely take it outside the office. Nessie is lovely but kind of strait-laced. She's living with her parents in Hertfordshire so she can save for a deposit on a flat with a maths teacher who she met at church. But right now, she is holding up her phone to show me what appears to be an AI generated image of herself with a perm.

'Wow,' I say. 'What am I looking at?'

Nessie smiles. 'It's the haircut I'm thinking of getting.'

'A perm?'

'A volume boost.'

I stare at the image. She looks like a sheep.

'What made you go with this look specifically?'

'I wanted something bold. Something fun.'

Nessie explains that she recently went on a hen party in Marrakesh. During a game, she got voted 'Most Boring'. The idea of spending hundreds of pounds to fly to Morocco only for a group of your supposed friends to declare you boring by popular consent is already too much for me to get my head round this early in the morning. But Nessie has decided that the way to prove her friends wrong is by getting a perm.

'What do you think, Max? I really like it.'

She looks so excited at the prospect that I can't bring myself to let her down.

'Totally,' I say. 'Go for it.'

As Nessie grins, I feel a tug of guilt. Sometimes I'm a little too good at telling people what they want to hear, but lying is a very useful skill in a job like mine. International governments are always committing the equivalent of getting a perm and needing to be told it's a great decision.

'Thanks, Max,' says Nessie. 'How was last night? Did you have fun with Edwin?'

I'm really starting to regret telling people I was bringing a date. Why couldn't I have left him to be a surprise – or not, as it turned out. As I tell Nessie that Edwin couldn't make it, I'm tempted to reveal the rest of my dilemma. She's not my dad. In fact, I've always thought that Nessie and I have the potential to be real friends. It's not like she had any shame in telling me about her humiliation in Marrakesh. But I can't do it. I come to work to put on my best self, not to display my failings. I offer Nessie a smile.

'The important thing is that the deal got signed.'

'Yeah,' says Nessie. 'I can't believe it. What are we supposed to worry about now?'

Since my department insists on hot desking, you never know when you're going to end up in a random corner of the office, miles from your colleagues. But today, that's exactly what I need. The minute I'm alone at a desk, I approach my problem like I would any other work task. First, let's establish my objective: I need to convince the British Embassy that I have a stable partner in my life, but I don't need to convince anyone to move to Greece with me. All I need is someone for the application process. For a position of this nature, partners are likely to be invited to participate, but only for one or two events at most. They're not the ones who will be signing a contract. The British Embassy might be biased towards hiring someone with a partner, but they can't suddenly fire me because I've had a break-up and Edwin the orthodontist or whoever is pretending to be him will no longer be joining me in Athens.

But where am I going to find this mythical person? Last night was only part one of an exhausting three-day state visit, which continues tonight with another high-profile reception at the British Museum. I need someone who's willing to accompany me.

I start googling escort agencies. There's one called Toy Boy Warehouse, which sounds lots of fun, but perhaps not quite right for this particular engagement. In fact, none of the sites geared towards women are very suitable, while the few that are aimed at gay men are all about sex. Either way, I have doubts about the guys being advertised. Even the ones who claim to offer stimulating conversation look like they are better equipped to stimulate me in other areas. They can hardly compete with the brilliant Flora Forbes.

Then it hits me – I don't need an escort. I need an actor. I can create the perfect boyfriend and hire someone to play him. All he needs to do is look the part and be good at acting. The one snag in this plan is that I only have a few hours to find this elusive man, but every actor I've ever met has been desperate for work. There has to be someone out there.

I find an online directory of acting agencies. As soon I get out of the office for my lunch break, I call them one by one, but the few that answer hang up the moment I explain what I'm looking for. Then one agency catches my eye. It's based in Kennington, unlike all the others which are in Soho. The description lists its founder as a legendary industry maverick. It's worth a shot.

I call the number, but it goes to voicemail. I leave a message, but as I explain that I'm looking to hire a fake boyfriend, I feel stupid. Why would anyone take me seriously? However, as I'm buying myself a meal deal in Tesco, the number calls me back. I pick up frantically.

'Hello,' says the woman. 'This is Doily speaking.'

'Sorry, did you say Doily?'

'Yes. I just had a call from this number.'

'Yes! Did you get my voicemail?'

Doily tuts. 'I don't listen to voicemails. I thought you might be calling about the Gummy Bear situation.'

'What? No, sorry.'

I take a beat, trying not to panic that this woman sounds completely loopy.

'I was hoping you could help me with something else. I'm looking to hire an actor.'

She lets out a sigh of annoyance, which I have to say is not a *great* sign for an acting agent.

'I'm rather busy,' she says. 'Have you filled out our contact form?'

'Er . . . no.'

'Could you do that?'

'I'd rather not.'

'Is there a medical reason?'

'What?'

'A medical reason you can't fill out the contact form.'

I take a deep breath. 'There is, yes.'

'Ooh. What's that then?'

'It's, er, it's . . . private.'

I'm sensing that Doily is disappointed, although even at this early stage of our acquaintance, I've learned not to assume anything.

'Yes,' I say, 'so it would be great if I could just tell you what I'm looking for, and you can tell me if you're able to help.'

'Fire away.'

I hesitate. What I'm about to ask is kind of insane, even for a woman who hardly seems like she does things by the book. Maybe I should keep it ambiguous.

'It's a bit of a weird one, Doily. I suppose you could call it immersive theater.'

'Ooh, I love a bit of that.'

'It's great, isn't it? I need an actor who can operate in a professional setting. And I need them tonight. There might be some foreign travel, but I'd cover expenses.'

'Expenses? Is there a fee?'

Damn. I hadn't thought that far. 'I can pay, obviously. But I'm not loaded.'

'Not to worry.'

I must have misheard her. 'What do you mean?'

'The only people with money these days are these godawful sequels and reboots. You wouldn't believe how many Oscar winners are doing the Hungry Hungry Hippos live-action feature. I'm a big believer in supporting real art. I'd be happy to waive my commission if the project's worth doing.'

'Wow,' I say. 'Thank you.'

'Don't thank me yet. Tell me what you're looking for.'

I'm liking her more by the second.

'I need someone talented, Doily. He has to be able to play charming, but no nonsense. A safe pair of hands.'

I recall my conversation with Mariam at Buckingham Palace.

'It would be great to find someone with a bit of an edge. Someone who's prepared to have the tough conversations. Oh, and it would help if he's handsome.'

Doily tuts. 'What does that matter?'

'It's always an advantage.'

'Acting comes from the soul.'

'Of course, it's just—'

'You want a hottie. Fine. Any other requirements?'

This is looking up. 'I mean, it would be wonderful if you have someone who's familiar with Greece.'

'Greece? Are you a fan?'

'You could say that.'

Just then, I hear a mobile ringtone on the end of the line.

'Bollocks!' says Doily. 'I'm going to have to go.'

'But we haven't even—'

'Yes we have,' says Doily. 'Leave it with me. I've got just the chap for you.'

5

Hunter

My prayers have been answered. Maybe. Potentially. I've been handed another lifeline.

Doily was unable to give me many details as she was too busy attempting to stop her client from suing Helena Bonham Carter, but I'm used to that by now with her. She couldn't even confirm if this job is for a company who will be able to sponsor me for a visa, but there's one thing giving me hope: Doily mentioned that there was a possibility of foreign travel. That makes me think that whoever this company is might be capable of providing the requisite documentation for me to stay in the country.

All is not lost. Not yet, at least.

I'm aware that I'm clinging to hope, but I have nothing to lose by taking the meeting. They've asked to meet me at a pub a stone's throw from Bloomsbury Square, ivy spilling down its red brick exterior, its Victorian sign immaculately restored. It's a warm spring evening, but I manage to grab a table outside the pub. It's a great spot for people watching. There's a well-dressed couple having an argument about the contents of a John Lewis bag. There are two women who look like sisters, with travel suitcases and a bucket of champagne. There's a man who could be here on a date. He couldn't appear more English if he tried – a scrub of reddish-brown hair and a smattering of freckles across his cheeks. He's cute in a butter-wouldn't-melt way that makes me think he's never seen the inside of a dark room at a gay club. I pity whichever poor soul he's here to meet. At least I do until he looks up and catches me staring at him.

'Hello,' he says. 'Are you Hunter?'

Hold on – this is the guy I'm meeting? He doesn't have a producer vibe.

'That's me,' I say.

He seems surprised.

'What?' I ask, a bit defensively.

'Nothing. I just . . . thought you'd be British.'

My heart sinks. Please don't tell me they want to cast authentically.

'Try not to sound so disappointed,' I say, attempting to make light of it.

'Oh, no, I'm not,' he says, blushing. 'Nice to meet you. I'm Max.'

Where does Doily find these people? He's acting like this is the first time he's ever met with an actor. Maybe he's the producer's assistant.

I glance around. 'Is it just you?'

He frowns. 'Why, were you expecting more?'

'To be honest,' I say, 'I didn't know what to expect.'

I'm regretting not insisting that Doily give me more details. Some of these production companies barely deserve the title. Now that I think about it, asking to meet at a pub isn't a great sign.

'How much did Doily tell you?' he asks anxiously.

'Immersive theater. Could mean anything.'

'Is that all she said?'

'She said you wanted someone who was familiar with *Grease*.'

'Yes. Are you?'

'I was in it.'

'Nice. For how long?'

'Six months.'

'Wow. What part?'

'Rizzo.'

He frowns. 'Is that near Athens?'

'What?'

'I've never heard of Rizzo.'

'It's usually a woman.'

'Sorry, what?'

'What do you mean, what?'

'How can a town in Greece usually be a woman?'

Suddenly I realise the source of the confusion. I let out a bitter laugh.

Max's cheeks heat up.

'What's so funny?' he asks hotly.

I scowl. 'Goddamn it, Doily.'

'What are you talking about?'

'Don't you get it? You're talking about Greece, the country. I'm talking about *Grease*, the musical.'

Max stares, his mouth hanging open. 'You were in *Grease* the musical?'

'Why would I be in Greece, the country? I'm an actor.' I tilt my head at him. 'Now, would you mind telling me what the job is?'

That came out wrong. This really is not going well. For a minute, I think he's about to get up and storm off. But instead, panic flashes behind his eyes.

'Of course I wouldn't mind,' he says. 'But first, let me buy you a drink.'

He heads inside to get our drinks and I have a moment to catch my breath. I need to start behaving. No, this guy doesn't seem to have a clue about anything, but he wouldn't be the first producer I've met like that. Plus, let's be honest – this is mostly Doily's fault. I love her, but she's not the best at providing the necessary information. She once got her wires crossed and had me emotionally preparing to shoot a commercial for a bereavement charity which turned out to be for cat food.

I still nailed it, which means I can pull off whatever this guy needs from me. Immersive theater with some knowledge of Greece? Maybe it's that *Mamma Mia* dining experience. Not exactly my kind of musical, but at this point, I'll take anything.

A few minutes later, we each have a gin and tonic in hand but Max still hasn't explained what the job involves. Instead, he's rambling on about his own job, which it turns out is working for the civil service.

'Wait, you work for the government?'

'Is that a problem?'

'I mean, I'm not the biggest fan of the British government right now, but no. I just . . . thought you were a producer.'

Max starts to sweat. He explains that he's applying for a job in Athens where having a partner would be an advantage. It all sounds very conservative, but I'm still not understanding where immersive theater fits into all this, so I ask.

'Maybe I shouldn't have said *theater*,' says Max. 'It's more just . . . acting.'

'As what?'

'My boyfriend.'

I almost choke on my drink. 'You want me to play your boyfriend?'

He blushes. 'Yeah.'

I put down my glass a little too abruptly. 'In what setting?'

'Um . . . real life, I guess.'

I cannot process what I'm hearing. 'There's no company involved?'

'Well, no.' Max looks sheepish. 'I mean, apart from where I work. There's an event I'm meant to be attending in about an hour.'

My stomach sinks in disbelief. The seriousness of the meeting, the hope it represented, evaporates in a puff.

'Goddamnit, Doily.'

I get up from the table, my chair scraping against the floor.

'Where are you going?' Max cries with a note of panic.

'I'm an actor,' I say, my voice tightening. 'Sounds like what you need is an escort.'

How does this keep happening? I thought I couldn't sink any lower than being rejected for playing the back end of a cow, but the acting profession keeps finding new ways to humiliate me. All I can do now is make a dignified exit, but I'm kind of trapped behind this table. As I try to squeeze out, Max looks frantic.

'Please. I'm desperate. I'll do anything.'

Right at that moment, one of the champagne sisters leaps up and squeals in excitement. The other sister is holding her hand out, showing off an engagement ring.

I look back at Max, and it hits me. Would he agree to it? Is he really *that* desperate? Would he marry me so I can stay in the country, and he can have a fake boyfriend to improve his odds of getting a job? When you put it like that, no one in their right mind would agree to it, but this isn't a man in his right mind, clearly.

Besides, what is marriage? It's a contract that unfairly grants certain privileges to some people above others. This would be a strict business arrangement. If it works out, he'll get this job in Athens and I'll get to stay in London and pursue my acting career. We'll literally be in different countries.

I'm about to propose this to him when I see him checking the time and I realise now is not the moment to have this discussion. I need to make myself indispensable and *then* tell him what my conditions are. If I go to this event and meet all his colleagues, he'll be stuck with me. Not that I would want to coerce him. But he came into this with a very clear plan. Now I'm coming into it with one of my own.

'Fine,' I say. 'I'm in.'

'Amazing,' Max says with relief, before having a blip of worry.

'I mean when I said I'd do *anything*, I obviously didn't mean—'

'Oh no, of course not,' I say with a smile. 'I'm not going to ask for anything unreasonable.'

6

Max

I can't believe he said yes. I've got a boyfriend. A fake boyfriend. My plan worked.

Admittedly, he's not quite what I was expecting, but I can't claim that Doily hasn't delivered what I asked for. Talk about a hottie. The man is outrageously handsome, tall and olive-skinned with a swoop of dark hair that tumbles over his jade green eyes. And he's definitely got a bit of an edge. I wonder if I made a mistake with that particular request. I'm unnerved by how direct Hunter is, something I can't imagine going down well in a diplomatic setting. He hasn't given the impression that he's the easiest person to work with.

But the second he agrees to my proposal, a switch flips. He becomes focused, snapping into gear and out of whatever mood he was in. As we get down to business and into the detail of what I want from him, there's a spark, an energy that radiates from him. He pulls out a notebook and pen and starts scribbling. There's nothing casual about this for him. This is serious role play.

We agree that we won't tell any lies unless strictly necessary. Still, knowing how nosy my colleagues are, we come up with a story for how we met and how long we've been dating. When I tell him he's going to have to pretend to be an orthodontist called Edwin, Hunter takes it in his stride. He tells me the best characters are created from real life, but suggests that he should only be a trainee orthodontist, so he's not expected to be too much of an expert on anything. He looks up a course on orthodontics, so he can picture what he's been studying this week. I tell him no one is going to be grilling him on brace moulds, but he says you never know, and in any case, it's more about getting into that headspace.

I'm not going to argue with the proccss. I'm feeling morc reassured by the minute. We decide that for Hunter to come across as a stable and dependable presence in my life, we need to have been fake dating for as long as possible. I figure the longest we can get away with is four months, since it was about that long ago that I recall telling Nessie about a trombone player I was stalking on Feeld, and it feels like we have enough to worry about without bringing trombones into the mix. The only issue arises when I suggest that rather than making everything up, we might use a few details from Hunter's life.

'Why?' Hunter fires back.

His defences have gone up instantly in a way that intrigues me.

'I . . . I don't know. I thought it might make it easier.'

'Do you understand what acting is?'

'It just feels weird that I don't really know anything about you.'

'You don't need to. You're dating Edwin. Forget about me.'

I'm getting the feeling I might find that difficult. Someone once told me that actors are always less interesting than the characters they play. I'm not sure that's true in Hunter's case. Edwin the orthodontist was not the most alluring of guys, but there's something about Hunter that has already got under my skin.

'Backstory isn't important,' says Hunter. 'What matters is how I meet people in the moment. Have you had any thoughts about costume?'

'What about it?'

'Does this work?'

He gestures at his outfit. I try to focus, but I can't help noticing that his pecs are straining to get out of his shirt.

'Yeah, that'll do.'

Hunter scowls. '"*That'll do?*" Do you want to get this job or not?'

I frown at him. 'Of course I do.'

'Then take it seriously. Costume is everything. Right now, I'm dressed as an actor going to a meeting at a pub. I need to be dressed like a trainee orthodontist who is accompanying his boyfriend of four months to a high-profile work event. What's the dress code? What conversations did you have about this?'

'With who?'

'Edwin! Me! Your boyfriend!'

As he looks at me with total conviction, something between us ignites. Just for a moment, I believe that we really have been dating for four months. That he's looking forward to supporting me tonight after missing the big event at Buckingham Palace. That the attraction between us is real.

But then Hunter gestures back at his outfit. I reassess the cotton shirt and slacks. Now that he mentions it, maybe it's not formal enough for a diplomatic event.

'Don't worry about offending me,' Hunter says. 'If it's not right, let's change it.'

'Isn't it a bit late for that?'

'Not at all.' Hunter finishes his drink in one swig. 'Oxford Street is right there.'

We march over there at double quick pace. I'm kind of bowled over by his professionalism. If he's this dedicated, maybe I really can mould him into a creation that can compete with the brilliant Flora Forbes. I suggest going to Primark to cut costs, but Hunter insists that Zara is more appropriate. He's so decisive that I don't argue.

We head upstairs to the men's section, where decade-old pop hits are playing on loop. Hunter flicks through the racks like he's Miranda Priestly, holding fabrics up to the light, testing textures between his fingers. He gathers a few shirts and pairs of chinos and heads towards the fitting rooms. I linger by the entrance, but Hunter glances over his shoulder.

'Come on, we don't have all day.'

The cubicle looked big enough from the outside, but inside there's barely any room. I smile at Hunter to acknowledge the awkwardness, but he ignores me. There are mirrors on three sides, reflecting both of us from every angle. Hunter drops his selection of clothes on the bench, unbuttons his shirt and slips it off, completely at home with being topless. I look away out of courtesy, only to see his reflection. His skin is marked with tan lines, his back and shoulders sculpted enough that he must work out, but not so much that he obsesses over it. His lower back has a downy sheen of hair that disappears into his belt. Hunter pulls on one of the shirts.

'I like it,' he says, examining himself in the mirror.

I murmur in agreement, too overwhelmed by our proximity to offer any kind of meaningful appraisal. I'm expecting him to try on another shirt, but instead Hunter reaches for his belt. The sound of unbuckling gives me a rush of adrenaline. I tell myself to look at the ceiling, the floor, anywhere else, but instead I glance down right at the moment he drops his trousers and I catch a glimpse of his Calvin Klein briefs and the clear outline of his package straining to be contained. I blush furiously, avoiding Hunter's gaze, but he doesn't seem remotely self-conscious.

'What do you think?' he asks, pulling on the new trousers. 'Too tight?'

He turns his back to me, which means it's my duty to look. The trousers are perfectly cupping his sculpted behind.

'They look great,' I say. 'But you need to be comfortable.'

I glance up and our eyes meet in the mirror. There it is, that same spark from earlier, only in a setting like this, it's far more loaded. The air between us crackles with electricity. Everything is telling me to look away, but those eyes won't let me. I hold his gaze for a beat too long, my lips unconsciously parting. A knowing smile flickers across Hunter's face.

What's he thinking?

My heart is racing, and then, oh god, I feel a twitch between my legs. I avert my eyes, turning even more red than before.

I feel like the floor has fallen out from beneath me, but not a word has been said. Hunter slips off the first pair of trousers and folds them neatly on the bench, then steps into the next pair. My gaze is fixed downwards, but as he bends his leg to pull on the trousers, I see a clear side view of his bulge in one of the mirrors. I could swear it's got bigger, tugging against the zipper of his trousers with impressive heft as he pulls them on and tucks it out of sight. It's only the briefest of glimpses, and yet those swelling contours against the white cotton are enough to make me unsteady on my feet. The evidence is unmistakable: not only is he very well endowed, but he's turned on by what just happened. We both are.

'Better?' Hunter asks.

He looks at himself in the mirror as he adjusts the waistband.

I swallow and do my best to assess him. The trousers fit like they were made for him, and now that the outfit is complete, it's shocking how much it has changed his look. I'm not sure if it's quite giving trainee-orthodontist-who-I've-been-dating-for-four-months, but only because I can't imagine someone this hot, this suave and assured, being part of my chaos. Admittedly, the look is only half the battle. The next few hours are going to be a minefield. But Hunter is committed, and I couldn't be more grateful.

'You look perfect,' I manage to stutter. I offer him my arm like some Regency gentleman. 'Let's do this.'

Hunter looks down at my arm with a smirk, then brushes past me and walks out.

7

Hunter

That came off a bit harsher than I intended. I had to get myself out of there before I got any more aroused. That took me by surprise. I told Max to come in with me because we were pressed for time, and I didn't want to mess around with his English politeness and going in and out of the fitting room. Even when I took off my clothes the first time, I was focused on the task at hand.

But then we caught each other's eye.

There was something so shy and innocent about Max's gaze, like he knew he shouldn't be looking but couldn't resist. Even as his cheeks flushed red beneath those adorable freckles, he didn't avert his eyes. Watching him battle against his own desires like that was enough to drive me wild. Not to mention hard.

I must have been sixteen or seventeen when I first noticed someone watching me in the locker room. I was never really into sports, but in my junior year of high school I got into swimming. There was this one senior who was always there at the same time as me, right at the point we were stripping off. It rapidly became clear that both of us liked it, him stealing furtive glances, me pretending I hadn't noticed. That was as far as it ever went. I was too scared of showing any visible signs of excitement in public. But that only added to the thrill.

When I got to college, I tried to put a lid on those impulses. I kept everything polite and vanilla with the guys I slept with, even though nothing truly excited me beyond the initial rush of the chase. I thought about joining the swim team until I found out they had open showers. Not to sound arrogant, but when I'm turned on, it's pretty hard to hide the evidence. I even passed on a role in a production of *Hair* because it had a nude scene, and I didn't want to get a reputation.

Then I met Rafferty. He took me to sex clubs, fucked me in Central Park at night, and I went along with it all, pretending I was only doing it to please him when I loved it more than anything. After we broke up, all bets were off. I wasn't interested unless there was something illicit about the situation. I hooked up with guys I met at the gym, at auditions, I even slept with the priest at my cousin's wedding.

Thankfully, Max appears to agree that nothing good can come from talking about what just happened. As we walk over to the British Museum, he brings me up to speed on tonight's event. Apparently, one of Greece's conditions for signing this trade deal was that Britain finally return the Elgin Marbles, or the Parthenon Sculptures, to give them their less problematic name. They're some of the most illustrious treasures of antiquity, and have been housed in the British Museum since 1816. Tonight, they will be symbolically handed back to Greece. Max tells me that the director of the British

Museum, Montgomery Pim, is heartbroken over having to return his most famous artefacts.

'Sorry, what?' I splutter. 'He's *heartbroken* over having to return sculptures that your country stole?'

Max nods apologetically.

'Then he can go fuck himself.'

Max recoils. 'Jesus, Hunter! Do you understand what we're about to walk into?'

I laugh. 'Don't worry, I'm not in character yet.'

Max swallows. 'You might want to get into character pretty quickly.'

'Why?'

Max gestures ahead of us. 'We're here.'

I look up and see the British Museum's imposing façade. You can't deny what a perfect venue it is for tonight's gala, being modelled on a Greek temple. I look back at Max. He's fidgeting with his cuffs as his eyes dart around nervously. I remember what I promised him and what I'm planning to ask him at the end of the night. It's time to switch it on. I go to the place in my mind where I've stored the details that will help me bring this character to life. I'm here to support my partner. I'll do anything to help him get this job. When I turn back to Max, it's not me that's seeing him, it's Edwin, the trainee orthodontist and dependable boyfriend. I reach down and take his hand.

Max flinches, so I give him a reassuring smile.

'*Now* let's do this.'

As we enter the museum's central atrium, its sheer vastness takes my breath away. Light spills down through a soaring roof of glass and steel, while the marble floor rings with the footsteps of hundreds of guests. I feel myself rising to the occasion, but Max has frozen.

'What?' I ask.

'That's him.'

'Who?'

'Montgomery Pim, the museum director. The guy I was just telling you about!'

Max points towards one of those British people you can't quite believe is real, and not only because his name is Montgomery Pim. He's one of the most flamboyantly camp men I've ever seen, wearing a purple pinstripe suit and blessed with a bald patch that looks like it's been polished for the occasion. Max tries to steer us away from him, but Montgomery spies us and his eyes light up. He abandons his conversation mid-sentence and glides over.

'Gentlemen, welcome,' says Montgomery. 'Have we met?'

There are times as an actor when you feel ridiculous. When you have to say a line you know is trash. When you're wearing an awful costume. Or when you've stepped into a role at short notice. But those are the times you really have to commit.

'I don't believe we have,' I say confidently. 'I'm Edwin.'

I glance at Max, but he's gone quiet.

'And what brings you here tonight, Edwin?' Montgomery asks.

'He does,' I say, gesturing to my side. 'This is Max.'

'Lovely,' says Montgomery, glancing down at our hand holding with a mixture of lust and envy. 'Please, help yourself to an amuse bouche.'

The way he says it sounds almost indecent. He points out a tray of canapés.

'I'm Montgomery, by the way. But call me Monty, please.'

I cannot believe this ridiculous specimen is the head of the country's most important museum. All I can think of is Max's comment that he's heartbroken over having to return the Marbles. But I'm not me anymore. I'm Edwin.

'This must be a difficult occasion for you,' I say sincerely. 'How are you holding up?'

Monty sighs dramatically. 'Thank you for asking. I'm persevering.'

Max still hasn't said a word. I'm having to suppress an urge to tell Monty how I really feel about this whole business.

'You'll be OK, Monty,' I say, batting my eyelashes. 'I know everyone appreciates what a sacrifice you're making.'

Montgomery gulps, then turns to Max. 'Goodness,' he says, wiping his brow with a silk handkerchief. 'This one's a charmer.'

As another guest arrives and commands Monty's attention, Max looks at me in awe.

'That was incredible. I . . . I believed you.'

There's something about Max's earnest gratitude that tugs at my heartstrings, but I can't get distracted by that.

I raise an eyebrow. 'It's called acting.'

8

Max

We've only been here five minutes and I already feel like I'm going to explode. I held my breath throughout Hunter's conversation with Monty. I don't think I was prepared for what it was actually going to be like to attend one of these events with a fake boyfriend. And we haven't even met anyone I know yet. Still, I can't deny that Hunter passed his first test, charming the socks off Monty without making him doubt for a second that we were a real couple.

One of the big points of contention about tonight was how the optics of returning such a controversial object would appear in the context of a bilateral trade deal. It was deemed easier for everyone if we could make it look like a mutual exchange, so the Greeks dug around in their museum collection and found a painting by a British artist called Sir Harold Barking. No, I haven't heard of him either. I don't think anyone had heard of him before this week, let alone ranked his work alongside the treasures of the Acropolis, but sometimes diplomacy is about maintaining a useful fiction. I'm yet to see the painting in question, and until I do, I'm afraid that the name Sir Harold Barking just makes me picture Sir Harold on all fours, barking like a dog.

As we enter the exhibition room and I see the painting, it makes me wish we had gifted the Greeks 'Sir Harold, barking', and convinced some cash-strapped aristocrat to get up there and woof. That would have been a lot more impressive than what's on display, which is a very mediocre watercolour of the Parthenon. Naturally, everyone is having to pretend it's a masterpiece, crowding around the painting and making pretentious comments about its colour palette. This is a far more interesting spectacle than the painting itself.

'Hello Max,' I hear from behind.

I turn to see Mariam in her trusty brown pantsuit.

'Mariam.'

My heart is in my mouth. Mariam glances at Hunter then back at me about four times.

'This is Edwin,' I say to Mariam.

'Ah,' says Mariam.

I can see the cogs turning in her mind.

'Is this—'

'The guy who couldn't make it last night.'

Mariam is still processing. She must be thinking about the conversation we had at the palace. I didn't even hint that the man who stood me up might reappear in my life. I think I even described myself as single.

'What a nice surprise,' Mariam says eventually. 'How's the jaw?'

I shoot Hunter a look. I completely forgot to inform him about that part of the lie. Hunter peers at me for guidance.

'It's fine,' I say. 'False alarm. Just dislocated.'

Mariam looks bemused.

'Is the ambassador here?' I say hurriedly.

'No, he couldn't make it. Apparently last night's seafood upset him.'

All the air goes out of me. I went to all this effort only for Wrettham not to show up? But before anyone can see the crack, I force a smile. There will be other events. In fact, knowing that Wrettham isn't here tonight allows me to relax. Maybe I can think of this as a dress rehearsal for me and Hunter.

'While I've got you,' Mariam says to Hunter, 'could I ask you a quick question about my overbite?'

'Absolutely,' says Hunter without missing a beat.

He warns Mariam he's not fully qualified, but this doesn't stop her from explaining her issue while biting down repeatedly. We're in dangerous territory, but just then Quentin strides up with the brilliant Flora Forbes on his arm. They've dressed perfectly for the occasion, he in a peach-coloured shirt, she in a polka dot dress, allowing them to fit in with the art crowd while still looking suitably formal. Thank god Hunter had the good sense to take us shopping.

Quentin peers at Hunter. 'Is this the famous Edwin?'

'It is,' says Hunter, flashing a grin.

Flora is staring at him like he's an exhibit at the zoo. I get that he's hot and me having a date is a novelty, but this is ridiculous.

'Do I know you?' Flora asks Hunter.

My pulse quickens.

Hunter is wrongfooted. 'No, I don't think so.'

Flora purses her lips. 'Gosh. You look so familiar.'

'I get that a lot,' says Hunter with a little laugh.

He's holding it together well, but I can tell that he's panicking. As Flora peers at him, trying to figure it out, I recall that she's a musical theater geek. Only the other day, Quentin was complaining that Flora had dragged him to Peterborough on their anniversary so they could catch a rare staging of *Once Upon a Mattress*. She must have seen Hunter perform somewhere. Why didn't I anticipate this?

'*That's* it,' says Flora eventually. 'Your TikTok.'

I cannot believe this. We've been busted within minutes.

'Oh,' says Hunter casually. 'You saw that?'

'Who didn't?' says Flora.

What the fuck? Please don't tell me Doily sent me an actor who's gone viral.

Flora frowns at him. 'But I thought you were called—'

'Hunter. That's my stage name.'

'Nice,' says Flora.

I'm amazed that she's buying it, but I suppose it rings true.

'I wondered why you'd stopped posting,' says Flora. 'Max said you're an orthodontist?'

There's not a shred of suspicion in Flora's voice. She's genuinely curious.

'Trainee orthodontist,' Hunter says with a smile. 'Every actor needs a backup career.'

How is he doing this? He's coming up with these lies without missing a beat.

Flora nods sagely. 'So true. Why the UK?'

'Cheaper,' says Hunter. 'Dental school in America would ruin me.'

Flora murmurs in agreement. I still can't believe they're swallowing this whole, but I guess they don't have any reason to doubt Hunter. A viral TikTok star who goes by a stage name and has a backup career as an orthodontist might not be someone you meet every day, but maybe it's more likely than me hiring an actor to play my boyfriend. I feel a rush of inspiration.

'It's funny,' I say. 'People are always surprised that a musical theater actor could go into orthodontics. But there are so many similarities. Think about it! They're both about transformation. Edwin has taught me that confidence is all in the jaw. He's really improved my selfies. And like, who else would be able to do that apart from an actor who's also an orthodontist? When you think about it.'

I smile at Hunter, but he doesn't smile back. I glance at Quentin and Flora and their expressions have turned confused. Hunter shoots a look at me.

'Hey babe, can you show me where the bathroom is?'

'Sure babe,' I say uncertainly. I turn to Quentin and Flora. 'Back in a minute.'

I lead Hunter off in the direction of the bathroom, but the moment we get away from Quentin and Flora, he yanks me into an alcove and gives me an urgent stare.

'What did we agree?' he says.

I frown.

'No unnecessary lies,' Hunter reminds me.

'What? You just told about fifty.'

'Those were necessary.'

'Aren't they all necessary?'

Hunter raises his eyebrows in surprise. 'I was responding to their questions. You said a load of stuff unprompted.'

'But surely that adds to the general picture?'

'No. The fewer lies, the better.'

'I thought acting was all about make-believe.'

'That's a common misconception. Good acting is about telling the truth.'

There's that conviction again. He's talking like this is scientific fact.

'This is diplomacy,' I say hotly. 'No one tells the truth.'

Hunter frowns. 'That sounds . . . unhelpful.'

'Not at all. It's how you get countries to cooperate.'

'Ah yes, the famously cooperative international community.'

I glance around anxiously. He's not wrong, but we need to be careful. Hunter is coming out of his shell. Time to reel him back in. Thankfully, he appears to understand.

'Look,' Hunter says. 'It's not a big deal. They clearly believed us. All I'm saying is, don't lie if you can avoid it. If you answer questions like it's nothing, people will believe the weirdest shit. But if you give them explanations they haven't asked for, they start to get suspicious.'

It's hard to argue with that. In fact, there's a part of me that quite likes Hunter taking charge of the situation like this. As we hold each other's gaze, there's that spark again, the one from the fitting room. But Hunter appears to take it as a prompt.

'Come on,' he says. 'Let's go turn some heads.'

The way he can switch it on and off is mesmerising. I'm going to need about a week to recover from this evening. Back out in the party, Mariam introduces us to a number of embassy staff, and each time, Hunter is charming, polite, and perfectly professional. It's not only that people are predisposed to like someone this handsome, they're also won over by every word he says, and I'm right there with them. This is an award-worthy performance.

There's only one problem, but it's not insignificant. Any time Mariam introduces us to someone, she makes sure to introduce Quentin and Flora too. On the surface, people have the same polite reaction to them that they do to me and Hunter. But beneath that, there are subtle differences in how they treat us, and I'm convinced I know the reason. It's because Quentin and Flora are a cookie cutter straight couple, while Hunter and me . . . well, we're gay. I'm not saying there's any outright homophobia. Some people seem genuinely delighted to meet a gay couple among the hordes of heterosexuals, and some do that thing where they immediately tell you about their gay cousin, which is misguided but probably well-meaning. But some react with just the slightest bit of hesitancy or discomfort. And what about the people we don't meet? What about the ones who actively avoid us?

The fact is, this is the gayest I've ever been at one of these functions. I've lost count of the number of times over the years when I've conspicuously avoided mentioning my sexuality in the diplomatic world, convinced it would count against me. But tonight, there's no hiding it. When people see me with a hot man on my arm, they know instantly. And what if that's as much a negative as a positive?

I think back to my conversation with Mariam. She was right – it's not an even playing field, but the answer is not as simple as acquiring a boyfriend. The role Flora plays for Quentin is time-tested and traditional. I can't claim that about Hunter, no matter how much he adds to my ticket. He's played his part flawlessly, and still Quentin has the advantage.

It's a relief when the schmoozing starts to wind down and everyone gets ready for the handover of the Marbles. Like everything else, this has been the subject of ridiculous levels of discussion. For a long time, there was a serious plan to light up the statues in white and blue, the colours of the Greek national flag. In the end, sanity prevailed, and everyone agreed on a simple handshake between Montgomery Pim and the woman who is breaking his heart, the director of the Acropolis Museum in Athens.

There's always anxiety in the air in the build-up to carefully choreographed moments like this, but as I look around, I sense that something more is going on. We're not being herded as planned to the room where the Marbles are housed. Various officials are darting around skittishly and talking in hushed tones, and then I spot Henry Herbert or Herbert Henry with his iPad, a clear harbinger of doom. I cross over to Mariam and ask what's wrong.

'It's Montgomery,' she says fretfully.

'What about him?'

'He's locked himself in with them.'

'Who?'

'The Marbles. He says they're leaving over his dead body.'

'You can't be serious.'

'See for yourself.'

I follow Mariam away from the main gathering to the locked doors of the room containing the Marbles. Hunter joins me, intrigued by what's unfolding. There's a small group of people crowded around the door, all trying to beg, plead, and reason with Montgomery. Someone even asks if he'd feel differently if she made him a nice cup of tea. Hard to believe this country once ruled the world.

Montgomery isn't responding. Everyone looks panicked. There's no question of Monty's plan succeeding. Whatever happens tonight, the Marbles will go back to Greece. But what we want to avoid is an embarrassment. There are members of the press here, some from newspapers who are furious that Britain agreed to this exchange. They'd love nothing more than a fuck-up. So far, it doesn't look like any of them have noticed the hubbub, but it's only a matter of time.

Before I can think of a solution, I hear a familiar voice and turn to see the brilliant Flora Forbes clearing a path for Quentin through the crowd. He asks to have a word with Montgomery on the grounds that a distant relative of his was on a fencing team with Lord Elgin. When they get to the front, I turn to Hunter.

'We need to do something.'

Hunter frowns. 'Like what?'

'I don't know, but Monty liked you. There must be something we can say to convince him.'

Admittedly, I can't think what. I just know we can't stand here and do nothing while Quentin saves the day. If he pulls that off, he'll have this job in the bag. But what can we possibly say to Monty?

As Hunter listens to Quentin's attempts to bargain with Montgomery, I sense that Quentin's courteous remonstrations are the kind of thing that rub Hunter the wrong way. After one particularly obsequious plea, something in Hunter snaps. He marches to the front and ushers Quentin out of the way. Not aggressively, but with such conviction that nobody questions him. Honestly, it's kind of hot.

'Monty?' says Hunter.

Silence.

'It's Edwin. We met at the entrance. Open the door.'

By some miracle, the door opens a crack. Montgomery's beady little eyes peer out. Hunter doesn't hesitate. He barges inside and I slip in behind him and close the door. I look at the back of the room and see the Elgin Marbles in all their glory. There's Athena, standing proud and headless in her billowing robes, and Dionysus, reclining nude in crumpled sheets. Next to their resplendence, Montgomery looks even more pathetic, like a toddler who has crammed all his toys into the potty so he doesn't have to share.

'I shan't give them up,' Monty says defiantly. 'Father would never forgive me.'

Hunter leans in. There's sympathy in his eyes.

'I get it,' he says gently. 'No one likes to feel like they're letting down their parents.'

He gazes off into the middle distance.

'I barely speak to my dad, and I still hear his voice in my head every time I forget to look both ways when I'm crossing the street.'

Hunter affects a New England accent a shade deeper than his own.

'*Use the eyes god gave you, kid.*'

He shakes his head at Monty with a bittersweet smile, as if the shadows of their fathers' legacies bonds them on a cosmic level. I can only watch in awe. The way Hunter is able to put aside his true feelings about the Marbles to conjure this level of empathy is something to behold.

'But Monty,' says Hunter, 'this is not open for debate. The deal has been signed. You've already lost.'

Monty's lip trembles. Hunter rests a hand on his shoulder.

'All you're doing now is delaying the inevitable,' says Hunter. 'Is that what you want? To be embarrassed in front of all your peers? Arrested? Fired? Dragged through the mud by the press?'

Monty crumples. Hunter has nailed this, presenting Monty with the brutal truth while still acting like he's on his side.

'Do you want that to be your legacy?' Hunter asks.

'No,' Monty says, his voice quivering.

'Thought not,' says Hunter. 'Then let's get out of here.'

As Montgomery stumbles out, shamefaced, a swarm of museum officials rush forward to secure the room as if this is a hostage situation. Hunter strides away as if he had nothing to do with it. Mariam approaches me and asks what happened, and I'm bursting with pride as I tell her what Hunter pulled off. But when I finish the story, he's almost out of sight. I race to catch up.

'That was incredible.'

Hunter shrugs modestly, but he knows what he did.

'Seriously,' I say. 'I can't wait to introduce you to the ambassador tomorrow.'

Hunter hesitates, his gaze wavering. 'I'm not free tomorrow.'

'Wait, what?'

'I have plans.'

'But . . . I can pay.'

'I said I'm not free. I'm doing a performance at the Menier Chocolate Factory.'

'You're performing at a chocolate factory?'

'Former chocolate factory. It's a theater now.'

'How much are they paying you?'

'Nothing,' says Hunter. 'It's not about that.'

I don't like this at all, but I can't lose Hunter now. Not only have I found someone to match up to the brilliant Flora Forbes, but he's the perfect match for me. He speaks his mind. He's good at handling tense situations. With him by my side, I might actually have a chance of beating Quentin.

'Fine,' I say. 'As long as you're free for the rest of the application process.'

Hunter takes a deep breath, then leads me further away from the crowd.

'Listen,' he says, 'it's actually kind of complicated. My visa is running out.'

My eyes widen. 'How? Why?!'

'Because that's what your great British government has decided. I have two weeks left here.'

I choke on my breath. 'That's . . . how can they—'

'Very easily, trust me.'

I cannot believe this. I thought I'd found my secret weapon.

'You never told me you were leaving the country,' I protest. 'This isn't fair.'

Hunter folds his arms. 'For me or you?'

I feel a flash of guilt. 'Mainly you, obviously. This sucks. Unless . . . would it help if I pay you more?'

Hunter holds my gaze. 'That wouldn't help, no.'

I frown. 'Is there another way?'

'There's one way, yes.'

I lean forward, my eyes alight with hope. Hunter doesn't flinch. 'I mean, if you really want to keep me in the country, you could marry me.'

I stare at him. My mouth opens then closes. I can barely comprehend what I've just heard. There's a lot I'd do to get this job, but marrying a stranger? That's a step too far. I don't even know how to word my response, but Hunter has got the message. He gives me a rueful look.

'Yeah,' he says, 'didn't think so.'

9

Hunter

'He didn't deserve you,' says Zosia, inspecting her jet-black ensemble in the dressing room mirror. 'If he didn't say yes, that's a him problem.'

'I love you, Zosia. But it's kind of a me problem.'

'Whatever,' says Thiago, draped over the arm of a battered sofa in a glittery shawl. 'You put yourself out there. That takes guts.'

I'm straddling a chair in the middle of the dressing room, picking at some noodles that I have no interest in eating. Zosia and Thiago have been my crew since we met at an open call for *Starlight Express* in a parking lot in Essex. I didn't have anything in common with a Polish cabaret singer or a Brazilian dancer other than us all being desperate for work and bad at roller-skating. None of us got the job that day, but we found each other. Since my conversation with Max, I've been longing to see these guys, and yet nothing they are saying is hitting.

In the mirror, I see Thiago share a glance with Zosia. They're aware they're not getting through to me.

'Who even is this man?' Zosia demands.

'He's no one,' sniffs Thiago. 'As *if* a random diplomat deserves to marry our Hunter.'

'Guys,' I say. 'I appreciate it, but forget about him.'

'Preach,' says Thiago. 'We can easily find someone else to marry you in the next two weeks.'

They really do mean well. But now that they're here, I'm realizing I don't want them to put a positive spin on everything. This situation sucks. All I can do is accept what's happened and channel it into my performance.

'It's too late for that,' I say to Thiago. 'Let's just try and enjoy tonight.'

Both of them have made an effort to be here for me, even though Thiago has a huge audition tomorrow for a breakdance version of *Pride and Prejudice*, and Zosia was supposed to be hosting a costumed sing-along screening of *Cats* on the other side of town. They're both so talented, but none of us have had that breakthrough moment, and I'm pretty sure that whether or not they'd admit it, Zosia and Thiago are wondering how long they are going to survive in London.

Zosia crosses the room and sits next to me. 'You're going to kill it on Broadway.'

The word hits me in the chest. I hadn't thought that far ahead.

'I mean, if that's where you choose to go next,' says Zosia. 'I have friends there, and people still talk about your performance as Rizzo. Don't let your ex keep you away.'

I'm well aware that my situation is nothing compared to the hardships some people I know are going through. It's not that I wouldn't be fine if I had to go back to

America. I could survive there. But if I want to achieve my dreams, it's really only here or Broadway, and over there, Rafferty is determined to run my name into the ground. Not only that, but he's put the flop of *Grease* behind him and convinced his dad to fund a metatextual reimagining of *Thoroughly Modern Millie* starring Millie Bobby Brown. I can't escape him in New York. London is mine. At least, it was supposed to be.

A voice crackles over the intercom: 'Five minutes until curtain-up.'

Thiago and Zosia leap up and bundle me into a group hug, then head out to find their seats. I hate to say it, but I'm glad they're gone. I should never have asked them backstage. When I said I wanted to try and enjoy this evening, I meant I want to lose myself in my performance. The place I'm planning to go in my mind is not most people's idea of enjoyable.

There was no question of my farewell performance being anything other than Sondheim. There's a reason that production of *Into the Woods* hit me so hard as a child. Sitting next to me as I listened to the Baker's Wife pour her heart out was my mom, a woman who was constitutionally incapable of expressing how she felt. I don't remember the details, but we were probably seeing a show that weekend because my dad was on another of his mysterious work trips that everyone except my mom could see through, even me at that age. Sitting there that day, I felt like that one song helped me understand my parents better – not only my mom, but my dad, who must have had a reason for going off and looking elsewhere for the things he didn't get from his marriage.

But it was my mom who my heart broke for that day. I remember wishing that she could quit lying to herself and express the things that her heart really sang for. Unsurprisingly, in the car home afterwards, she told me she found the musical weird and silly. Looking back, it probably hit her in the same way it did me, but I guess when you're stuck in a failing marriage, you process it differently.

For me, however, that was the day I became committed to telling the truth through performance. It might not have secured me a London stage career, but I can at least go out with a bang. As part of my final warm-up routine, I like to visualise my performance from start to finish. It helps me get over my nerves. But as I run through my lines, a funny thing happens. I don't picture Zosia and Thiago in the audience, cheering me on. I see Max.

I imagine him in the front row, a playbill resting in his lap. He's not one of those people who sit there looking too cool for school. His eyes are bright and he's unabashedly enjoying my performance. His hand drifts towards his pocket as if he wants to get his phone and take a photo, but then he decides against it, perhaps worried about distracting me. His gaze fixates on me, pure and adoring.

Whoa, where did that come from? Max isn't going to be here tonight. He's got his event. I'm never going to see him again. Last night ended so weirdly. Before we had a chance to really talk about my crazy proposal, his boss approached us. Apparently everyone was worried that Montgomery's freak-out would get leaked to the press and certain newspapers would have a field day with it. I agreed to keep it quiet, but I really didn't care by that point. I could tell Max felt bad about my situation, but there was still no way he was going to say yes to marrying me.

So why do I feel ten times worse than I did before I met him? Why can't I get him off my mind? It can't be anything to do with him, because I just met the guy, and from what I did get to know of him, he's hardly on my wavelength. I know what it is. It feels crazy to say it, but it's the same feeling I get every time I stop playing a role I've really enjoyed. I had fun stepping into the shoes of Edwin, the trainee orthodontist. I liked being Max's fake boyfriend. We made sense together. And yes, it was only a role, but when you really inhabit a role, it feels real. For those few moments, it *was* real, at least on some level. And now, just like that, it's all over. Max has probably already moved on.

10

Max

It doesn't mean anything that I'm googling him. If you looked at my Google history, you'd find all sorts of random searches: 'Can dogs eat tiramisu?', 'Julie Walters puppy farm rumours', 'horseradish sauce stain removal'. And that's just the last five minutes.

But here I am, on the District line on my way to the conclusion of Greece's state visit, and I'm looking up the performance that Hunter is doing tonight.

Hunter Moretti. Trust him to have such a hot name.

The Menier Chocolate Factory is a venue near London Bridge that is hosting some sort of musical revue. Hunter is performing a song called 'Being Alive' from the musical *Company*. This must be his farewell to the London stage. His bio lists all his plaudits for this gender-flipped *Grease* that he starred in.

I google the production and I'm hit with a flood of results. It's immediately apparent that it was kind of a big deal. The show got reviewed in the *New York Times*, and Hunter was singled out as the highlight. Apparently, male Sandy and female Danny produced mixed results, but Rizzo was a masterstroke, sultry, brooding, and mesmerising. That's not hard to imagine. Being off-Broadway meant the show was ineligible for the Tonys, but I discover a whole forum of people who believe that Hunter should have been a dead cert for a nomination following the show's Broadway transfer. Except that Hunter wasn't in the Broadway transfer. He was the only original cast member who wasn't. The forum posters are mad, convinced this would have been his big break. One forum user claims to have heard through the grapevine that it was entirely Hunter's decision.

What happened? How did Hunter go from being on the verge of Broadway stardom to living in London and struggling for work? Something must have gone seriously wrong. I do a bit more googling, but if the answer was online, you'd better believe those forum posters would have found it.

In any case, what does it matter? There's no way I can marry Hunter. There's just no way.

We'd have to lie to the government, the same government that pays my salary. This Athens job will involve security checks at the highest level. It's not a workable plan, so there's no use thinking about these what ifs. Time to put on a brave face and forget about him.

By day three of a state visit, everyone is ready to jump into the Thames to avoid having to engage in any more excruciating small talk. At least they've chosen a fitting venue for a send-off. As I enter the gate of the Royal Botanical Gardens, I see the Temperate House standing majestically against the sunset – an ornate, painstakingly restored Victorian greenhouse, twenty metres in height, and housing over a thousand plant species.

Stepping through the arched double doors, the green-house rises around me like a glass cathedral. Sun beams catch the mist, a gentle humidity brushes my cheeks . . . and it occurs to me what a stupid place this is to hold a cocktail party. The Greeks are barely breaking a sweat, but their pasty-faced hosts – my fellow countrymen – are wiping their brows, unbuttoning their collars, and glugging so much cucumber-flavoured water that there's already a long queue for the bathroom. I spot a woman taking refuge in a mist sprinkler as if she's midway through a trek across the Amazon rainforest. Gradually, her familiar features emerge through the miasma.

'Mariam!' I exclaim.

'Hello Max,' says Mariam, wiping her brow and looking around in surprise. 'Edwin not with you?'

I feel a pang in my chest. 'He couldn't make it.'

'Oh,' says Mariam, as if this confirms a suspicion.

'Yeah. I was hoping he'd be able to support me through this job application, but it doesn't look like he's going to be available.'

Mariam can barely hide her delight. 'That *is* a shame.'

I have never understood why Mariam favours Quentin over me for this promotion. But you can't say she's tried to hide it. Mariam excuses herself so she can hose down. I'm not sure if she's speaking metaphorically or if she's planning to ask a gardener to whip out the power hose. As she scoots off, it hits me how disappointed I am to be here without Hunter. I've been to dozens of these events without a date, and I've never felt so alone.

Still, I can't do anything about it. I need to find the ambassador and get some more face time with him without Quentin and Flora in my way. I wander through the greenhouse. The plants are arranged in a grid, with all manner of towering palm trees and exotic ferns separated by a series of paved walkways. I start searching the walkways, but after getting lost near a Chilean wine palm, I realise this method is not going to work. At each end of the greenhouse is an iron spiral staircase that coils up to a viewing balcony. Once I'm up there, it doesn't take long before I spot Wrettham and Topsy.

I run down the stairs and race straight up to them.

'Ambassador,' I say, a bit too abruptly.

Wrettham looks up and excuses himself and Topsy from a woman who is the chair of the Friends of the Hellenic Society, if memory serves correctly.

'Max,' he says. 'Glad we caught you. I hear your partner saved the day last night.'

Damn. How do I take credit for this so it doesn't seem like I'm nothing without Hunter?

'Yes,' I say. 'At my suggestion. It was a great team effort.'

'Really?' says Wrettham. 'That's not what I heard from Mariam.'

I'm regretting telling her what happened, given how easily I could have got away with lying, but how was I to know we'd end up here?

Wrettham smiles. 'I'm just glad to know he's feeling better. Can't be fun, being attacked by a baboon.'

It was Topsy's friend, not Hunter, who had the run-in with the baboon, but I don't bother to correct Wrettham.

'It's such a shame we keep missing him,' says Topsy. 'He sounds wonderful.'

'He is,' I say with regret.

It occurs to me that I could attempt to pull off some sort of *Weekend at Bernie's* situation where Hunter remains my boyfriend even though he never makes it to another event with me. Maybe his performance at the British Museum is enough. But I can't commit to that before running it past him. I decide that I need to keep things ambiguous.

'Maybe we'll get to meet him at Chevening,' says Topsy.

'Where?'

'Shh,' says Wrettham to Topsy.

'It's hardly a state secret,' says Topsy.

Wrettham turns to me stiffly. 'Please keep this to yourself, but the first part of this job assessment, should you make it that far, is going to be hosted by the Foreign Secretary at Chevening House. We're making a weekend of it. And partners are welcome.'

I knew the British embassy had delusions of grandeur, but I'm not sure why they're running this job hunt as if it's a reality TV show. A weekend at the Foreign Secretary's countryside retreat makes it sound like Judges' Houses on *The X Factor*. And partners are welcome? I'm devastated at the thought of doing that without Hunter.

'It should be very jolly,' says Topsy. 'Flora is going to perform selections from the *Oristeia*.'

'*Medea*,' says Flora from behind me. '*Very* different.'

I turn to see Quentin and the brilliant Flora Forbes slide into our conversation. Flora is wearing a dress covered in bold sunflowers, while Quentin's shirt carries a subtler pattern of daisies in similar shades. For once, they haven't quite nailed it, looking just a little too much like a newly upholstered set of armchairs.

'There you two are!' says Topsy. 'Thank you *so* much for this afternoon.'

I pull a quizzical expression.

'They needed someone to show them around the Greek pottery exhibition at the V and A,' says Quentin. 'Since Flora did her dissertation on the iconography of women's labour on water jars, it just made sense.'

'We had a lovely little afternoon, the four of us,' says Topsy.

I cannot deal with this. The four of them sitting together at dinner was bad enough, but now they've been going on excursions together? It's like they've cloned themselves.

'I was just saying we were hoping to meet Max's partner if Max is shortlisted for the Athens job,' says Topsy.

'Oh,' says Flora, glancing around. 'Could Edwin not make it?'

'No,' I say. 'Not tonight.'

Quentin looks relieved. I missed his reaction to Hunter's triumph last night, but I presume he wasn't happy about it. I don't know why I'm not admitting they're never going to see him again.

'Is he committed to a career as an orthodontist?' Flora asks.

My heart skips a beat. 'I think so. Why?'

'It's just, he's such a brilliant performer,' says Flora. 'I've never seen him live, but his TikToks are amazing. I always thought he could do anything.'

Her words hit me right in the gut.

He *could* do anything. I know he could, because he did it last night. Who else could have jumped in at short notice like that, handled all those questions that Flora threw at him, then saved the British government from a major humiliation? Hunter did all that without breaking a sweat. He was everything I needed and more. And there's no reason he couldn't continue to be.

Actually, there's one reason. One reason that felt so extreme, I never seriously considered it. But what if that's the answer? We're always being told to go the extra mile at work, push ourselves to the limit and expand what we're capable of. Honestly, that's what the prospect of marrying Hunter is starting to feel like. It's not just a hoop to jump through to get me where I need to be. It feels like an adventure. A crazy project that Hunter and I could do together. Untraditional, yes, but thrilling. Maybe even life-changing. An incredible gift to each other. What is that if not the essence of marriage?

'He hasn't given up performing,' I say to Flora. 'In fact, he's performing tonight.'

'Gosh,' says Wrettham. 'Very brave. But a good way to stick it to the baboon.'

Nobody says anything.

'Shame you're having to miss it,' says Topsy.

'I'm not,' I say decisively. 'If you'll excuse me, I'm heading there now.'

11

Hunter

It's a beautiful place for a farewell. Standing in the wings, I can only see part of the Menier Chocolate Factory's gorgeous proscenium arch, but you can feel the history in these floorboards. There really is nowhere like London to perform. I haven't had nearly as many chances to be on stage here as I would have liked, but it's time to go out with a bang.

As I hear the applause for the previous number, my heart starts to race, but that's a good thing. Nerves always make a performance better. The lights go down. The audience falls quiet.

I take a deep breath, then step into the spotlight.

The theater dissolves around me as the first few notes of *Being Alive* ring out from the piano. My voice is raw and trembling at first. As I sing about wanting someone to hold me close, it catches on something painful. Damn you, Stephen Sondheim.

The song is a slow unfurling, a confession of loneliness wrapped in the plea to be seen, to be held, to be known. As the song builds, my voice gains strength, aching and resolute at once.

I close my eyes as I hit the final note, my voice cracking but all the more powerful for it.

The room is silent.

I hold my breath until I hear the first claps, a ripple that quickly swells into a tidal wave of applause punctuated with wild whoops that I know are from Thiago. Usually, I love this moment – what performer doesn't? – but after that, I feel spent.

Those words I sang were too close to the truth even for me, capturing what I long for more than anything, the kind of love I don't believe I'll ever find. I peer into the crowd, searching for my friends, wanting to see their smiling faces.

Then I see Max.

From the moment our eyes meet, I don't need to ask why he's here. I can see it – he's on board. He looks at me, searching for a reaction. I nod at him. He gets up from his seat and starts walking towards me.

That wasn't what I meant, but what the hell. If we're going to do this, we might as well go for it. The audience is starting to notice him getting up on stage, but they don't know what's going on.

Until he gets down on one knee.

There's a collective gasp. I look down and see Max removing a signet ring from his finger.

'It's only temporary,' he says. 'I didn't have time to buy one.'

People are losing their minds, filming on their phones and squealing.

'Hunter,' Max says, 'I don't want you to leave. I want to finish what we started.'

He takes my hand and offers me the ring.

'Will you marry me?'

The audience holds their breath, but my eyes remain locked on Max. What passes between us is more than a pact. There's an understanding. A connection. Something neither of us could describe but both of us feel. I pull him up to a standing position.

'Sure, why not? Fuck it. Let's get married.'

12

Max

It's all fake. That wasn't a real proposal. I have to keep reminding myself, because it's been three days and I still haven't come down from that high. I used to think that public proposals were kind of tacky, but now I get it. My crazy impulse was completely legitimised by the roar of the crowd. If they bought our love, why won't everyone?

I didn't plan on giving Hunter my mum's ring. I saw myself slipping it off my finger before I knew what I was doing. But in that moment it felt right. I felt my mum shaking her head and grinning at me in approval.

And yet, when I look back on that night, the proposal isn't the part I remember most vividly. How could it be after sitting through *that* performance? Hunter stood up there and tore his heart out. I now understand what he meant when he said that acting is about telling the truth. As he sang about wanting someone to hold him close, it felt like it was coming from deep within. Except it wasn't, was it? That was acting, just like the moment he looked me in the eye and accepted my proposal. Just because I felt that spark again doesn't mean it was anything other than the latest acclaimed Hunter Moretti performance.

I mustn't let myself get caught up in the emotion.

It's all fake.

It's all fake.

It's all fake.

Except that today is the day it becomes all too real. My bags are packed and I'm in a taxi with Mr Peanut on the way to move in with my fiancé.

It feels insane to say that. The past few days have gone by in a flash. The morning after the proposal, Hunter got in touch to check that I actually meant what I'd done. I didn't hesitate. It's not that I haven't thought about all the ways this could go wrong or generally be a bad idea. I'm not completely delusional. But all I have to do is go back to that moment in the greenhouse with Wrettham and Quentin when I realised that if I want to have a shot at this job, I need to take drastic action.

Yes, it's an extreme thing to do to get a job, but knowing that Hunter is prepared to go to the same lengths for his career makes me feel better. From what I know of him, he's not someone who takes anything lightly. And no, we might not be a pair who would get married in real life, but in a way, that makes everything easier. There's no chance any lines will get blurred. This is a strictly professional arrangement.

Living with the person you're marrying turns out to be an essential step to getting a visa approved, and it rapidly became clear that Hunter had more space to accommodate me than vice versa. Luckily, my landlord had me on such an insecure contract that I was able to give up my room with very little notice and only lose a few hundred pounds of rent. The polyamorous furniture restorers were surprisingly sad when I told them I was leaving. I don't think they had any affection for me, but they quite liked Mr Peanut. Terrifying how fast that place can go from being the centre of my life to somewhere I'll never see again.

The taxi pulls off the main road onto one of the most beautiful squares I've ever seen. I double-check the address – yep, this is where Hunter told me to come. I've always dreamed about living somewhere this beautiful. No house I've ever lived in has been beyond average at best. From the terrace in Surrey where I grew up to the dingy flat-share in Manchester where I studied for university to the various horrible rentals in London I survived before landing on the windowless room, I'm not sure there's been a single angle that would make for a flattering Instagram shot. But it looks like that's about to change.

Hunter's house is the biggest of them all, a double-fronted red-brick mansion with multiple wrought-iron balconies filled with pot plants and its own private courtyard in front. Hunter told me he lived with Doily, but he didn't say she lived *here*.

'Mr Peanut,' I say, 'I've got a feeling we're not in Kansas anymore.'

As the taxi pulls up, I text Hunter to tell him we're here.

'We?' he replies.

A few moments later, a side door swings open and Hunter steps out. He's dressed casually, light slacks and a navy T-shirt, his hair still damp from the shower, his eyes as piercing as ever. Mr Peanut bounds up to him. Hunter's expression darkens.

'You have a dog.'

Shit. How could I have forgotten to mention Mr Peanut? There's been so much to organise, I somehow just assumed Hunter knew about him.

'Yeah, did I not—'

'No,' says Hunter. 'You did not. I didn't clear this with Doily.'

Mr Peanut is attempting to clamber up Hunter's legs and lick his face.

'Aww, I think he likes you,' I say with a grin.

'Down!' Hunter snaps at Mr Peanut.

Mr Peanut isn't bothered, but my hackles go up.

'Don't shout at him!'

'I didn't shout. I gave a command.'

'He doesn't know that one.'

Hunter stares at me. 'He doesn't know *Down?*'

I can't help but be personally offended. Hunter folds his arms and I do my best to restrain Mr Peanut.

'You shouldn't let him jump up like that,' Hunter insists.

'He's saying hello!'

'Have you thought about teaching him to say it politely?'

I'm not used to this reaction. Most people act as if Mr Peanut is the cutest thing they've ever seen.

'If you don't like dogs, just say that.'

'I do like dogs,' says Hunter. 'I've fostered dogs. First thing I learned is that discipline is a form of kindness.'

I hate being lectured, but there's something undeniably noble about fostering dogs, damn him. I need to reel it in. It must be a shock to invite a stranger to move into your home and end up with a dog as well.

'I'm sorry,' I say. 'I completely forgot. This has all happened so fast.'

Hunter takes me in.

'Is that all you've got?' he says, pointing at my suitcase.

'Yeah. I've been kicked out of so many rentals that I learned to pack light.'

As I look at Hunter, I feel like he must understand. He's an immigrant. Surely he knows that feeling of being shunted from place to place across an unforgiving city? But if he does, he's not in the mood to bond over it. He gives me a weary look.

'Follow me.'

The house is no less impressive on the inside. The hallway is vast and echoing, sunbeams from a fanlight spilling across a tiled floor. High above, a dusty chandelier dangles precariously. The walls are lined with faded silk panels and a scattering of framed playbills and oil portraits. There are piles of unopened post on a side table.

Hunter leads me down to the basement flat where he lives. Unlike the rambling splendour of upstairs, it's calm, spare, and tidy, only a few carefully chosen paintings on its white walls. He points out his bedroom but keeps the door closed. My room is small but does the job. There's a bed and a few dusty moving boxes stacked in one corner, next to a yoga mat and a folded drying rack. A lopsided bookshelf holds some stray paperbacks. It's clearly been used as a spillover room, but there's a quiet charm to it.

As Hunter shows me the bathroom, I catch my breath. We're going to be sharing. Sure, we're unlikely to be in there at the same time, but it's a kind of intimacy I hadn't considered. Hunter, however, is already striding past it.

The living room is large but minimalist: a few books neatly stacked on a low shelf, an upright piano tucked into one corner. Hunter gets out a stainless steel Moka pot and packs coffee into it like he's storing rations. There's so much to say that I don't know where to start, but Hunter seems more than happy to stay in the silence. I listen as the pot goes through the motions, from a slowly growing hiss to an unruly gurgling. Hunter pours us each a cup, then takes a seat opposite me at the kitchen table.

'I'm really sorry about Mr Peanut,' I say. 'I don't know how I forgot.'

Hunter frowns. 'You sure you didn't choose to forget because you were scared it was a deal-breaker?'

'No!' I exclaim. 'I wouldn't do that.'

Would I do that? I hope not. Thankfully, Hunter is over it.

'It's OK. I just don't want Doily to think I'm taking advantage.'

He looks pained at the suggestion.

'What are you going to tell her?'

'About what?'

'Us.'

'I already told her.'

My eyes widen.

'I can't lie to her, Max. Anyway, you spoke to her on the phone last week. You think she'd buy us meeting and moving in together and getting engaged this fast? Even four months is hard to believe.'

I'm reeling at the thought that someone else has been brought in so casually on this deception. 'What did she say?'

'She was thrilled. She's looking forward to meeting you. So are my friends.'

'Hang on a minute, who else have you told?!'

Hunter explains that two of his friends have been aware of everything from the start. He promises that's it. He reveals that footage of my proposal has been shared by a few people online, but says he's brushed off everyone's enquiries. He asks me who I've told.

I stare at him. 'No one!'

Hunter sits up in surprise. 'You got engaged and you've told no one?'

'I . . . no. I was waiting until we'd spoken. I can't believe you've told three people what we're doing.'

'Like I said, we shouldn't lie unless we have to.'

'I don't think we should tell the truth unless we have to.'

'Wait,' says Hunter. 'Are you seriously telling me there's no one you're planning to be honest with?'

I'm really not sure who I would tell. Most of my university friends stayed up north after we graduated, and although we're still in touch, I can easily go months without seeing them. I obviously feel strange about pretending I've fallen in love and got engaged, but I feel equally strange telling my friends I'm faking a marriage to get a job. I think I'll leave them out of it for now.

'I'm not trying to pressure you,' says Hunter. 'I mean, it's great if you think you can keep this a secret. I just don't want you to lose your mind.'

I smile to myself. It's not like I've got a track record of honesty.

'I think I'll be more comfortable keeping it secret.'

'Cool,' says Hunter. 'But there is one person I need you to be straight with.'

I frown.

'Me.'

I feel a jolt of fear without knowing why. 'You? About what?'

'Everything. If this is going to work, we need to be completely honest with each other. Is there anything you're hiding?'

Right at that moment, a ray of sunlight peeps through the clouds and shines through the kitchen window, catching Hunter's jade green eyes and setting them alight. I'm transported back to that moment in the fitting room when something sparked between us. Something real. Something mutual. But Hunter must know that. So the fact that I find him attractive doesn't count as something that I'm withholding from him.

I look him in the eye. 'No,' I say. 'No secrets.'

Before Hunter can say anymore, I hear a voice behind him. Someone is calling from the corridor, but it's not a request to enter. It's an announcement. A moment later, Doily walks in.

'Hunter,' she says, 'you won't believe this. Emma Thompson is in talks for the *Mrs Tiggywinkle* origin story.'

Doily is dressed in a red velvet coat and a turban with a diamond pin. She looks like a cross between a seaside pier fortune teller and a queen at her coronation.

Mr Peanut leaps up and starts pawing at her.

'And who's this handsome gentleman?' Doily asks.

'This is Max,' says Hunter. 'I told you about him.'

'I meant the dog.'

'Mr Peanut,' I say.

'Mr Peanut! Wonderful.' Doily bends down and pets him. 'A very warm energy. Does he have an agent?'

I trip over a response, but Doily bursts out laughing.

'I'm joking,' she says. 'I always ask that to dog owners, and they're always secretly keen. Do you remember what Olivia Colman was like with her labradoodle, Hunter?'

This woman is not disappointing. Two name drops within a minute.

'Is that OK?' asks Hunter.

'Is what OK?' asks Doily.

'If Mr Peanut moves in with Max.'

'Of course it is. *Tu perro es mi perro*, as they say.' She turns to me. 'Oh Max, I can't thank you enough for stepping into the breach like this. I'd have married him myself if he'd asked.'

I can't cope with how casual we're being about this.

'It happens all the time,' says Doily, reading my mind. 'Not many people know this, but in the nineties, Imelda Staunton was briefly married to a Kazakh warlord. Tax reasons. They never got busted, though they did face questions over why they married so fast.'

Hunter and I share a look. Another detail I hadn't considered.

'Don't worry,' says Doily, 'you can come up with a reason. Terminal illness of a close family member?'

'No,' I say instantly. That's a lie too far, even for me. We start brainstorming excuses, from bureaucratic necessity to inheritance benefits, but nothing feels credible.

'I know,' says Doily. 'Why don't we say I'm selling the house? I've had an offer I can't refuse, and it's always been Hunter's dream to get married here, so the wedding has to be soon. People will believe any old nonsense if it's romantic.'

Hunter pauses. 'We can't get married here. You're not licensed.'

'I certainly am,' says Doily. 'And ordained. It's a long story, and if you want the details, you can ask that bitch Julie Andrews. Ask her for my snood back while you're at it.'

She smiles at me, but my mouth is hanging open. I can just about cope with a fake wedding, but Julie Andrews slander might be where I draw the line.

'We can do the ceremony in the garden,' says Doily. 'Just let me know when you have an idea about the guest list.'

She heads back down the corridor, muttering to herself in excitement. I watch her go, not entirely convinced she wasn't an apparition.

Hunter smiles. 'You'll get used to her.'

I shake my head in amazement. 'I just . . . is she serious? Wedding? Guest list?'

Hunter's brow furrows. 'What were you expecting?'

'I don't know. I hadn't thought that far ahead, but I guess I imagined we might sneak off to a registry office.'

'We can't sneak anywhere. We need this to look real. Who do you want to invite?'

This hardly seems fair. Hunter already has Doily and two friends in on the scam. Since I've ruled out telling the truth to anyone I know, I'm going to have to invite people who believe it's real. I refuse to drag my friends into it. But my colleagues? They've met Hunter. They bought him as my boyfriend. Much as I hate the thought of Quentin and Flora at my wedding, that feels like the easiest solution.

'Great,' says Hunter. 'What about family?'

'What about them?'

'Mine are all in America, but it might look suspicious if none of yours are there.'

Oh god. I hadn't thought about what I'm going to say to my dad.

'I can speak to my dad.'

'And your mum?'

I see the moment it clicks. Over the years, I've received every possible reaction to this news, from pity to nervous laughter to the most deafening silence imaginable. If anything, Hunter's reaction is worse.

I sense he instinctively knows that I don't want his sympathy, but from that alone, I feel like he sees me more now. And it's terrifying.

'Sorry,' says Hunter. 'I didn't—'

'It's fine. It happened a while ago.'

I know that Hunter and I agreed to be honest with each other, but this is one topic I have no interest in getting into. I let out a yawn.

'God, the last few days have been exhausting. I might unpack.'

Hunter must know it's only an excuse, but he doesn't push.

'Sure,' he says. 'I'll let you get settled.'

There's a reason I don't tell people about my mum unless I can't avoid it. They always get weird, wanting to ask questions they know they shouldn't, shower me with hugs, or find some other way to treat me differently. I appreciate the fact that Hunter didn't pry.

I go to my room and slump down on the bed with Mr Peanut. It's a relief to be alone. It's not only because of that sting of grief just now. It's the promise I made to Hunter to be honest with him. I can avoid topics or I can walk away from a conversation. But we're living together. This is the first time I've ever lived with a guy I'm dating. And yes, it's fake, but it's still a proximity that I'm not used to. There are only so many places I can hide.

I'm realising that I didn't think through all the consequences before agreeing to move in. Lying to my colleagues isn't an issue, but lying to my dad? Letting him think his son has fallen in love when he hasn't? That's insane. But how can I tell him the truth? He'd worry himself sick. And I can't keep the whole thing a secret from him. He likes to send me newspaper clippings, so I'm going to have to tell him my change of address. There are going to be lies one way or another, so I might as well go all in with the big one.

Difficult as it may be, it's better than telling people the truth. There's a reason Hunter has told three people so easily and I haven't told anyone. He needs to stay in the country, which is something that people will sympathise with. I'm doing it for a job. It sounds so silly when you put it like that.

But I know one person who would understand. I open my suitcase and carefully pull out the book with my mum's letter folded inside. I've read it so many times in the past five years that it's in danger of falling apart, but I can't stop looking at it.

There's a world out there full of people ... never forget that.

I haven't forgotten, Mum. And I know there's only one way I can reach it. My mum knew better than anyone that if we want to escape the grey little lives that have been lined up for us in this country, we have to step out of our comfort zone. We have to take some risks. But it was easier to take those risks when I had her as my safety net. Without her, this is a leap into the unknown.

I look up and see Hunter standing in the doorway. I hurriedly fold the letter and snap the book shut.

'Hey,' he says. 'Just wanted to check you're OK.'

As I look at him, I don't feel remotely equipped to tell him everything that is running through my mind, and yet there is something about his open expression, his bracing honesty, that makes me not want to lie to his face. Maybe I can share just a hint of what I'm feeling.

'Yeah,' I say. 'Just nervous. Nervous, but excited.'

13

Hunter

What is it about being in the shower that makes it so easy for your mind to drift? I used to stay in the shower for hours when I was a teenager. I kept expecting my mom to flip and demand that I get out of there, but she never did. She's never been that bothered about what I'm doing. We talked on Sunday for the first time in weeks, and I could swear she was glad to hear I would be staying in London. No need to explain the details. Now she doesn't have to worry about me randomly showing up and judging whatever awful guy she's dating. At least we spoke. My dad is still drifting around Thailand, both of us using time zones as an excuse for why we never get around to catching up. You can't blame me for wanting to stay in this country. I really don't have any reason to go home.

Still, there have been plenty of times these past few days when I've had to pinch myself. I'm really doing this, huh? Getting married to a virtual stranger for a visa. If I'm caught, I'll be deported. I'll have a criminal record. I'll be seriously restricted from traveling in the future, let alone living and working where I want. It's no joke.

Just then, Max says something from outside the bathroom door.

'What?' I shout.

He replies, but I can't make it out. I turn off the shower, throw a towel around my waist and open the door. Max is standing there.

'What did you say?' I ask.

Max shuffles and averts his gaze. 'I said are you going to be much longer?'

'Not that long, no.'

'It's just . . . our guests will be here soon.'

Max and I decided that to create as realistic a wedding experience as possible, we should have a bachelor party. We settled on Ancient Greece as the theme. Since it's going to be stressful enough putting on a show at the wedding, we agreed that tonight, we would only invite the people who know the truth, namely Zosia, Thiago and Doily.

'I need the mirror to do my make-up,' I say to Max.

'That's fine.'

'What do you mean?'

'You can use the mirror.'

'What, while you're in here?'

Max shrugs. 'I don't mind.'

I'm immediately returned to that moment in the fitting room when we locked eyes in the mirror. The thought of doing my make-up while Max is in the shower is so thrilling to me that I can barely breathe. How is he acting like it's normal? But maybe it is for him. I can't drag Max down to my level. He doesn't deserve that.

'It's OK,' I say. 'There's a mirror in the hallway. I'm done. The bathroom's yours.'

I shut myself in my bedroom, feeling the blood rush to my cheeks. What's wrong with me? I didn't think living together would be this hard. With Rafferty it lost its spark so quickly. But that's the problem with this arrangement. We're not a real couple. We're not sleeping together. Which means that situations like sharing a bathroom are charged with curiosity and possibility. For me at least.

I try to put it out of my mind and focus on my costume. I've decided to keep it simple and dress as Hercules – a toga and sandals, a baseball bat as my club, and a bit of gold eyeshadow for fun. But as I knot my toga, I picture the scene that might have unfolded if I'd stayed in the bathroom like Max suggested. I'd be looking in the mirror, trying not to steal glances through the steam on the shower door. It doesn't help that I can hear Max humming as he lathers himself as if he doesn't have a care in the world.

Before I know it, I've dropped my toga to the ground and I'm lying naked on my bed, jerking off. I close my eyes and continue the scene in my mind with Max – how he would step out of the shower, butt naked and dripping wet. I'd let my towel fall to the floor.

We'd stand there for a moment, look each other up and down, then hold our gaze. I'd stroke Max's cheek, noticing a freckle I hadn't before. Then, as he looked at me with those innocent eyes, I wouldn't be able to resist any longer. Our lips would meet, Max's mouth damp with steam, his hair scented with shampoo. I'd reach down to grab hold of his dick and let him do the same to me, getting rock hard the moment his hand closed around me. We'd want to take it slowly, but we wouldn't be able to. Instead, we'd stand right there, kissing with ever more urgency as we worked ourselves to a climax.

That's all it takes for my fantasy to catch up with reality. I bite down to muffle my gasps and jet all over my chest.

Around 6 p.m., the bell rings and I answer the door to Zosia and Thiago dressed as Hades and Persephone. Zosia makes an imperious Hades, dressed in a black toga and clutching a skull as a prop, while Thiago has brought Persephone to life with a crown of flowers and a white toga that flows around him as he bounds up and embraces me.

'I cannot believe this!' squeals Thiago.

'I cannot believe this,' drolls Zosia.

Usually when Zosia and Thiago visit, we stick to my part of the house, but tonight, Doily has offered to host. Her living room is a jungle of clashing botanical prints, vintage velvet cushions, and antique armchairs. On the sideboard, she has left out the champagne glasses that were gifted to her grandfather by the Duke of Rutland. The bookshelves spill with ivy and ferns, and there's a tall rubber plant in one corner. Piles of scripts and Nancy Mitford novels are spread across her reading desk, and fairy lights hang over a Tiffany-style lamp. On the mantelpiece, for some reason, is Jacques Cousteau's honorary BAFTA.

'I can't wait to meet this woman,' says Thiago.

'You've met her before,' I say. 'At the Oliviers.'

'For like two seconds. We were both drunk. I cried. Can't remember why.'

'I'm more interested in meeting the husband,' says Zosia.

Thiago shrieks in excitement. Zosia reclines on the chaise longue.

'Come on then,' she says. 'Tell us everything.'

I pour us each a glass of champagne and fill them in. The three of us have a WhatsApp group that is more or less a triple stream of consciousness, so they're already up to date on the basics. I tell them I've discovered there's no way I can pretend to be even a trainee orthodontist without fully faking degree certificates and so on. An assistant orthodontist, however, is a viable alternative, and we'll just have to gaslight anyone who heard the original story. I've already signed up for an online course for dental assistants. That's the type of character research I genuinely enjoy, and I'm already confident enough to show off my knowledge of radiography equipment and dental dams. But what I really want to talk about is Max. Thiago shares so many details of his sex life with us that it's like we have front row seats, but I don't feel like telling my friends I just jerked off to the thought of Max. Instead, I talk about the weirdness of domesticity with someone I'm not sleeping with.

'Yet,' says Thiago.

I roll my eyes and laugh.

'It's not against the rules,' Thiago says.

'He's not exactly my type.'

Zosia laughs out loud.

'What?' I say.

'You love them.'

'Who?'

'Posh little English boys.'

'He's not posh.'

'Fine, but you know the kind. Rabbit in the headlights, wouldn't say boo to a goose. Am I right or am I right?'

She knows me too well. There have been more than a few like Max since I moved to London, but none who I've dated seriously, let alone moved in with.

'Touché,' I say. 'But that's fine for a bit of fun. This is different. I'm scared I'm going to ruin him.'

Zosia laughs again. 'Hunter, I love you. Do you think actual fuck boys go around worrying they're going to ruin the guys they sleep with? Did Rafferty ever worry about that?'

It's a fair point.

'I get it,' says Zosia. 'But I really don't think you have to worry. Anyway, he agreed to this marriage. How innocent can he be?'

Not long afterwards, the door is nudged open. I'm expecting it to be Max, but it's Mr Peanut who greets us. He has been transformed into Cerberus, the three-headed dog, courtesy of a DIY collar and some Furbies, making him the cutest guardian of the underworld I've ever seen. Mr Peanut is swiftly followed by Max, who has dressed as Hermes, wearing a toga, a streak of silver paint along each cheekbone, and a pair of wings that Doily rescued from an all-male production of Peter Pan.

'You must be Max,' says Thiago.

'How do I look?' Max asks nervously.

As Thiago leaps up to compliment his outfit, Zosia turns to me.

'I get it now,' she says with a grin. 'You keep your hands off this angel.'

Soon after that, we are joined by Doily, who has dressed as Helen of Troy, her usual eccentric ensembles replaced by the simplest white dress and a single gold cuff. Zosia and Thiago swarm around her, as Doily cracks open a bottle of Pol Roger and starts telling them how much James Corden is getting paid for the *Humpty Dumpty* miniseries.

Max throws himself into the conversation, but I can't relax, not with Zosia's comment ringing in my ears. I know she was only joking, but I'm worried I've dragged Max into a scheme that he's not prepared for. Tonight is a night off, but whenever we're out in public, we're going to have to pretend. We're going to have to lie to everyone we know. I'm really not sure Max is ready. I'm an actor. I don't have many friends or any family in the country. I'm lost in these thoughts when I look up and see Max approaching me.

'Are you OK?' he asks.

I smile at him. 'Just processing everything.'

'Fair,' says Max. 'But come on. Your friends are here.'

He leads me over to the group, and the moment we get there, Thiago claps his hands in excitement. 'Right, girlies. Who wants to play a game?'

Doily suggests every parlour game she can think of. She succeeds in convincing us all to play the Minister's

Cat, on the grounds that it was the highlight of a turbulent Hogmanay she spent at Sean Connery's castle, but the plan is abandoned because Doily can't remember the rules.

Thiago smiles. 'I was thinking more like . . . truth or dare.'

There's a collective *ooh*. No one can resist a good game of truth or dare.

'Fine,' says Doily. 'But can we have a no filming rule? I've never lived down that footage of me scissoring Prunella Scales.'

'No phones,' says Zosia. 'Done.'

Thiago kicks the game off. He chooses truth, and is asked about the craziest place he's ever had sex. He proceeds to list six, including a helipad and backstage at the Balsamic Vinegar Awards. Zosia also picks truth, and she's asked to tell us the worst thing she's ever done. She tells the story of psychologically manipulating her school bully to the point that the bully became convinced that Zosia was a witch. Doily opts for dare, so Thiago dares her to remove her underwear without leaving the room. Doily announces that she's not wearing any, prompting the biggest cheer so far. Now it's my turn.

'Truth,' I declare.

'Boring!' cries Thiago.

'I don't care. I'm not doing any of your dares.'

The others get into a huddle and discuss what to ask me. As always in these games, it takes a while for them to hit on anything that feels juicy without being completely inappropriate, but eventually a smile spreads across Thiago's face.

'What's Max's best feature?' he asks me.

Everyone whoops, delighted at anything remotely suggestive. I look over at Max. How am I supposed to pick? There's his chest hair, which is peeking out of his toga invitingly. Or his thighs. His thighs are great. But really his best feature is – what would you call it? His essence. His aura. His innocence.

Except that as I hold his gaze, I could swear there's a cheeky glint in his eye, almost as if he wants to be led astray. Whether it's that or the fact that I'm on my second glass of champagne, I turn to the others with a smile.

'I can't say yet. I haven't seen all of him.'

My answer draws a scandalised whoop, even if it's technically a cop-out. Max blushes, but I can tell he enjoyed that. I feel a rush of blood between my legs and rapidly cross them. This toga doesn't leave much to the imagination.

Thankfully, it's now Max's turn.

'Dare,' he declares without hesitation.

Everyone cheers in approval. We launch into a frenzied discussion of what we could get him to do. As Thiago and Zosia whisper to each other, I'm secretly hoping they're going to ask Max and me to retire to a darkened cupboard, but then Doily pipes up.

'I've got it. This is perfect.'

She turns to Max with a wicked grin. 'I dare you to steal Elton John's gnome.'

Max stares at her. 'His what?'

'His gnome.'

'Elton John has a gnome?'

'He's very proud of it. It's from when he did the soundtrack to *Gnomeo & Juliet*. Awful film. Anyway, Elton loves that gnome. I've been meaning to steal it for years.'

When asked for an explanation, Doily embarks on a lengthy story that begins in the 1980s, backstage at a Wham! show, and ends with a client of hers going up for a Timon and Pumba spin-off series that never ended up happening. It's debatable how much of this saga Elton John is personally responsible for, but the important part is that Doily has long had a vendetta against him and has chosen tonight to act on it.

Or rather, for Max to act on it.

'That's not fair,' I protest. 'He could get in trouble.'

'I'm up for it!' Max declares.

'I'm not,' says Thiago. 'Where the fuck does he even live?'

'We don't all have to go,' says Doily. 'It's Max's dare.'

'We can't make him go on his own,' I insist.

'I agree,' says Doily with a smile. 'Why don't you go with him?'

I'm pretty sure this has been engineered so Max and I can head off on a mission together. I wouldn't put it past any of them. Doily gives us directions to Elton's house in West London, where the gnome is located. She claims Elton is likely to be at his mansion in the countryside and it should be a simple smash and grab, but as Max and I jump into a cab, all I can think about is all the ways this could go wrong. I was determined not to corrupt Max, and now we're in a situation where we could legitimately get caught and arrested, our faces plastered across the tabloids, our reputations down the drain, our plan in ruins.

And then there's the devil on my shoulder. The one who's drawn to danger. Who seeks it out. Who thinks Max might be able to see up my toga as I sit opposite him in the cab. Who secretly hopes he can. But this isn't about me. I might take risks sometimes, but only because I'm prepared for the worst. I'm not sure Max is like that. I get the impression he always thinks everything is going to work out. It makes me feel like I need to protect him.

The house is on a street of enormous detached mansions. If this was America, it would be a gated community, but here you can walk right up to them. Elton's house is the largest of all, a vast double-fronted home with a path down one side. Max and I share a look, then sneak down it. My heart is pounding.

The garden is filled with manicured hedges and stone statues. It's cloaked in shadows, but light is spilling from the house. We look up, and it's apparent that Elton is not only home, but hosting a dinner party.

'Fuck,' I mutter under my breath.

We peek inside, momentarily transfixed by what appears to be a who's who of the British creative industries. Doily would be having a field day. I actually can't name half of these people, but they're the type who have third billing in those *Best Exotic Jersey Potato* films that Doily claims can't get funding these days, which I didn't realise was a bad thing. Tonight, they're all dressed in Hawaiian shirts and sipping pina coladas.

I turn to Max, but his sights are on the garden. He gasps, then gestures at a flowerbed. There, lit by moonlight, is a diminutive garden gnome. It hits me what we're about to do. If we get caught, we'll be dragged to the police station, right at the moment we're trying to stay under the radar. This whole charade could come crashing down.

'Wait,' I say to Max.

He turns back, frowning.

'I really don't think it's worth it. It's too risky.'

'It's a dare,' says Max. 'That's the point.'

If it was just me, I wouldn't hesitate. But I can't do this to Max. I can't deal with his lack of fear.

'Max, I'm worried.'

'It's only a gnome.'

'It's not about the gnome.'

Max looks confused. I'm not sure how much of this I really want to share, but we did agree to be honest with each other. I take a deep breath.

'I'm worried about what we're doing. Not tonight. The whole plan. I know it was my idea, but we're breaking the law. It could end badly.'

'We've talked it through,' says Max.

'Yes, but you're so convinced it's all going to work out. Life's not like that.'

Max laughs. 'Who do you think I am, Hunter?'

I don't know how to respond.

'I'm not eight years old,' says Max. 'My mum is dead. I've worked with countries who are at war with each other. I know bad things happen. I just don't let it rule my life.'

His eyes are ablaze. 'At some point, which we don't get to choose, it all just stops. None of this means any-thing. So the only meaning I have ever been able to find is in trying to enjoy it while we can.'

I look at Max uncertainly. 'And that includes stealing Elton John's gnome?'

'Especially that.'

'Why risk it?'

'For the story. For the memory. For the hell of it. For the people who aren't alive to do it with you. And because if you had the chance, why *wouldn't* you steal Elton John's gnome?'

I feel like I know Max better from this one conver-sation than from everything else we've discussed since we met.

'You are going to be the death of me,' I say.

Max grins. 'I thought you were meant to be the bad influence.'

I shake my head in disbelief. 'We're really doing this?'

When Max proposed to me on stage, it was a shot in the dark. Now the full extent of what we're doing has been dragged into the spotlight. But Max doesn't flinch.

He takes my hand. 'If we go down, we go down together.'

I feel a rush of something I haven't felt in a very long time. Sure, Doily and my friends have my back, but the idea that my partner does too, even my fake partner – that's new. It's a feeling so unnerving that I can't look Max in the eye.

Thankfully, his mind is on the prize. He gives me one last nod of confirmation, then, still holding hands, we turn towards the gnome and run.

The next few moments are a blur. A security light goes off, but we make it away from the house before anyone sees us. We race around the corner and hail a cab. Before I know it, we're hurtling back towards home with Elton John's gnome nestled in Max's lap.

As we zoom over Vauxhall Bridge, the city lights speed past us. Maybe for the first time since moving to London, my world feels alive with possibility. Max might not be my real fiancé. He might not be my soulmate. But I think I've found my new partner in crime.

14

Max

I should steal from celebrities more often. It's a remarkably guilt-free exercise, although in the days since, I've been paranoid every time the doorbell rings. What we got out of that night was so much more than a gnome. I had the sense when I met Hunter that he didn't respect me. Since the bachelor party, that's changed. I feel like we're equals. As the wedding has come together, we've actually listened to each other's opinions. Sometimes he's freaked out and I've had to calm him, other times, I've been unreasonably optimistic, and he's reeled me in. It's all been surprisingly harmonious, apart from one little detail.

I've got a crush on him.

Who can blame me? The guy is ridiculously sexy. When I suggested I'd be fine sharing a bathroom, I was trying to play it cool, but obviously I secretly liked the idea. He barely made an effort with his Hercules costume, and he still looked incredible. I'm glad I didn't have to answer that question about what his best feature is, although based on what I glimpsed in the fitting room, I suspect it may be a part of him I've yet to see.

Yet. That's a crazy thing to contemplate, but I'm riffing off the answer Hunter gave.

I can't say yet. I haven't seen all of him.

That was the hottest possible way he could have answered that question. He must have known what he was doing.

The thought of crossing that line with him is terrifying. Yes, it would be unimaginably hot, but I don't know if I could cope. I don't know if I'd measure up. Hunter is so bold and sure of himself that the idea of going to bed with him, taking off all our clothes together, being that vulnerable . . . I'm not sure I'd ever recover. But what am I thinking? Why would we let things get that complicated? It's never going to happen. A guy who looks like Hunter can have his pick of men. Why would he go for someone who has no idea what he's doing? It was probably just a throwaway comment. I need to forget about it.

Today at least, I'll have enough on my plate. We told our guests to arrive for drinks at noon, but at 9 a.m. sharp, my dad messages to say he's outside. I hurry out front as he emerges from his pristine Skoda Octavia. It looks brand new, and you'd never know it's a two-year-old model he purchased because he calculated that was the ideal sweet spot between depreciation and performance.

'Max,' says my dad. 'I can't believe it.'

Telling my dad I was getting married was the worst part of this whole experience. I ran over all the reasons it was better this way, but nothing could take away from how weird it felt. He didn't say much in response, because he never does, but even over the phone, I could tell he was emotional. I've been dreading seeing him, but my first reaction isn't guilt. It's sadness.

Maybe it's because he's aged. His grey hair is thinning, and his face is drawn into wary lines, like he's not quite sure where to put himself. His suit doesn't fit very well, but he wears it with stubborn dignity. He looks better rested than the last time I saw him, since he's now settled into retirement. But without that purpose that comes from work, there's something missing behind his eyes – direction, maybe. Or confidence.

Then it hits me – the last time I saw my dad in a suit, we were burying my mum.

It knocks the breath out of me. My dad gives me a puzzled look.

'Are you all right?'

'Yeah, I just . . . wasn't expecting you this early.'

Now that I'm close, I can see he's in a weird mood too, possibly for the same reason.

'Max,' he says, then hesitates as if he's not sure what he wants to say. 'I know this is going to be an emotional day. But I just . . .' His voice breaks. 'Your mum would be happy.'

Oh Jesus. I wasn't ready for that. I nod and bite down hard. As I lead my dad inside, he starts mumbling about how he made good time thanks to the completion of the road works near Dorking and the removal of the temporary lights at the M25 junction. But the damage has been done. I've been telling myself my mum would approve of this plan, but would she approve of me lying to my dad? I try to put it out of my mind as I show him into the flat, offer him a seat on the sofa, and go to boil the kettle. Then I hear footsteps.

I hadn't prepared myself for seeing Hunter in his wedding suit. The dusky blue is accented with an iridescent silk pocket square, patterned with tiny sea creatures and presumably borrowed from Doily. His hair is gelled, making him look like the lead in a 1950s Neapolitan melodrama.

Hunter walks up to my dad and shakes his hand. I don't think I can take any more sincerity. My dad starts fiddling with his cuffs, and I feel like he's about to burst into tears and welcome Hunter to the family.

'Right,' says my dad. 'Shall we get on with the pre-nup?'

I'm momentarily speechless. 'What?'

'I emailed you about it,' says my dad.

'No you didn't.'

'Yes I did. 12.42 p.m. on Wednesday.'

My dad doesn't make mistakes about things like this. He frowns. 'Don't tell me you were planning to get married without a pre-nup?'

I stare at him. 'What are you talking about, Dad? Pre-nups are for millionaires.'

'No they're not. Anyone can get a pre-nup.'

'No one I know gets a pre-nup. I don't have any assets.'

'Well, I do. Not a lot, but there's something for a rainy day, plus I own a house. When I die, it'll be yours. We need to protect that.' He turns to Hunter. 'What about you, lad?'

'What about me?' Hunter asks. He seems more amused than offended.

'Do you have any assets?'

'No. I wish.'

'What about your parents?'

'I mean . . . they both have homes, but I'm not worried that Max is going to put a claim on my mom's heavily mortgaged duplex in Rhode Island.'

My dad looks doubtful. 'Do they have a will?'

'Er . . . I don't know.'

'Do you want to check with them?'

'No need,' says Hunter. 'I'm happy to sign a pre-nup.'

'No!' I exclaim. 'We don't have to buy into this madness.'

'It's not madness,' says my dad. 'You never know what's around the corner.'

That stops me short. It's a sentiment that carries a lot of weight in our family.

'I've had it drawn up by a lawyer,' says my dad. 'All you two need to do is sign.'

He hands over the document as if we're going to do it then and there.

'Dad,' I protest. 'Can I read it first?'

'You've had three days to read it.'

'I thought we established—'

'Ah yes. Well, go ahead.'

Hunter stands over my shoulder as we flick through the document. I have to admit, everything it says sounds very sensible. Then I spot a potential roadblock. I look up at my dad.

'We need a witness. And it can't be you.'

Doily's garden is looking even more enchanting than usual. Flower beds of lavender and rosemary spill into gravel paths beneath ancient fig trees and a rusted sundial on the lawn. Her cherry tree is in full bloom, and she's draped the pergola with strings of lace and bunting that might have last fluttered at a fete in the eighties. Rows of mismatched vintage chairs form a wonky semicircle around a makeshift aisle. Doily is wearing a gardening apron and placing bunches of wildflowers into an assortment of random vases and pots. She turns to us.

'I'm having to substitute cornflowers for meadowsweet,' Doily says gravely. 'Don't tell Lesley Manville or I'll never hear the end of it.'

I smile. 'Your secret's safe with me.' I step back and gesture at my dad. 'Doily, this is my dad, Alan.'

Doily surveys him with suspicion.

'They're signing a pre-nup,' my dad announces stiffly. 'We need a witness.'

'Absolutely not,' says Doily. 'I hate those things.'

My dad frowns. 'Pre-nups get a bad rap, but—'

'Not pre-nups,' says Doily. 'Contracts.'

I stare at Doily. 'You hate contracts?'

'Horrible concept.'

'But . . . you're an agent.'

'That's why I hate them. Whatever happened to a good old-fashioned gentlemen's agreement? I can't tell you the number of problems that contracts have caused me. I realised early on that they were something to avoid wherever possible. I've done well enough for myself, haven't I?'

She gestures around as if she's claiming that the house and garden are the spoils of her agenting career when in fact they're the result of her great-great-grandfather inventing a cheap way to manufacture custard.

'I'm sure you've done very well for yourself,' says my dad, 'but I spent thirty years as an air traffic controller, and we had to plan for every eventuality.'

Doily and my dad are a match made in hell. Both of them are convinced their careers have been the making of them, and neither of them have any ability to see beyond their own perspectives. I turn to my dad. 'Why don't you walk Doily through the contract so she knows what she's actually witnessing? If she has any issues, I'm sure we can find someone else to do it.'

Miraculously, Doily agrees to this. Hunter and I head back to our flat to finish getting ready. As soon as we're alone, I turn to Hunter with an apologetic look.

'I hope you weren't expecting me to have a normal dad.'

Hunter laughs. 'I actually think he's smart. We should have thought of this.'

I can't help loving how cool he's being about this. It would be easy for him to take offence. But that's not Hunter's style.

He peers at me. 'How about you, are you OK?'

I frown. 'Why wouldn't I be OK?'

'You just had to lie to your dad's face. And we're about to stand in front of a bunch of other people who know you and lie to them.'

I could be honest. I could tell Hunter how the guilt is flickering at the edges of my mind and threatening to catch fire. But I feel like if I do that, there will be no going back. The only way to keep it in check is by not giving voice to it. I look Hunter dead in the eye.

'I'm fine. Seriously. You don't have to worry about me.'

* * *

When I go to check on my dad and Doily, she's explaining how contract stipulations have kept Celia Imrie's *Mad Madam Mim* prequel in development hell for the better part of a decade, while my dad counters with practical solutions that could solve everything. That should keep them both occupied for a while. I retreat to my room to finish getting dressed, and before I know it, our guests start to arrive.

Hunter and I managed to come up with a few more people to make it look a bit like a normal wedding without having to drag in anyone I'd rather not involve. There's my ex-housemate Gunter, who quite literally owes me for a utility bill from 2017. There's a woman I met at a conference in Birmingham who has been incessantly messaging me on LinkedIn ever since, suggesting we hang out, who I have finally been able to oblige. There's a personal trainer who I had one free trial session with then never went back, but who still leaves motivational comments on all my social media posts. All these people give the impression of being my friends, while allowing me to keep my real friends, or at least what's left of them, safely out of the picture.

In fact, as I see this group of disparate people, I wonder why I didn't come up with a few more random stragglers to fill up spots at the wedding instead of inviting the quartet who I am looking at on the far side of the garden. Too late now. I take a deep breath, then cross over to say hello to Quentin, Flora, Nessie and Mariam.

'Max!' they call in unison.

I greet them one by one and take them in. You can tell that Quentin and Flora are seasoned wedding guests.

Quentin is scanning the gathering, trying to figure out who's worth talking to and where the canapés are located, while Flora looks less enthusiastic but ready to play the role that's expected of her. Mariam is wearing that same brown pantsuit, and Nessie . . . holy shit.

'Oh wow,' I say. 'You did it.'

Nessie grins. She did it. She got the perm. It looks awful. Worse than I feared, if that's possible. The hair has gained volume, but not in a good way, clinging to her head like a helmet. She has gained about twenty years and thirty pounds. I can confidently say this is the biggest glow down I've ever seen.

'What do you think?' Nessie asks.

I glance at my colleagues, but they all stay quiet. What do I think about the fact that Nessie has got a terrible perm that I explicitly encouraged? I don't think my real opinion has any right to be aired. It's hardly the biggest lie I'll tell today.

'I love it, Nessie. It's incredible.'

Nessie places a hand on her heart. 'That means a lot, Max.'

I can't look her in the eye.

'We're so honoured you invited us,' says Mariam. 'This is very exclusive.'

Was that a pointed comment? It's hard to tell.

'It's a last-minute thing before Doily sells the house,' I say. 'This place means so much to Edwin. And he means so much to me.'

'So who else is here?' asks Quentin.

I glance over at the man who gave me a single free personal training session four years ago, who is deep in conversation with the man who owes me £86 for a gas bill.

'London friends, mainly,' I say casually. 'And my dad.'

'Nice,' says Quentin. 'So are you thinking of doing a bigger thing at a later date?'

'Potentially.'

I'm trying to stick to Hunter's rules and not lie any more than necessary. If it was up to me, I would start over-compensating and commit myself to a ceremony for two hundred people in Manchester Town Hall.

'Don't bother,' says Flora. 'I don't know why people blow all their savings on a wedding. This is much more sensible.'

As far as I can tell, she means it. In fact, as I leave my colleagues and go to greet the rest of the guests, I feel bad about how much they are all buying into this. Quentin may have his suspicions, but everyone else appears to be completely convinced by what we're doing. Yes, it's a little crazy of us, but love makes people crazy, and weddings make everyone sentimental. Shit – now I'm really feeling guilty.

I head over and start shovelling down canapés. After a while, Hunter crosses over to me.

'Max, are you OK?'

'Of course I am.'

'What do you mean of course? Anyone would be stressed by this.'

'Not me.'

I gobble down another canapé.

'Max, I'm serious. You helped me the other night when I needed it. I'm happy to do the same for you.'

I force a smile.

'That's kind of you. But I don't need it.'

Before Hunter can press further, Doily invites everyone to gather on the semi-circle of chairs – everyone aside from Mr Peanut, who has located something of immense importance beneath a lavender bush. Someone has reserved a seat for Elton John's gnome, which feels like the kind of bravado that's going to come back to bite us, but I have to admit it's also quite funny. At least, it would be, if my heart wasn't pounding out of my chest.

This is really happening.

Hunter and I decided against walking down the aisle, so we go and stand in front of the pergola that is acting as an altar while everyone takes their seats. In any case, the star of the show is Doily. She's dressed low-key by her standards, wearing a dove-grey silk shirt dress with a soft vintage shawl and a wide-brimmed straw hat.

'Quick bit of housekeeping,' says Doily. 'Phones off, unless you're expecting an urgent call from an ambassador or a midwife. Loos are through the French doors and to the left – don't open the door with the pink ribbon. Please only biodegradable confetti, out of respect for the birds. The conservatory has been designated as a quiet zone, should anyone feel faint or overcome by emotion. Finally, and most importantly, in about fifteen minutes, a brass band will pass the garden gate en route to Dulwich. Do *not* acknowledge them.'

You can't say she's not keeping our guests entertained. I find myself desperately relieved any time Doily draws attention to herself and away from me. I didn't anticipate feeling this guilty. Even my one-time personal trainer looks swept up by the occasion. I'm desperate for this to be over.

But Hunter and I came up with all sorts of ways to make it feel like a real wedding. Mariam reads an extract from *All's Well That Ends Well* that goes on forever. Zosia and Thiago sing an a cappella version of 'It's Raining Men', slowed down in a way that is meant to be sultry, but makes it feel like a funeral march. Throughout all of this, my dad won't stop taking photos.

'Right,' says Doily. 'Now for the legal part.'

I feel a drop of sweat trickle down my cheek. My armpits are damp and my throat is dry. We're about to get married. Legally married. If I felt sick before, I now feel like I'm going to collapse. Doily invites Hunter to say his vows.

'Max,' says Hunter. 'Before we met, my love life was a disaster. My last relationship ended so badly I had to move continents.'

This prompts a sympathetic laugh.

'I stopped expecting anything,' Hunter continues. 'I thought romance novels belonged in the science fiction section.' He pauses for effect. 'Then you walked in.'

People are hanging on his every word. He really is a flawless actor.

'You see life like a movie where you're the hero,' Hunter continues. 'Where everything always works out. And the plot twist I never saw coming—' He looks at me, open-hearted. 'Is that I get to be your co-star.'

The crowd aahs. My dad sniffs and swallows hard. This is a man who didn't cry at his own wife's funeral. But I'm not far behind him. My eyes are locked on Hunter, and I'm feeling every word he says as if he means it. It's honestly kind of disorienting.

'Max, I would call you my golden retriever, but I wouldn't want to upset Mr Peanut.'

Everyone chuckles and looks over at Mr Peanut, who is gleefully chewing on an old croquet ball. Hunter turns back to me, smiling.

'You're my sunlight. My source of warmth. And if you ever see me squint when I'm looking at you, it's not only because I'm secretly mapping your freckles like they're the Milky Way. It's because my eyes are still adjusting to your brightness.'

There's an audible sigh from the audience.

'Lovely,' says Doily. 'Max?'

My heart drops like a stone. How can I match that? How is anyone going to believe me? I thought I could do this, but now that the moment has arrived, I feel like I'm going to faint. I stagger around the back of the pergola and fall to a crouching position. I hear people gasp, but I can't look back. Hunter follows me round.

'Max,' he says, rubbing my back. 'What's the matter?'

He looks at me like he's done something wrong. His only crime was being so convincing that it's brought home the gravity of what we're doing.

Will I ever get to exchange vows like that with someone I truly love? If I do meet someone, I can't not tell them about Hunter. But at what point do I tell them? What will they think of me? Will anyone honestly want to get involved with someone who treats love and marriage this casually, lying in front of friends and family? Or am I doomed to taste only a fake version of true love, never the real thing?

Hunter gives me a sympathetic look. 'Tell me what's going on, Max.'

'I can't do it.'

Hunter frowns. 'You want to call this off? Because we can.'

Simply hearing him say it fills me with relief. He's on my side. In fact, knowing that allows my fear to clear a little. I don't want to pull out. But I also don't want to rub what we're doing in people's faces.

'No, I want to do this. But I don't think I can stand up there and tell them I love you.'

Hunter looks surprised, but he holds steady.

'You don't have to use those words. I didn't.'

'You nailed it. Did it not feel weird to you?'

'Not really.'

'Why not?'

'Because, Max, it wasn't all lies.'

It hits me like a freight train. No wonder I bought it. He was speaking from the heart. There's no time to process what this means, but as I look at him, belief runs through me. I have no idea where the words are going to come from, but I feel like I can do it.

Hunter takes me by the hand, and we head back out. There's an audible sigh of relief from the crowd as we emerge and Hunter explains that it was simply a case of nerves. Doily invites me to say my vows. I take a deep breath.

'Today is a weird day,' I say. 'And I think we all know why.'

Hunter shoots me a look, but he needn't worry – I'm not going to be *that* honest.

'It's because my mum isn't here.'

It's only as I say it that it hits me how true that is.

'She would have loved today. She would have loved the chaos. The spontaneity. But most of all, she would have loved Hunt— I mean, Edwin.'

Shit. That was close. But only because there was not a word of a lie there.

Hunter nods at me, urging me on.

'And yes, it hurts not to be able to share this with her. But there's one thing that's getting me through it, and that's the man opposite me. Even in the short time I've known him, he's changed me. He holds me to account. He never indulges me. He doesn't let me put any walls up. He sees the real me.'

Hunter wipes away a tear. I'm not even sure he's acting. He was right – the truth is enough. That's the key to selling this relationship. It isn't real love. Our destinies will send us in different directions. But there's something real at the heart of it.

'Gosh,' says Doily with a tearful smile. 'That was beautiful.'

She proceeds with the marriage vows. Thankfully, the legal part of the marriage is the paperwork, so we can get away with calling Hunter Edwin in the ceremony. Before I know it, Doily has declared us husband and husband.

'You may now kiss.'

My breath catches. I forgot about this part. It has all the potential to be awkward. Not because we're faking it, but because of the way I just laid myself bare.

I hold Hunter's gaze, wondering if he's as wrapped up in the moment as I am. Can he separate fact from fiction? Because I no longer can.

I close my eyes and lean in. The first thing I sense is the woody scent of his aftershave. Then his breath, warm and minty, which sends a shiver down my spine. Finally, his lips find mine, softer than I was expecting, just the gentlest touch. Heat surges through me.

I reach up and put my hand on his cheek as if to stabilise myself. We're barely touching, but my knees have gone loose and my pulse is racing, sending a rush of blood to my head. I feel like if we kiss any harder, it will burn straight through me, unleashing a passion we won't be able to contain.

But I also don't want it to end. The taste of him is addictive. This was meant to be a kiss for the cameras, yet it feels like the start of something dangerous and exciting.

Or is it just me?

Applause rises around us, and I open my eyes. Hunter's mouth curves into a smile, and I find myself smiling too. It's not just relief, but gratitude, a dash of conspiracy, a hint of affection. More to the point, it feels utterly genuine on both our parts.

For the first time since we met, we're not faking anything.

15

Hunter

I was in high school the first time I had to kiss someone on stage. We did it every night for a week in front of my parents and the whole school. It was so convincing that people asked if we were dating. I had to do it again in college, and most recently in a short film that I shot with friends in Brooklyn. Each time, whether I felt zero attraction to my scene partner or something more, I was able to lock in and inhabit the character. If there was one part of the wedding I thought I was prepared for, it was the kiss.

I was wrong.

Maybe that was inevitable. After the episodes in the fitting room and the bathroom, the spark between me and Max has been threatening to catch fire. Still, I went into the kiss expecting to be in command. I wasn't. The moment we kissed, I felt like I was losing control. Like if I didn't cut it short, I would lose myself entirely. I can't speak for Max, but if we hadn't been standing up there in front of everyone, I would have gone on for longer.

Much longer.

Now the sun is dipping below the horizon, casting the garden in long shadows and golden light, and I can't take my eyes off Max. The anxieties of the day have given way to something much more languid. At one point, Doily disappears into the kitchen and emerges with a spread of slow-roasted vegetables and salads. Everyone gathers round the garden table, naturally saving the head seat for Elton John's gnome. Since we're not really doing things traditionally, Max and I end up opposite each other. As wine is poured and the food is served, unexpected pairings emerge. Doily and Quentin share a long rant about the declining quality of butter, while Flora and Nessie rank the different casts of *Hamilton*. Max remains in my line of sight throughout. We spend most of the meal distracted by our guests, but as we reach dessert, Max looks up and locks eyes with me right as I take a bite of lavender crème brûlée. The sensations blur into each other and the kiss comes flooding back to me. I can't look away.

Soon after that, someone throws on some Whitney Houston, and everyone leaps up to hit the dance floor. I dance with Thiago, with Flora, with some guy who keeps giving me tips on how to maximise my deltoids, but Max and I keep looking each other's way and exchanging little smiles or nods. As it nears midnight, someone cues up 'Wonderful Tonight' and declares it the final song. Max and I step towards each other for our first dance.

I'm glad we didn't make more of a thing of this. I much prefer it this way, when the garden is dark, and everyone else is swaying alongside us. As I place my arms around Max, I smell his aftershave, the wine on his breath, the beads of sweat on his neck. I feel a rush of desire so intense that I might fall over if I wasn't clinging to him so tightly.

I mustn't get over-excited. This is not the first time I've had a crush on a scene partner. It happened during a production of *Spring Awakening* in college, in a role where our characters didn't kiss or even interact that much. But that only added to the longing. The crush ended soon after the production did because it wasn't real. It's so easy to get confused when you're acting, especially when you're as committed to the performance as I am. So the fact that I'm longing for Max more than ever doesn't mean anything. It's simply me doing what I've been asked to do. Still, I've had enough wine that I can admit that this feels good. A little too good, if I'm honest.

'Are you OK?' Max asks.

I snap back to attention. 'Yeah. All good.'

Max looks unconvinced. 'You were a million miles away.'

I give him a soothing smile. 'Just thinking about a show I was once in.'

As I hold his gaze, the melody of one of my solos rises in my throat. I sing a line or two, quiet enough that only Max can hear.

Max gulps. 'You know, you're a very convincing performer.'

I smile as we continue to sway to the beat. There's not a single part of me that is acting in this moment, but I'm not going to admit that.

'Thanks,' I say. 'Have you ever acted?'

Max thinks back. 'I played a sheepdog in my primary school nativity play. But I don't think I'm very good at acting.'

'Really?'

'No. I give too much away.'

As I look at Max, I can't help but smile in recognition. I feel like I can see every single one of his thoughts. The little crush he has on me. The way it makes him nervous and excited at once. But maybe that's wishful thinking. In any case, his performance today has been exemplary. I lean in and whisper into his ear.

'You were perfect today. I believed every second.'

I don't notice when our last guest leaves. I must be more drunk than I realised. All I know is that, at some point, it's very late and only the two of us are left. As we head inside, I have every intention of going to bed. Instead, I collapse onto the sofa in the living room. I look up and see that Max has joined me.

I couldn't tell you why we start to giggle. Relief, I guess. Disbelief. Pure pleasure. What starts out as giggles soon becomes full-chested laughter. Eventually, it dies down. Max smiles at me.

'We did it.'

'We sure did.'

I sit up and look at him earnestly. 'Seriously though, how did you find today?'

Max hesitates. 'Harder than I thought. But it got better. I meant what I said in our vows. I couldn't have done it without you.'

I'm suddenly very aware of how close we are sitting. I swallow hard.

'That's what I'm here for.'

It feels strange to say it. With Rafferty, I never had any sense that we were there to support each other.

I was his assistant, his mascot, his accessory, while he was what – my keeper? He cast me in my first role and paid my rent, so I definitely benefitted from our arrangement. In many ways, my deal with Max is just as mutually beneficial. But not even I can pretend that it's as cynical.

'Damn,' says Max, shaking his head in disbelief. 'We actually got married.'

'Yep,' I say.

Our legs are touching and our eyes are still locked.

Max smiles. 'Technically, I could apply for an annulment.'

I laugh. 'We're not in Vegas.'

'Yeah,' says Max, 'but there are still circumstances where you can get out of it.'

I raise an eyebrow. 'Are you planning to get out of it?'

'No, I just mean . . .' Max trails off. 'Obviously we haven't, you know . . . consummated it.'

I feel a tingle down my spine. How can that word, so technical, so sexless, give me such a thrill? Maybe it's because I can feel the heat of his thigh against mine.

'Sorry to disappoint you,' I say, 'but you clearly haven't done your research. That only applies to straight couples.'

Max stares at me. 'You're kidding.'

'Nope.'

'Wait, so . . . if one of us wanted to seal the deal by getting it on, there would be no point?'

Our eyes remain locked. I feel like he must be able to hear my heart pounding.

'No point,' I say. 'No reason to do it.'

Before I know it, his lips are brushing against mine. It's like we're picking up where we left off at the ceremony, except that this kiss has nothing in common with that one. It isn't scripted. We're not doing it to keep up the charade. This kiss is breathless, wild, fired by passion. I can taste the wine we've both been drinking.

I run my hands through Max's hair, then slide them down his chest and reach for his belt. Max pulls back.

I smile at him. 'We don't have to.'

'No, I want to. I'm just . . .'

He can't find the words. I try to read it in his expression. Nervous? Tired?

'Max, I mean it. Let's go to sleep.'

He looks me dead in the eye. 'I don't want to go to sleep yet.'

His breath quickens and his lips part. He no longer has to explain. He's up for it, just as long as there's not too much pressure. I remember that feeling, even if it was a while ago. But this can be whatever we want it to be.

'Should I turn out the light?' I ask.

Max's eyes fill with gratitude. He nods in a way that leaves me breathless. I get up and press the light switch.

The room is plunged into darkness. Instantly, the mood shifts. In the early days with Rafferty, he was obsessed with looking at me during sex. He took a lot of photos, which I enjoyed until I realised he showed them to his friends.

Here in the dark, we're free to enjoy the sensations. I return to the sofa and fumble my way towards Max. Our clothes come off in a hurry, but Max leaves his shirt hanging open. Amid the shadows, I can see the hint of a treasure trail. I would love to turn on the light and see the look in his eyes, but simply imagining it is enough to drive me wild.

I straddle Max and lean in, kissing up his neck until my mouth finds his ear. I give it a little nibble. He moans, his body twisting towards me.

'Do you like that?' I ask.

Max murmurs with pleasure.

I continue biting and kissing his ears. I can feel him relaxing. He pulls my lips to his and we're kissing again. His tongue enters my mouth, his breath warm against mine.

We reach down and take hold of each other's dicks, both equally hard. Max clutches my thigh with one hand as we jerk each other off. I press my forehead against his.

My mind goes back to that moment in the fitting room. What if we had acted on our impulses that day? If I had turned to face Max front on, let him see the effect he'd had on me, whipped it out right there and watched him fall to his knees.

Oh god. I want to do that now. That and a whole lot more. My body aches for it, but I don't want to scare Max. Tonight at least, I'm going to follow his lead. There's a strange pleasure in holding back, letting the anticipation build as Max takes the reins.

I can feel myself getting close. Normally I would ease off, slow things down, mix it up, but Max is moaning as if he's close too. I give in to the inevitable. It blooms and spreads through me. Every nerve is alive, my pulse racing. I surrender completely, letting the wave rise until it comes shooting out of me and all over Max's chest. He chuckles in delight as I feel him spilling over my hand, hot and sticky.

We share a few more gentle kisses, our breath mingling, heart rates gradually calming. I collapse onto the sofa next to Max, our legs entangled. I could sleep like this, but since Max wanted to take it easy, we should probably head off to our separate rooms in a moment.

But not yet. Not just yet.

16

Max

I always thought that sex on your wedding night sounded like a terrible idea. If you'd been sleeping together for a while, surely you'd just be exhausted? And if it was your first time, isn't that the worst possible moment to do it? But now I think I get it. Last night, sleeping with Hunter felt like the most natural thing in the world, the only way to capture the magnitude and intensity of the day we'd just lived through together. I was so terrified to go there, so relieved when he turned the light off. Still, if that's what taking it easy is like with him, I dread to think how I'll cope with anything more than that.

Everything I've done until now pales in comparison. With other guys, fumbling around felt casual and inconsequential. This was the opposite of that. Being so close, feeling his skin against mine, his breath in my ear, was intoxicating. He was hard as a rock throughout. My hand barely fit around it. A part of me wished I could see him in all his glory, but I also loved the darkness, how it allowed me to enjoy the experience without worrying about how it looked.

It felt strange to part ways after that, but it was also a relief. It took me forever to get to sleep. My whole body was infused with the memory of what we'd done, not to mention the emotions of the day. I thought when I woke up, the lust would have faded, but if anything, it's stronger this morning. I'm not lying here thinking about the fact that I got married yesterday. I'm thinking about what Hunter and I did on that sofa.

And how I want to go further.

I want to do it with the lights on this time. I want Hunter to teach me everything he knows. I'm sure we can trust ourselves not to overcomplicate things. It's only sex. And it will be easier to fake being a couple if we're actually sleeping together. We might as well enjoy this process. In fact, I wonder if Hunter would be interested in picking up where we left off right now. Everyone's horny in the morning. But I can't just jump into bed with him. I need an excuse. Then it hits me: breakfast in bed.

I don't think I've ever made anyone breakfast in bed, but surely that's the kind of thing you do for your new husband? I'm envisioning a beautiful tray with painted china, a bunch of wild flowers, maybe one of those cute honey pots with a wooden dipper. In a house like this, I'll be able to assemble something along those lines.

It's the food part that's the challenge. I can't cook. Famously. For the past few years, I've either microwaved meals or scrambled together some pasta and pesto, whatever it took to get the food in my stomach as quickly as possible. Mr Peanut is a fussy eater, and I'm always having to prepare him raw liver or smoked fish to convince him to consume something. By the time I'm done with that, I don't really care what I eat.

But I'm married now. I'm cohabiting. And getting Hunter back into bed with me is going to take more than a Pop Tart. I survey the contents of Hunter's fridge. It's all very healthy – oat milk, grapes, courgettes. The store cupboard is slightly more promising, and I realise I have everything I need to make pancakes. Pancakes! Who doesn't love pancakes? What a charming thing to make my husband the morning after our wedding.

However, once I begin this great culinary endeavour, admittedly for the first time, it's not as easy as I was expecting. I produce a batter the rough consistency of vomit. I presume that won't matter once the pancakes are cooked, but I somehow manage to burn them on one side and undercook them on the other. That's actually quite impressive if you think about it. Let's not talk about the pancake that ends up half stuck to the ceiling and half on the floor.

Listen – I tried. You have to start somewhere. And what it lacks in taste, appearance, and all-round finesse, it makes up for in, um, a dandelion. I can't go into the garden without alerting Hunter to my plan, so I'm reduced to what I can find out front. I recall seeing some yellow dandelions that would really brighten up a breakfast tray. Unfortunately, the only dandelion that Doily hasn't picked for the wedding has turned into its spores. A dead dandelion, effectively. So really my offering consists of some lumpy half-cooked batter decorated with a dead flower. But hey, it's the thought that counts.

As I walk into his bedroom with my tray, Hunter looks up.

'I made you breakfast,' I announce.

Our eyes meet, and I'm overcome with a desire to jump into bed and pick up where we left off. Hunter surveys the tray doubtfully. 'Thank you.'

He sits up and takes a bite of pancake, making a noise of approval.

'Well?' I ask.

'Delicious.'

My face lights up. 'Are you serious?'

Hunter hesitates. 'Do you really want to know what I think?'

'Yes!'

Hunter frowns. 'Honestly, they're not the best pancakes I ever tasted.'

My expression crumples.

'What?' Hunter says. 'You asked for the truth.'

'I wasn't serious.'

Hunter stares at me. 'You were lying about wanting me to be honest?'

I shrug. 'You could be honest without slagging off my cooking skills.'

'How?'

I pause to think. 'You could have said, wow, thank you for going to all this effort, this is such a lovely idea. I'm always going to remember that you cooked me pancakes the morning after our wedding.'

Hunter offers a guilty smile. 'You're right. I could have. Seriously, Max, I would love to live in your head sometimes.'

As he holds my gaze, I feel another rush of desire for him. That was definitely a come-on. Hunter turns and places the tray on the bedside table. Oh my god, he's going to kiss me. I purse my lips in preparation. But when Hunter turns back, his expression is grave.

'I think we should talk about last night.'

My breath catches. That doesn't sound good.

'Er, sure.'

'I feel bad,' says Hunter. 'I should have been more responsible.'

My heart sinks like a stone, but I try not to let it show on my face.

'It's OK,' I say. 'We were drunk.'

'I know. I just think it might be easier if we don't do that again.'

I try to look casual. 'I agree.'

'Really? Awesome.'

I feel like a fool. How did I let myself come skipping in here, thinking that a tray of disgusting pancakes would make him want to sleep with me? I'm such an idiot. Once was clearly enough for him. He doesn't want to go there again with an amateur like me who couldn't even bring himself to leave the light on.

My face flushes red and I look away. This is so humiliating. What if he had my number from the moment I walked in here? What if he saw straight through my ruse with the pancakes? What if the honest feedback was a way of breaking it to me gently? I want to run away and hide, but I can't slink off now or he'll know how crushed I am.

I need to act as if hanging out in bed together like this is the most natural thing in the world. I reach for my phone and check my emails. I barely use my personal account, since there's little in my life that doesn't revolve around work. I cringe when I see the email from my dad with a copy of the pre-nup. Then I see the next email, and my heart stops.

'OK, don't panic,' I say to Hunter.

'I wasn't until you said that,' says Hunter. 'What is it?'

I can't bring myself to tell him, so I show him the email. Our application for a marriage visa has been processed but not yet approved. Instead, we've been invited to an interview. And when I say invited, I mean summoned.

The interview is tomorrow.

17

Hunter

If I was being an optimist, I would say that the email came at a convenient time. I could tell Max was disappointed by our conversation. I felt awful, but what other choice do we have? Sleeping together again would be fun, but it wouldn't be a good idea. Something tells me I'm the more experienced one here, so it's up to me to be responsible. I was worried that Max wouldn't be able to treat it as just sex, but honestly, I'm not sure I could either. We've got way too many other things on our plate without adding any more complications.

Case in point: the interview.

I can't say it was a surprise. I've done my research and I'm well aware that plenty of people get invited for an interview as part of the application process. What's less clear is why that happens. The authorities insist it's random, but the consensus online is that it likely indicates some sort of suspicion concerning your application. So excuse me while I panic just a little.

The system is set up precisely to catch people like us. We're lying. We're not in love. And our ability to lie is about to be put to the test by the government's ability to catch us. Luckily, this is where Max's positive attitude comes in useful. He announces that what we need is a whiteboard and a set of wipeable marker pens. Doily seems more likely to possess a blackboard salvaged from the local orphanage that closed down, but we manage to find a whiteboard that is scrawled, for reasons best left unknown, with a list of Vanessa Redgrave's most irrational phobias. I prop it up on the living room sofa, then Max and I sit on the floor and begin to brainstorm every possible question we might get asked.

Treating our relationship like a work exercise is remarkably satisfying. Why didn't we do this sooner? We could have avoided so many stumbles. With the whiteboard's help, we quickly turn a bunch of random anecdotes into a comprehensive relationship timeline. We search online, cross reference with our diaries, and plot out our first, second and third dates, conceiving all sorts of romantic and considerate gestures, even if I suspect that Max is getting his ideas from Hollywood films rather than real-life relationships.

Our past histories are not quite as open to creative licence. The guidelines state that we may be asked questions about our lives before we met, and while they insist it isn't a test, I've found forums online where past interviewees claim it can amount to an interrogation. I ask Max to tell me his full dating history. I'm not surprised when there doesn't seem to be much of one.

'So you've never been in love?' I ask.

'I guess not.'

'That makes sense.'

Max looks hurt but tries to laugh it off. 'What, you think I'm unloveable?'

I smile. 'It makes sense in the narrative we're trying to sell. Getting married fast is quite an immature thing to do.'

'So you think I'm immature. Got it.'

'Romantically speaking! It's not an insult. But I'm the first person you've ever been in love with.'

'Fake in love.'

'Yes, Max, fake in love. But first love is incredibly overwhelming. You're really going to have to sell that in your interview.'

Max looks at me, intrigued. 'Sounds like you're speaking from experience.'

I clam up.

'Come on then,' he says. 'Dish the dirt.'

'I have been in love.'

'With who?'

I really don't want to talk about Rafferty. It's not that I'm not prepared to put that time in my life under the spotlight and see it for what it was. But I don't want to bring those clouds into Max's sunlight. I'll talk about it in my interview if necessary, but that doesn't mean I have to do it now.

'It doesn't matter,' I say.

'We promised to be honest with each other,' Max says.

'I am being honest. I just don't want to talk about it.'

'So what do I say if they ask?'

'Be honest! Say I won't talk about it.'

Maybe one day I'll be ready to talk about Rafferty with Max. There's a part of me that thinks he'd take it well. When I told Zosia and Thiago, all they wanted to do was cuss him out, which was no less than he deserved. But that never feels as good as I think it's going to.

'Fine,' Max says. 'You're private. Tell me what I need to know.'

'I thought I just said—'

'I'm not talking about the details. Help me understand what being in love *feels* like.'

How can I communicate this to someone who hasn't been there? The highs and the lows. The small humiliations. Max doesn't need to know that part. He's asking as a matter of character research, and when it comes to that, I'm not sure how helpful my experience with Rafferty is. I'm not even sure that Rafferty loved me. I think he had the hots for me and he loved what dating me said about him, but I don't think it went as far as love. Did I love him? Or was I just young and naive?

I believe in telling the truth, but I'm starting to see that the truth isn't required in every situation. I don't want to turn Max into a cynic. Not when we're on the verge of having to sell our love. I want to protect what's pure about him. So I'm going to break my rule and lie just a little.

'It feels amazing,' I say. 'It's the best feeling in the world.'

18

Max

I could tell he was lying. Takes one to know one. What's he hiding? What happened in his past? He clearly thinks I can't handle the truth. I respect his right to privacy, but I got the sense that a part of him did want to tell me. More than wanting all the answers, I find myself wanting to look after Hunter. Wanting to help him in the ways he can't help himself. I think of what he said about me in his wedding vows. How my attitude inspires him. Maybe I can help him discover a different side to himself. Maybe I can be what he needs.

It's only as the first rays of dawn peep through my window the next morning that I start to think about the interview. You can't say our preparations haven't been comprehensive. We've invented a whole life for ourselves. I've run over the facts so many times that I'm starting to believe them.

Doily has volunteered to look after Mr Peanut while we're out, specifically by taking him along to her charitable initiative teaching calligraphy to disadvantaged youths. I've dropped him off with her and I'm making myself a good luck quadruple strength coffee when

Hunter walks into the kitchen. His hair has been tousled dry, and he has a small shaving cut on his chin. How does he keep getting more beautiful? I feel a rush of lust, but it comes with a bittersweet pang in light of our conversation yesterday. Still, it has to be a good thing that I'm attracted to my husband on today of all days.

As Hunter and I step onto the street, he takes hold of my hand. I give him a quizzical look, but he simply smiles. I'm not sure if he's comforting me or vice versa. We barely talk on the way to the immigration office. I can't think what to say other than test each other on everything we've agreed, but getting a question wrong might throw us.

The immigration office is a dull, musty-smelling building that looks like it has been in bad need of refurbishment for years. The receptionist is a bald Eastern European man who laughs intermittently as he checks us in, a habit that becomes less mystifying when I realise that he's watching an endless loop of cat videos on a phone propped up in front of him. He informs us that we may be in for a wait, but it's only a few minutes before someone approaches us, a woman in her fifties with hair cropped so short it feels almost military, and an unreadable expression. She sizes us up without a flicker of warmth.

'Hunter?' she says.

Hunter nods. She peers at him blankly.

'Janet Pilcher. Would you like to follow me?'

19

Hunter

Honestly, Janet Pilcher, I'd rather not, but I'm pretty sure that was a rhetorical question. As I'm led down the corridor, my chest tightens, and I feel like I'm walking into a courtroom, not an office. My palms are damp. Overhead, the fluorescent lights hum and flicker. I don't want to be over-dramatic, but I really feel like I might never return.

It's one thing to know that what Max and I are doing is illegal. It's another thing to come face to face with the authorities who could choose to ruin our lives. I'm really having to summon my acting abilities, since this experience is making me resent the power that governments have over us. Why should they get to make arbitrary rules about who is and isn't permitted to stay in the country? Sure, being in love with someone who lives here is a good reason to be allowed to stay, but there are many other reasons, like wanting to pursue a career. I don't see why some people should have their dreams crushed but not others.

But that's not an issue that's going to be resolved in the next twenty minutes. My fate has been placed in the hands of Janet Pilcher, who hasn't said a word since she invited me to follow her. She leads me into a drab little office with nothing in it apart from a desk, a couple of chairs, and a tea station in one corner. It contains various types of tea, and, for some reason, Marmite, even though there's no sign of a toaster. Janet catches me looking at it.

'Would you like a cup?'

'Of Marmite?'

'What? No. Tea.'

'Oh. Right. No thanks.'

My voice cracks. Damn, I'm nervous. A surprisingly common problem with actors. So many of us are nervous wrecks in real life. You'd think we'd be able to act our way out of anything, but that's not really how it works. I realise that despite all our prep, I've walked in here as myself, not Edwin, the trainee orthodontist's assistant, a man who would have no reason to lie about anything. But I'm going to have to get there pretty fast.

I pause and try to get in the right headspace. I like to use the Stanislavski technique, where you draw on real emotions you've experienced. In the past, when I've had to play a romantic scene, I've thought about the start of my relationship with Rafferty. But that no longer feels right. Without planning it, I go to a place I'm not expecting: sitting opposite Max at our wedding, gazing at him over my lavender creme brûlée.

'Right,' says Janet. 'Shall we begin?'

As she starts asking me questions, I'm on high alert. I don't even consider saying something unless I'm sure that Max and I went over it together. I'm scared that Janet is going to notice my hesitancy, but as I settle into it, I have to admit this isn't as bad as I feared. We did our homework, and it's proving helpful.

Things get a little trickier when Janet asks about my past relationships. Not that I'm worried about slipping up, but does the government really need to know this? I say as little as I can about Rafferty. I have no desire to churn up those memories. But as I talk about him, a funny thing happens. I realise how far I am from that experience. Max and I might be faking it, but we're also genuinely looking out for each other. We're far more of a team than Rafferty and I ever were. So I tell that to Janet.

'And what do you two do for each other in your relationship?' Janet asks.

Damn. What we've done for each other is very simple: Max has given me a way to stay in the country, and I've given him a chance to get his dream job. But I can't say that, obviously. I rack my brain for anything I can offer without contradicting what Max might say.

'Uh . . . we're good for each other. Max helps me relax and have fun. And I keep him honest.'

'Max is dishonest?'

Jesus, Janet. That was meant to be heartwarming.

'Not like that,' I say with a laugh. 'But sometimes he's too optimistic for his own good.'

Janet doesn't look as if she's personally acquainted with that concept.

'Right. And how does he help you relax and have fun?'

She's really holding my feet to the fire. The only example I can think of is stealing Elton John's gnome. But I can't tell that story. I'd be marched straight over the road to the police station. How can I put it in a way that is truthful but not?

'Well, Janet,' I say, 'we like to acquire rare pottery.'

The best I can say about my answer is that it has Max written all over it. Having said that, I can picture him happily telling his officer the gnome story, naming Elton and everything. But if he does, I haven't contradicted him. Janet makes a note, then looks up.

'That's all.'

'Did I pass?'

For the first time, Janet smiles, but there's nothing friendly about it. 'Your answers can't be right or wrong. They just have to match your husband's.'

20

Max

I only have to wait a few minutes before I'm summoned myself. My officer is a man in his forties with a head of tight curls and a tie covered in roses, who looks like he's suppressing the urge to tap dance. I'm expecting to be shown to one of those interrogation rooms you see on a police procedural, but this office is warm and cosy. On the desk are a large number of snow globes.

'Have a play,' the man says, gesturing at the snow globes. 'That one's actually a sand globe, and look at this one! Confetti.' He picks up a globe containing a bride and groom and shakes confetti all over them.

'Very topical,' he grins. 'My name is Malcolm Lovejoy, and I'm here to make this experience as comfy as possible for you. Can I offer you some tea and bickies?'

This is a trap. This has to be a trap. They can't possibly have hired someone called Malcolm *Lovejoy* to interrogate me. But if he's being played by an actor, Malcolm is giving the performance of a lifetime. He pulls out my file and skims it.

'Just reminding myself of the basics,' says Malcolm. 'Ooh, Pisces! Snap.'

150

He offers me another grin. 'Right, here's the deal. I love love. I'm a right old romantic, me. But we just have to make sure everything is hunky-dory with you and, er—'

'Hunter.'

Was that a test? Hunter and I debated this question, since there's no getting around the fact that some people out there know him as Hunter and others as Edwin. In the end, we decided to tell people that his names are used interchangeably, as that avoids the risk of any slip-ups. Thankfully, Malcolm doesn't seem bothered.

'Now,' says Malcolm. 'Why don't you tell me the story of your relationship?'

I'd be delighted, Malcolm Lovejoy. I didn't realise I was going to be given such free rein. I thought I was going to be tested on how many birthmarks Hunter has on his left butt cheek, which come to think of it, I probably should have asked to verify. I start to talk effusively about how Hunter and I met, then stop myself. The more I go off on a tangent, the more chance there is of mine and Hunter's stories diverging. I reel myself in and stick to the facts that Hunter and I agreed on. Malcolm listens, smiling and occasionally chuckling with delight, as if he's tuned into his favourite podcast on a Sunday morning.

'And what do you two do for each other?' Malcolm asks.

Shit. We didn't prepare for this one. But the first part of the answer is easy.

'Hunter is incredibly supportive of my career,' I say. 'I'm applying for a new position, and he has made it clear that he'll help me any way he can.'

'Aww, bless. And what do you do for him?'

For a moment, I'm stumped. There's no way of spinning the fact that my main use to Hunter is helping him stay in the country. But I have to say something. Then it hits me.

'I cook for him!'

'Ooh, scrummy. What do you cook?'

I visualise the lumpy pancake that Hunter so valiantly ate.

'Mainly pancakes.'

Malcolm makes a note of this. I guess that lumpy pancake is now part of my official government record, but hopefully Hunter said the same thing if they asked him.

'That's all fabby dabby,' says Malcolm. 'One last question.'

He leans forward on his desk as if particularly curious. 'Why haven't you been in a relationship before?'

I pause. 'I, er, what?'

'You say in your application that this is your first serious relationship. Why haven't you been in one before now?'

There's no hint of menace in Malcolm's question. He's just trying to make sure everything adds up. He's not even the first person to ask me this. A couple of men I've dated in the past have posed the question, always with a note of suspicion, and while I brushed them off at the time, it prompted me to reflect on the answer.

I look at Malcolm and my first instinct is to lie. Make up some excuse, tell him I've been too busy with work. But I don't want to do that. I want to commit to the new path I've been taking with Hunter. I lean forward.

'To be perfectly honest, Malcolm, I think I've been scared of letting people see the real me. Sharing how I feel deep down. But I'm starting to change, and it's all thanks to one man. It's all thanks to Hunter.'

21

Hunter

The end of the interview was a big anti-climax. We weren't told if we'd passed or failed. We were simply allowed to leave, and informed that we'd hear back soon whether our application had been successful. That was it. No triumphant celebration, no dramatic arrest.

As Max and I walked away from the test centre, we compared notes. When I found out we'd given different answers to the question about what we do for each other, I was convinced it would be our downfall, but Max promised me we'd think of something if they ever tried to call us out on it. For once, I decided to go with his optimism.

No, that's not very me of me. I've always thought that optimism skates too close to delusion to really trust it. But in moments like this, when you don't have any control over your fate, what's the point of thinking negatively? I'm going to believe everything will work out until I'm proven wrong.

Even so, I'm not the best company when I'm waiting for news, which is a shame, since that's most of my life. Until my visa is confirmed, we are basically in limbo.

Waking up the morning after the interview, I'm relieved at the thought of Max going back to work today. Passing his bedroom, I see that it's empty and I figure he's already gone into the office. It's only as I walk into the bathroom, half-awake and desperate to pee, that I realise Max is in the shower.

My heart almost stops. My first instinct is to walk straight back out again. I can hold it in until he's done. But I stop myself. Max must have already seen me enter. He made it clear that he's fine with sharing a bathroom. The toilet is on the other side of the room from the shower, it's not like he'll have a clear view of me. Guys pee next to each other in public all the time. This is the perfect way to show we can live alongside each other domestically without making it sexual. I can totally do this.

Thank god I didn't walk in here naked. That's how I sleep, but since Max moved in, I've got in the habit of pulling on some underwear when I leave my room to avoid situations like this. Unfortunately, there's no avoiding the fact that peeing involves standing there with your dick in your hand, which is not ideal when you're trying not to think about sex. My mind goes to all the times I've been at men's urinals and got turned on as I noticed men clocking me. Plus, needless to say, I woke up with a boner.

I stand there waiting for it to go down so I can do what I came in here to do. Eventually, I succeed. But no sooner have I finished and I'm washing my hands than the shower cuts off and steam drifts out as the door swings open.

'Morning,' Max says, casually reaching for his towel like it's the most natural thing in the world to be standing there dripping, naked, inches away from me.

I catch myself glancing at him, just a flicker, but it's enough to know too much. A line of water runs down through his chest hair and disappears into a wispy treasure trail. His torso has a softness that feels inviting, human, and absurdly hot. How are we going to survive living together? With Rafferty, intimacy blurred into routine until the erotic edge dulled. But with Max, it's the opposite. Because we've decided not to sleep together again, everything is impossibly charged.

'Morning,' I say, far too brightly to sound natural.

'You're up early,' says Max.

His towel is now safely wrapped around his waist, which in theory makes this whole encounter less awkward but in practice only draws attention to a prominent dick print that looks like it wants to burst out.

'I'm always up early,' I say defensively.

'Any plans for the day?'

'Not really.'

I don't know why I'm not telling him what I'm planning to do today. Actually, I do know, but I'm not going to get into it with him. I'm worried he's going to judge me or think I'm lazy, but he just offers me a breezy smile.

'Nice.'

I wish he hadn't done that. It hit me in a very specific place. When I lived with Rafferty, there were days when I had nothing happening, and he always made me feel bad about it. When you're an actor, it's pretty hard to control your destiny. The fact that Max is so non-judgmental about it is hardly helping to limit this inconvenient attraction I've developed towards him.

Ten minutes later, he enters the kitchen in his work suit and hands me a sheet of paper.

'What's that?'

'Instructions for Mr Peanut. I wrote them down last time I went away. Thanks so much for looking after him today.'

I scan the sheet, which is dense with text.

'Let him off lead when you get to the park?'

'He loves to run around.'

'I'm not going to do that. I'm scared he'll run off.'

'He's never run off.'

'That's because he's attached to you. He's not attached to me.'

But Max smiles, unable to conceive of anything going wrong.

'He'll be fine, Hunter, trust me. You guys have fun.'

He collapses to his knees and launches into an extravagant farewell with Mr Peanut, stroking him all over and working him up into a frenzy.

'You shouldn't do that,' I say.

'What?'

'Make your departure such a big deal. No wonder he gets upset when you leave.'

Max smiles at me. 'Are you jealous?'

I scoff. 'No, I am not jealous of a dog.'

Max cocks his head playfully. I could swear he's flirting, which feels like a terrible idea and therefore irresistible.

'Could have fooled me,' says Max. 'If you're going to miss me today, just say that.'

I hold his gaze. 'You wish.'

'Please,' says Max. 'I can't wait to leave.'

'Then why are you still here?'

I need him to walk out right now. I'm overwhelmed with the urge to tear off all his clothes, bend him over the sofa and bang the hell out of him.

For a brief moment, I really think we might be about to throw it all away and have sex at 8.30 a.m. right here in the living room. Instead, Max smiles at me innocently, leans in to give me a gentle kiss on the cheek, then leaves.

22

Max

Why did I kiss him? What the hell was I thinking? I was acting like he was some 1950s housewife, but the truth was, I didn't know what to say. That man is too hot to handle. I don't know why I claimed I was cool with the idea of sharing a bathroom. Look how relaxed he was, striding in there and peeing in front of me without blinking. And there I was, trying to conceal the fact that I had a hard-on.

Even the sound of his stream turned me on. I tried not to look, but at one point I caught a glimpse through the shower door and a side view of his dick, long and thick. I was so overcome with lust that I thought I was going to faint. I don't know how I'll cope if I run into him in the bathroom again.

Better avoid it at all costs. Hunter has made it clear that nothing is going to happen between us. Except . . . he did get a bit flirty back there. What was that about?

I mustn't read too much into it. He was clearly hiding what he's planning to do today. I bet it's a hookup. We haven't talked about that, but it would be silly to think he wasn't going to sleep with other people.

In fact, it would probably be good for us. Not that I like the thought of him with other guys. It will be a relief to arrive at the office and focus on work.

'Here he is!' exclaims Linda from Accounts. 'The blushing groom.'

Conveniently for Linda, I turn red.

'I assumed you wouldn't be in this week,' says Linda. 'Aren't you supposed to be on your honeymoon?'

'Oh, I, er—'

'Come on then,' says Sunita from HR, swooping in. 'Tell us everything.'

For the next five minutes, we're like some sort of AI simulation of a happy, harmonious office. We stand around chatting and laughing while I tell everyone about my wedding. Hunter and I agreed to tell people we're going away for a proper honeymoon in the autumn when work has calmed down. I'm poorly equipped to remember the details that my colleagues want to hear, the outfits and menus and how many people cried. But nothing can dampen people's excitement over a wedding.

I can't help noticing that my colleagues are treating me differently. It's not just because they're excited to have something to gossip about. I feel like they see me as a success now, simply because I'm married. Which I have to admit feels nice, but it does beg the question: how did they see me previously?

Eventually, I drag myself away from them so I can get on with my work. At least, that's the idea. Mariam looks up as I take a seat.

'Good bash at the weekend,' she says. 'Did you get my wedding gift?'

'Er, I don't think so.'

'Damn, then I forgot to send it. I was hoping I'd remembered.'

Classic Mariam.

'That's OK. You really shouldn't have.'

'I didn't.'

'Well don't.'

'Salad tosser.'

'Pardon?'

'That's what I'm getting you. Horrible, isn't it, when lettuce goes soggy.'

'Oh, it's the worst.'

We both know she's never going to get around to giving me a salad tosser.

'I had a great chat with that Napkin lady,' says Mariam.

'Who?'

'Edwin's agent.'

'Doily?'

'That's the one. I'm not surprised Edwin needs a back-up career, the way the industry's going. Did you know Benedict Cumberbatch is doing a Ronald McDonald biopic?'

'What's that?' asks Quentin, coming over.

Great. This is the last thing I need.

'Just talking about all the lovely people I met at Max's wedding,' says Mariam.

'Ronald McDonald?' asks Quentin, deadpan.

'Thanks so much for coming,' I say to him earnestly.

'Not at all,' says Quentin, smiling slyly. 'Lovely ceremony. Beautiful house.'

I nod politely. I'm not giving this man an inch.

'Funny little slip-up in your vows,' says Quentin.

My breath catches. 'What do you mean?'

'You called him Hunter. Then you corrected yourself.'

Fuck. Trust Quentin to spot that.

'Easily confused,' I say, my heart pounding. 'That's the problem with stage names.'

'Yes,' says Mariam. 'Look at Reginald Dwight.'

'What?'

'Elton John to you and me.'

I feel a jolt of pure fear, and it takes me a moment to realise Mariam hasn't somehow made the connection to the garden gnome. I'm going to have to deal with this for the rest of my life every time someone casually mentions one of the world's most famous singers. Thankfully, Mariam has been distracted by her emails.

'Ooh Quentin, you might want to check your email,' says Mariam. 'You've made the shortlist for Athens. Congratulations.'

My heart sinks. I'm not sure why this information is being shared with Mariam, but if she's telling Quentin he made the shortlist, then presumably I didn't. I pull out my phone and see an email telling me I've also made the shortlist. I give Mariam a wounded look.

'I made it too. No congratulations for me?'

Mariam looks at me wearily. 'Honestly, Max, I got you a salad tosser. How much more do you want from me?'

I force a smile and turn away to find myself face-to-face with Quentin.

'Well done, Max,' he says. 'It will be nice to spend a bit more time with Hunter. I mean Edwin.'

He's scanning me, looking for a reaction, but I refuse to give it to him. 'Call him what you want,' I say casually. 'We can't wait.'

I really don't know what I did to make Mariam prefer Quentin to me for this position. She never seemed that biased towards him in the past. I should be excited that I made the shortlist, but it's all too much, what with lying to everyone about the wedding and waiting to hear back from our immigration interview. All I want to do is sit in the corner and get on with some work. Unfortunately, the one remaining desk is next to Nessie.

'Thanks for coming this weekend,' I say.

As Nessie looks up at me, all I can see is that perm.

'My pleasure,' says Nessie. 'Were you all right?'

I freeze, then recall my dizzy spell.

'Yeah. Just overwhelmed. Edwin looked after me.'

Nessie looks touched, and I feel a tug of guilt. Not for the first time, I have an urge to confide in her the way that Hunter does with Zosia and Thiago.

'Max, can I ask you something personal?' Nessie says tentatively.

Shit. Why is she being so coy? Could she tell something was up at the wedding? Has she sussed me out? I don't know why I thought I could pull the wool over everyone's eyes. All of a sudden, I don't want to confess anything.

'Er, sure,' I say. 'Can't promise I'll answer it, but fire away.'

Nessie shifts from foot to foot. 'It's my hair.'

I feel a flood of relief that this is about her, not me.

'Everyone keeps telling me how much they love it, but . . . I feel like they're lying.'

She knows. She knows how bad it looks. But it can be hard to be honest with yourself when everyone else is lying to you. And even though I have been lying about this to Nessie from the start, a lot has changed since then. I made it through my wedding vows. I survived the immigration interview. I can tell Nessie the truth about her terrible hair.

'They are lying,' I say. 'We all are.'

Nessie's mouth drops open.

'The perm is bad. It doesn't suit you. And you did it for the wrong reasons. You're not boring. You just have friends who don't appreciate you. You looked great as you were.'

Nessie is lost for words. Her eyes have filled with tears. I'm convinced I've blown it, but she throws her arms around me.

'Thank you, Max.'

I'm taken aback. 'It's nothing.'

'It's everything.'

I know what she means. True honesty can feel like a gift.

'Happy to help,' I say, brushing it off.

'Seriously, Max, I owe you. Let me know if I can help with anything.'

I think of all the other things I could be honest about with her. The stress of faking it. My fears that Quentin is becoming suspicious. My crush on Hunter. I have no doubt that every one of these would feel a little lighter if I talked them through with someone like Nessie.

But now is not the moment for such a momentous conversation. I give her a smile.

'Thanks, Nessie. I definitely will.'

For the first time, it's not something I'm scared of. In fact, I'm already looking forward to it.

23

Hunter

Mr Peanut is fascinated as he watches me set up the tripod in the living room. I feel like he's going to somehow find a way to rat me out to Max. It's not like me to be dishonest. The reason I didn't tell Max what I planned to do today is because I'm so used to Rafferty belittling me for pursuing my dreams.

Sondheim may have been the writer who made me fall in love with theater, but it was Shakespeare who convinced me I wanted to be an actor. I was fourteen, in my first year of high school and hating every minute when halfway through the semester, our English teacher went on maternity leave and we got a new teacher, Ms Nelson.

Every gay kid has that one teacher they dream of tearfully thanking in their Tony acceptance speech. Ms Nelson is mine. She was an artist in her spare time and often came to school in paint-splattered overalls. I heard there were parents who complained about that, but personally I found everything she did impossibly cool and glamorous. That first semester, we studied *Twelfth Night*. Ms Nelson didn't shy away from its queer subtext. More than that, she brought the text to life in a way I have never forgotten. Ever since then, it has been my dream to appear in a Shakespeare production.

Shakespeare's Globe, a reconstruction of the original Globe Theatre, was one of the first places I visited when I arrived in London. You can buy tickets to stand at the front for only ten pounds and experience theater almost exactly as people did in Shakespeare's day, with the roof open to the stars. I promised myself I wouldn't leave London until I managed to step on those boards, and I'm finally within touching distance. Even though my visa is still only provisional, I've decided to think positive and start auditioning. The Globe is holding an open casting call for the greatest play of all: *Hamlet*.

I don't want to get ahead of myself. They claim it's an open call, but they probably have to do that because of their funding. Wait for them to turn around and cast Paul Mescal. But I still get a chance to try. For the first round of auditions, they're having actors send in tapes of a scene that's not from *Hamlet*, but is in some way thematically related. I have the whole of today to pick something and get it on tape.

The problem is, I don't know where to start. I need to wow these producers. I need to show off everything I can do in a two-minute performance. But that's a hell of a lot of pressure to put on one audition tape.

My first attempt is the 'tomorrow and tomorrow and tomorrow' speech from *Macbeth*, but I can't get past the fact that those lines are now the title of a bestselling novel about computer games. I try *King Lear* to show off my range, but it feels ridiculous. *Dr Faustus* is too melodramatic, *The Seagull* too self-conscious. I get all the way to Tennessee Williams and Sarah Kane and still nothing's working.

At lunchtime, I'm in need of a break, so I take Mr Peanut out for a walk. It's been a while since I had a dog in my care. The last one I fostered was a hyperactive dachshund with a kamikaze streak who gave me palpitations every time I took him outside. For the first ten minutes, Mr Peanut is a similar nightmare, pulling on the leash, attempting to greet random strangers, and eating anything and everything he finds on the sidewalk. Every time he misbehaves, I stop and make him sit. To my surprise, it works, although it slows our progress to a crawl.

When we finally reach the park, I don't dare let him off the leash. The thought of having to tell Max that Mr Peanut has bolted is too horrifying. But there's a dog park that is gated off, and Mr Peanut is desperately straining to enter. Even I can't conceive of how he could come to any harm in there.

I shut the gate behind us and let Mr Peanut off the leash. As he dashes away from me and launches himself at a schnauzer, I'm convinced it's going to end in tears. But I force myself to remain calm, and it soon becomes clear that there's nothing to worry about. Watching Mr Peanut run around and play with the other dogs, I get a serotonin boost that honestly makes me understand Max a little better. No wonder he's so relaxed and carefree about everything if this is how he starts each day. As I stand here and bask in the feeling, it's as if a little bit of his spirit rubs off on me.

I meant what I said about Max at the wedding. The last few years have not been easy. But I'm realizing I've been pushing away anyone who might make me think another way is possible. What if Max is who I've been needing all this time? Just because we're not romantically involved doesn't mean we can't be what the other person needs. I don't have to worry about things between us turning sour because it will never get that far.

As I walk home with Mr Peanut, I'm no closer to figuring out what I'm going to do for my audition. But I've made a decision. I'm not going to stress over it. I'm not going to assume that Max will have the same reaction as Rafferty. I'm going to ask for his help. For him to turn his trademark optimism towards this problem.

For us to do this together.

24

Max

The work day turns out to be surprisingly busy, keeping me in the office until late. This trade deal being signed was supposed to be a moment of triumph, but now everyone is preparing the long-form agreement that will be released to the public, and it's throwing up all sorts of complications.

When I get home, the lights are dimmed and Hunter is on the living room sofa, a glass of red wine on the side. Mr Peanut is curled into the nook of Hunter's legs, snoring softly against Hunter's bare thigh. It's only then that I notice what Hunter is wearing – a pair of boxer shorts and my old university hoodie. I can't remember the last time I wore that old thing, but on Hunter, it's painfully hot.

I feel a surge of desire that catches in my throat. Mr Peanut wakes up and sees me. He leaps up and runs over. On any other day, I would fall to the floor and writhe around manically with him, but I want to show Hunter I can be responsible. Strange as it feels, I reach down and pat Mr Peanut on the head as if we're meeting for the first time.

'That's more like it,' says Hunter.

I shoot him a wry look. 'Coming from someone I just caught snuggling him.'

'I was very strict with him on his walk! We did some training.'

He looks down at Mr Peanut.

'But yes,' Hunter says. 'I will admit that we bonded.'

It shocks me how much I adore the image of the two of them spending the day together, Hunter trying to be strict while secretly falling for Mr Peanut.

Hunter asks me how my day was, and I inform him that I've been shortlisted for the Athens job. He congratulates me, but he's subdued, and it's clear there's something on his mind.

'How was your day?' I ask.

Hunter sighs and tells me about the *Hamlet* audition. As he walks me through what they've asked for and how much he's been struggling with it, I see what it means to him. I can imagine few things more exposing than having to constantly put yourself on the line in auditions. Yet Hunter is so talented and self-assured that seeing him this vulnerable is a surprise.

'I really want this one, Max,' Hunter says. 'I don't want to make the same mistakes I've made in the past.'

I frown at him. 'What mistakes?'

Hunter's expression darkens. 'I think I have a tendency to take these things a bit too seriously.'

'Then do something fun.'

'It's Shakespeare.'

'Shakespeare's fun.'

'Not his tragedies.'

'Doesn't matter. What's the most fun you've ever had on stage?'

Hunter stops to think. 'Probably Rizzo.'

'Then do something from *Grease*.'

'How is that thematically related to *Hamlet*?'

Fair point. I pause to think. 'What about *The Lion King*? Isn't that based on *Hamlet*?'

'Kind of, yeah.'

'That's it! It's perfect.'

'What is?'

'"I Just Can't Wait To Be King".'

Hunter bursts out laughing, but I'm serious. I make my case. Hunter is already an outsider. If they want to cast a celebrity, they will. He needs to take a risk. More than that, he needs to have some fun with it. What's the point of any of this if he's not enjoying it?

Eventually Hunter agrees to try it. I'm grinning like a stage mum as I prop my phone on a chair and cue up the karaoke track. The music swells. The lyrics tumble out. And instantly it's wrong. I stand in the corner reading Zazu's lines from my phone in a ridiculous posh accent which isn't helping. Hunter tries again. And again. Each time it feels thinner, more hollow. Soon the laughter's gone, and I can see his shoulders slumping.

I step forward and place a hand on his arm. 'What's the matter?'

Hunter looks up, surprised by my gesture but comforted. He sighs. 'It's just not working. It's a nice idea, but . . . Hamlet never wanted to be king.'

I pause to think. 'So sing it ironically.'

Hunter's eyes flicker with inspiration. We roll again. This time, he sinks into the lyrics. Every grin is brittle, every 'I just can't wait' hysterical. The joy teeters into mania. He claws at the words, letting them spiral into something unhinged. His performance at the Menier Chocolate Factory was stunning, but this? This is inspired.

When the track cuts out, the room hangs silent. Hunter is panting, his chest heaving, dizzy from the effort. I'm no longer laughing.

'Was that OK?' Hunter asks tentatively.

'OK?! That was incredible!'

Hunter doesn't dare believe it. 'Are you serious?'

'Yes,' I say earnestly. 'I'm so proud of you.'

It's only a throwaway comment, but Hunter looks like my words have knocked the breath out of him. He glances away, then looks back, disarmed.

'Are you OK?' I ask.

'Yeah. Thanks, Max.'

'Any time.'

Hunter hesitates, collecting his thoughts.

'I'm serious. Thank you. You really pushed me.'

I hold his gaze. Something unsaid hangs in the air. I'm unnerved by the intensity of feeling between us.

'I'm sure you'd do the same for me,' I say. 'It's nothing, really.'

But it's not nothing. We both know it.

The job assessment is not until next weekend, but we decide to go ask Doily if she's free to look after Mr Peanut while we're away. Doily always tells us to treat the whole of her house as if it's our own, but Hunter insists on knocking. When there's no answer, we let ourselves in, Hunter announcing our presence loudly. Doily calls us into her office.

We enter and find her crouched on the floor, attempting to put a binder of crumpled invoices in order. The room is littered with half-drunk cups of tea in Doily's finest china. Standing over her like a drill sergeant and clutching his trusty Thermos is my dad.

'Hello Max,' he says casually.

'Dad? What are you doing here?'

My dad looks surprised by my bemusement.

'I'm helping Doily digitise her files.'

Doily sighs, resigned. 'Not that I think it's necessary, but HMRC is on my back, and your father insists I don't want to mess with them.'

Hunter and I share a look of intrigue. Mr Peanut wanders over and nibbles on some leftover custard creams.

'That's a great idea,' I say to Doily. I turn to my dad. 'When were you going to tell me you were here?'

'At some point,' my dad says, completely unapologetic. 'I got distracted. There's a *lot* to be getting on with. Look at this mess!'

'Oh stop it,' says Doily. 'It's just a bit of clutter.'

'It's carnage,' says my dad. 'Total and utter carnage.'

As he surveys it, he looks gleeful. Bringing order to chaos is what he lives for. He picks up a random piece of paper. 'Is it really necessary to keep the receipt for an animatronic rat?'

'It certainly is,' says Doily. 'I brought that so my client Gerald Boswell could audition for the new Bubonic Plague 4D experience at the London Dungeon, but I shall be returning it if he doesn't get the role. He's not very good. And that rat was expensive.'

My dad tuts, but I can tell he's enjoying the back and forth.

'Are you boys all right?' asks Doily.

'We're going away next weekend,' says Hunter. 'Max has a job interview.'

'Oh!' says Doily, turning to my dad. 'That's wonderful.'

'Yes,' he says, which trust me, is the most we're going to get out of him.

'We were hoping you could look after Mr Peanut while we're gone,' I say.

'Of course. You don't mind, do you, Alan?' Doily asks my dad.

'It's next weekend,' I say. 'You won't still be here, will you?'

'I'll be here every weekend until Christmas at this rate,' scoffs my dad.

I share another glance with Hunter. I suddenly feel like Mr Peanut is going to be interrupting something.

'You know what?' I say. 'Don't worry about it. I can get a dog-sitter.'

I could swear that my dad and Doily both look pleased.

'I'm surprised you're not taking him with you,' my dad says, raising an eyebrow at Doily. 'Didn't I tell you he's attached at the hip to that dog?'

Doily gives us a pointed look. 'Alan was asking how you coped, Hunter.'

Hunter frowns. 'With what?'

'With sharing a bed, all three of you.'

I notice the smallest glimmer of panic flash across Hunter's face, but he recovers quickly.

'We don't,' he says smoothly. 'Max and I sleep in separate beds.'

'Oh,' says my dad, flushing as if he's intruded on an intimacy. 'Fair enough.'

He turns to Doily. 'Secret to a long-lasting marriage, I've heard!'

Hunter and I leave my dad and Doily to their business and head back to our flat. As soon as we shut the door, we turn to each other excitedly.

'Did you have any idea about this?' Hunter asks.

'No! My dad doesn't tell me anything.'

'Do you think—'

'I mean . . . that's what it looks like.'

'Right? I thought it was just me.'

'No. I think we might get back from the Cotswolds and find them married too.'

Hunter laughs and starts making our dinner, but I feel a flash of fear as I'm reminded of my dad's question.

'Do you think he suspects something about us not sharing a bed?'

'No,' says Hunter. 'I think he was curious and bought my explanation.'

'You really just . . . told him the truth.'

'Yes, Max, I hate lying. Do you not hate lying to your dad?'

His question hits a wound that I'm in no mood to pick at.

'It's just . . . what we do.'

The truth is I'd love to be honest with my dad, but I don't know what I'd say. This situation with Hunter is complicated. We've agreed not to have sex, but if anything that's only increased the tension. And it's starting to get to me. My instinct is to keep it to myself, but I know it's better out than in. I turn to Hunter. 'Do you think we *should* share a bed?'

Hunter looks surprised.

'I don't mean . . . I mean literally just sleep together. We're going to have to do it at Chevening, and it might be a good idea not to do it there for the first time.' I hesitate. 'But also . . . it just might be good for us.'

Hunter pauses, thinking it over. I know there's a risk of this looking like I'm trying to get him into bed with me, so I need to be clear, however awkward it is.

'Seeing you cuddling up with Mr Peanut,' I say. 'Those are the kind of moments that really bond you. And yes, we've managed to convince people this is real so far. But we're going to come under a lot of scrutiny next weekend. They don't need to know we're not having sex. But I don't want them to pick up on any distance between us.'

Wow. That felt surprisingly good to get off my chest. I wait for Hunter's reaction.

'You might be right,' he says. 'But so is your dad.'

I frown in confusion.

'There's not room for three of us.'

Hunter points at Mr Peanut. 'If I'm in, he's out.'

I feel it like a blow to my chest.

'But . . . I've always shared a bed with him.'

'Exactly. It's time to change it up.'

I look at Mr Peanut. I hate the idea of not having him to cuddle all night. But if I have to choose between him and Hunter . . .

'Fine,' I say. 'Let's try it.'

'Tonight?'

'Why wait?'

'I'm ready if you are.'

'Let's do it.'

I turn to leave, but I see Hunter hesitate. 'What?' I ask.

'Nothing.'

'Yes there is. Tell me.'

Hunter shakes his head. 'It doesn't matter.'

I fold my arms. I've never seen Hunter so awkward.

'It's just . . . I sleep naked. Always have.'

A shiver runs down my spine. Why did I suggest this? How am I going to cope with having Hunter naked in my bed? I should say no. Tell him that's too much.

Hunter frowns. 'But, I mean, if you're not comfortable—'

'I'm fine with it.'

'Really?'

'Really.'

I don't think either of us believes me. But this isn't going to work unless we both commit to the idea that we can handle it.

'Seriously,' I say, doing my best to sound casual. 'Let it all hang out.'

25

Hunter

Why didn't I lie? Why did I have to tell him I sleep naked? There he was trying to bond us, and I had to ruin it. Not that there's necessarily anything sexual about sleeping naked, but who am I kidding? This is me we're talking about. Just the thought of it sends a rush of heat through me. My mind is racing with images: stripping down in front of Max, sliding under the covers, turning over in my sleep and pressing into him. There's no way I can lie next to Max in bed and be normal about it. But I have to try. We managed to share a bathroom the other day. I can do this.

I'm convinced Max knows exactly what I'm thinking, but luckily he's focused on Mr Peanut's first night alone, fussing with his bed under the kitchen table, coaxing and soothing him. I worry I'm incapable of walking naked across the room in front of Max without getting turned on, so I decide to get ahead of the problem by getting into bed first. I head into the bedroom, slip off my clothes, and jump under the covers. I pull a random book from the shelf, as if Max is going to believe I have a sudden interest in *The Complete Works of Shackerley*

Marmion. I switch it for my phone and scroll aimlessly, absorbing nothing. This is my worst acting performance in a while.

Moments later, Max enters. Neither of us says a word. He drops his trousers and gets into bed in a Snoopy T-shirt and boxer briefs. Damn, he looks adorable.

'Should I turn out the light?' I ask, trying to keep my voice steady.

'Do whatever you normally do,' says Max.

'Cool. Night.'

I turn out the light and roll onto my side. I really didn't think this through. I can't do what I normally do, the thing I've done every night since I was fourteen. Even if I waited until Max was asleep, it would feel wrong, because I know what I'd be thinking about: the man lying inches away from me.

God, what I would do to him if given the chance. Sliding down those briefs and pleasuring him every way I know how until he was ready to take me. My breath quickens at the thought of it. I could go to the bathroom to knock one out, but I'd better wait until Max is asleep. I roll onto my back to check and see that he's wide awake, staring at the ceiling.

'Are you OK?' I ask.

Max hesitates. 'I'm fine.'

But he seems to want to say something. I wait.

'It just feels weird,' Max says eventually. 'I got Mr Peanut a few weeks after my mum died. He's been a bit of a comfort blanket.'

I feel a rush of guilt. Here I am having dirty thoughts while this is what's on his mind.

'Oh my god, Max. You should go sleep with him.'

'No,' says Max firmly. 'Thank you, but no. I want to do this. It's good for me.'

I feel so grateful that he would share this with me. I'm no longer thinking about wanting to fuck him. I'm seeing the boy who lost his mum and has been searching for comfort ever since.

'Do you want me to hold you until you fall asleep?' I ask.

Max looks a little surprised, and I guess I am too. Rafferty never liked to cuddle, but with Max, it just feels right. He pauses, then smiles.

'Actually, yes,' he says. 'I'd love that.'

26

Max

Hunter and I have been sharing a bed for a week now. We only planned on doing it once. Or maybe we didn't have a plan, but the first night went so well that it made sense to continue, at least until this assessment weekend. I've spent so long sharing a bed with Mr Peanut that I'm used to having another warm body beside me. And Hunter has been in a relationship, so he must be used to it.

Still, that first night was like nothing I've ever experienced. *Do you want me to hold you until you fall asleep?* I've never wanted anything more. It could have been so awkward, but it wasn't at all. As his warmth enveloped me, I tried to remember the last time I'd felt so held. Sure, a lot of people have hugged me in the last five years, but this wasn't like that. With Mr Peanut, it's always me doing the holding. But with Hunter, it felt so natural and soothing that my body gave in without protest. I fell asleep almost instantly.

After that, the second and third nights were a little more uncertain. Mr Peanut turned out to sleep fine without me, so there was no need for Hunter to offer to put his arms around me again. We both danced around the fact that he was naked. I told him it wasn't an issue because I didn't want to seem like a prude, but my god, knowing he was lying there with no clothes on drove me wild.

The fourth night was unseasonably hot. We were sharing a single sheet, but that morning, I woke up at dawn and gazed over in the half-light to see Hunter asleep on his back, fully exposed. What was previously suggested in the fitting room, in the dark on our wedding night, and through the steam on the shower door, was now in full view. I couldn't take my eyes off it, hanging there between his legs, soft but heavy. It wasn't even the size of it that took me aback. It was the feeling it inspired in me, urgent and ravenous. I wanted to reach out and take hold of it, trace its curves with my tongue, feel it swell in my mouth. But with Hunter asleep, it felt wrong to even look. I rolled onto my side and lay there awake until my alarm went off and I could jump into the shower and jerk off.

From then on, I was determined. Don't look. Don't think about it. Don't give any opening for those thoughts to enter. More than once, I thought I was out of the danger zone only to meet Hunter in my dreams. There, all bets were off. We did things I've never done with anyone in real life, things that have always felt out of reach but are now at my fingertips. One time, I woke up feeling flushed with ecstasy and sticky in my underpants. I looked over at Hunter, and it felt impossible that he could be lying there asleep and unaware.

Maybe it's because today is the day we head to the assessment, but my sleep was unusually bad. I was aware of Hunter's presence in the bed all night, how much space he takes up. I was irrationally annoyed at him and at myself for being unable to get him off my mind. I finally got to sleep in the early hours, which means that as the sun rises, I'm still in bad need of rest. I'm drifting in and out of sleep when I feel it – a gentle pressure against my butt. What is that?

Oh.

Hunter's breath is even. Is he asleep? He's probably dreaming about some actor he once railed on Broadway. Then he shifts, a low murmur escaping his throat, the words indistinct.

I want to turn and look at him, to know for certain if he's awake. Instead I lie there, rigid in more ways than one. I'm not used to this kind of ambiguity.

Sure, maybe on a first date, you're unsure if you're boring them, how much you're into them yourself, whether it's just the wine talking. But once you've made up your mind to go home with someone, it's pretty clear what's going to happen.

Here, in the dawn light, I don't know anything. Except that I'm hard, and feeling Hunter's dick against my butt is making it worse.

By which I mean better.

This can't be accidental, can it? Would it be wrong to press back, just the smallest amount, to see if he notices? My hips tilt before I can make up my mind, as if my body is deciding for me.

Another mumble. I don't catch the words. I don't even know if they are words. But Hunter doesn't move away. I can feel that he's hard too, his dick resting gently against the gap between my cheeks. I can't take much more of this.

I roll onto my back as if that will solve the problem, but it places Hunter within my peripheral vision. His eyes flicker open. He gazes at me dreamily. We're dangerously close.

I should say something. Anything to cut the tension. But my mind is blank. I open my mouth, assuming that the right words will come out.

That's when my alarm clock goes off.

As we rouse ourselves, I'm convinced it was another dream. It's impossible to believe that minutes earlier, I was on the verge of asking Hunter – what? If he wanted to have sex? Now that the moment has passed, it feels unimaginable. But I didn't imagine that. Did I?

There's no time to wonder, because it turns out that's the third time my alarm went off. I must have hit the snooze button in my sleep. In fact, now that I'm properly awake, I'm remembering what a terrible night's sleep I had. I don't know what I was thinking, sharing a bed the night before a job interview.

There's no time to pack properly. Hunter says he'll grab some clothes for both of us, so I race into the bathroom, bleary-eyed, and throw a random collection of toiletries into a wash bag. I can't stop thinking about what happened just now. I'm sure Hunter was at least partly aware of what was going on. Which means . . . maybe he's no longer against the idea of us sleeping together. Or maybe his subconscious wants what he knows he shouldn't have.

I can't decide which is hotter.

We make it onto the train with seconds to spare, spilling a coffee I insisted on picking up. The train is packed with people heading to an opera festival, and I'm relieved when I find two free seats. I plonk down just as the train sets off.

'Hello, hello,' says a horribly familiar voice.

Quentin and the brilliant Flora Forbes are seated across the aisle from us. Fuck these two, honestly. Everything about them is immaculate, from their single leather suitcase to their casual sweaters in complementary shades to their Tupperware containers of yoghurt and granola topped with hazelnuts that have, it is reasonable to presume, been hand-toasted by Flora. They're sharing a travel flask of tea and each has a book for the journey, the latest Kate Atkinson mystery for Flora, some historical non-fiction for Quentin. The only thing ruining the picture is, for some reason, a pungent smell of cheese.

'Don't let us interrupt,' I say, gesturing at their books.

'Not at all,' says Flora, closing hers decisively. 'It's not Atkinson's best.'

She turns to Quentin. 'Have you finished your granola?'

Not waiting for a response, she confiscates Quentin's Tupperware, gets out her travel bag, and hands him a tube of Aesop hand mist. They both clean their hands, the product's sophisticated floral scent filling the air.

I can't bear these two, I really can't. The way they are so embedded in their routines as a couple . . . they must think Hunter and I are total frauds. How do we compete with this? I pull my wash bag from my case and rummage around in it.

'Hey babe,' I say to Hunter. 'Do you want your . . . er . . . Bonjela?'

I've plucked out a crusty old tube of Bonjela cold sore gel. Hunter stares at me.

'I'm good.'

Why isn't he playing along? Quentin and Flora are watching us like hawks. I put back the Bonjela and search for something more suitable, but I packed in the dark, and it's not like I even own anything on a par with Aesop hand mist. I'm only now realising that everything I chucked into my wash bag was from the medicine shelf. Throat pastilles. That'll do. There's something very intimate and domestic about carrying your partner's medication for them.

'Sorry,' I say to Hunter. 'I meant these.'

Hunter frowns. 'What are they for?'

'Dry, tickly cough,' Quentin reads from the pack.

I give Hunter an urgent look. Cough, motherfucker! How hard can it be to produce a dry tickly cough? I thought he was supposed to be an actor.

'I'm good,' says Hunter, in a tone that's clearly designed to make me stop whatever I'm playing at. But I'm committed now. And Quentin is still watching in gleeful fascination. I peer back into the wash bag, and it can only be sheer desperation that leads me to produce a slender red tube of Anusol.

'Here you go, darling,' I say to Hunter. 'Here's your—'

'Anus Oil?!' Quentin exclaims.

'That's not how you pronounce it.'

Hunter looks at me as if I'm insane. 'That's not mine, babe. It must be yours.'

I hold his gaze. 'Oh. Silly me.'

Hunter turns to Quentin and Flora. 'He slept badly, poor guy. Hey Max, why don't we go find the quiet carriage so you can have a nap?'

27

Hunter

I had to get him out of there. What was the point of sharing a bed for a week to bond us if he's going to ruin it with a performance like that? That boy has made progress, but he slips into old habits far too easily. We gather up our belongings and shuffle through the train. As soon as we're in the next carriage, I turn to Max with a frantic look.

'What the hell were you doing back there?'

'What do you think I was doing? Trying to make us look like a couple.'

'By pretending I have cold sores and anal fissures?'

'Yes! Do you not think Flora would bring Quentin's medication on a trip if he needed it?'

'That's not the point. Literally no one asked.'

Max gives me a sheepish look. 'I just feel like such a fraud next to them.'

My heart floods with sympathy. 'I don't know a single real-life couple who travels like those two. If anything, Quentin and Flora are the ones putting on a performance.'

Max looks surprised by this. I forget how inexperienced he is in relationships.

'Look,' I say, 'I know it's nerve-wracking to be on show. But I thought we agreed we wouldn't lie unless we had to.'

Max glances away, embarrassed. 'I told you, they make me feel inferior.'

'I don't think that's it.'

Max frowns.

'Trust me,' I say. 'Our real-life relationship is a lot more authentic than whatever you were doing back there. I think you're just used to performing around these people.'

Max looks like he's received a bullet wound to the head. But sometimes people need to hear the truth, plain and simple.

'You're not going to convince anyone this weekend with lies,' I say. 'I think we make a pretty convincing couple as we are.'

As I look at him, my mind drifts back to this morning in bed. Could Max tell I was awake? I was so close to acting on my impulses, but how can I do that when it was me who suggested that we shouldn't have sex?

I think Max and I can agree that particular experiment has failed. We're incapable of being friends who cuddle in bed. It's clear we both want something more to happen. But I'm scared of where that would leave us. Scared of how we would come back from that. There's no good answer – except for the fact that the tension between us is so electric, so charged with unspoken desire, that there's plenty of material for Max to use without having to make anything up.

I lead him through the train to find some new seats. We're passing through the next carriage when I catch sight of a middle-aged man dressed in a velvet jacket and cravat, snootily observing a woman seated opposite him reading a tabloid newspaper. He's so busy judging that he doesn't notice me. But I know exactly who he is.

That's Gerald Pope.

He's one of Doily's clients, a wannabe Shakespearean who ended up doing walk-on parts in soaps and commercials and now he's bitter. He must be going to the opera festival, which is exactly the kind of high-minded thing he'd do at the weekend. I quicken my pace until we reach the final carriage, which is almost empty. We take some seats.

'What was that about?' Max asks.

'What?'

'Back there . . . there was someone you didn't want to see.'

Sometimes this guy notices more than I give him credit for.

'Oh,' I say. 'Gerald Pope, one of Doily's clients. He's the worst.'

'Wait, isn't he the one who auditioned with the animatronic rat?'

'No, that's another Gerald. Doily has a thing for them.'

'A what? A thing for Geralds?'

'Yeah. She thinks they have an inherently tragic quality. She's got about twelve on her books. Some of them are lovely. But Gerald Pope . . .' I shudder. 'He's everything I hate about actors. I'm terrified that will be me one day.'

We're interrupted as an attendant comes along with a snack cart and makes an uninspired attempt to sell us her last KitKat. I'm hoping that Max will drop this line of questioning, but once the cart has passed, I see that he's looking at me with curiosity.

'Why did you come to London?' Max asks.

I'm surprised at the question. 'For my acting career.'

'Yeah, but you had a career in New York. You left right after your big break. You turned down a role on Broadway.'

I look alarmed. 'Who told you that?'

'Broadway_Baby_86.'

'Who?'

'There's this forum—'

'Max!'

'I was curious.'

I can hardly be mad at him for googling me. This was going to come up eventually. I look out the window for a moment, then turn back.

'I was dating the director. When I got all that attention for *Grease*, he couldn't cope. It killed him. Not that he would ever admit it.'

I pause. These memories are painful, but it's time for Max to hear this.

'I was so desperate not to let it ruin us that in the end, I did the only thing I could think of. I gave up the role. I honestly thought it would save our relationship. But because he hadn't been honest with me, I couldn't tell him why I'd done it. He definitely couldn't tell me how grateful he was. And then our relationship was built on a whole pack of lies. It was doomed. After that, I promised myself two things. I would never lie in a relationship again. And I would never, ever put a man ahead of my career.'

Max swallows hard. Does he think I'm talking about him? *Am* I talking about him? Are we not letting our relationship progress because we both know that ultimately, we're not prepared to give up our dream careers? I'm no longer sure. Everything about Max is one big question mark.

'I'm so sorry that happened to you,' says Max. 'He punished you for shining.'

I'm momentarily speechless. Whenever I tell this story, people's reactions focus on Rafferty. Thiago announced that he wanted to punch him in the face, then stood up and jumped around like a boxer. That felt good at the time. But nothing has hit me like Max's words. That's precisely what Rafferty did to me.

'Thanks,' I say, hearing my voice quiver.

'How long ago was this?' Max asks.

'A few years now.'

'So you were young. In a new city. You must have felt so alone.'

I nod at Max. 'I did.'

Why is this such a revelation? My therapist must have said similar things to me. But Max isn't being paid. More to the point, he's been there himself. I can't imagine all the ways that people have talked to him about his mum dying. How often he must have longed deep down for them to recognize his pain rather than try to make him feel better.

'Thank you for telling me,' says Max. 'No one deserves that.'

He smiles at me with such tenderness that I feel like my heart is going to explode. He's not trying to console me, and yet it's as if a crack of light is bursting through. It's the same feeling I had watching Mr Peanut run around in the park, only this time it's clearer.

When Max is in my corner, life is less dark. New things are possible. And maybe, just maybe, my wounds can heal.

28

Max

Sometimes it hurts to do the right thing. I could see what Hunter needed from me in that moment. But my god, it pained me to give it to him. His words were a punch in the gut. It was only then I realised how much I had been starting to believe that he and I might one day be a real couple. That he might decide to follow me to Athens. I don't know how I thought that would work, since I've always known his ambitions are focused on London. But in any case, there was confirmation if I needed it that not only is he not considering it, it's the last thing he'd ever do.

We sit in silence for the rest of the journey. When we arrive at our destination, there are enough cars at the station that at least we're not obliged to share with Quentin and Flora. I catch my first glimpse of some of the other candidates, including Priyanka Patel, a sharp-tongued Oxford graduate from the trade deal's negotiating team, and the inimitable Herbert Henry or Henry Herbert, who looks naked without his iPad. I'm jolted by the reminder that it's not only me and Quentin going for this job. This is the crème de la crème of the civil service.

Chevening House is only a few miles from the station. Our car turns through a tall metal security gate and we begin to wind down a long private drive through manicured parkland. As we crest a gentle rise, the stately red-brick façade of the house comes into view. Hunter leans forward in his seat, wide-eyed. He's so cool about everything that it hadn't occurred to me he might be over-awed by a place like this.

We get out of the car, crunch across the gravel and enter the house's vast hallway. The first thing I notice is the smell of wood polish that has presumably been freshly applied. Oil paintings loom from the walls. I hear the click of heels. Maybe it's because I'm focused on the sound of her shoes, but I see her from the feet upwards, like some government-edition Jessica Rabbit. The leopard print stiletto heels that must be giving palpitations to whichever housekeeper is charged with maintaining the floors. Wide-legged trousers, a silky blouse, and a perfectly tailored blazer. Manicured nails clutching a can of beer. Gold hoop earrings and bright red hair – not natural ginger but post-box red – cut in a distinctive bob. Her eyes flicker with mischief.

'The Right Honourable Baroness Willis of Dewsbury,' a butler announces.

'Oh stop it, Barry,' says the Right Honourable Baroness Willis of Dewsbury. 'It's Baroness Sharon, and you know it.'

The butler is no doubt using the correct form of address that he learned at whatever snooty training college he attended, but Baroness Sharon is how everyone knows her, and she has embraced it. Part of it is definitely snobbery that a working class woman has been able to ascend to the upper echelons of society, following in the dubious tradition of British people with titles that no one can quite explain. Part of it is simply that her nickname has a ring to it. And no politician is better at marketing herself than Baroness Sharon, the Foreign Secretary. She has managed to be one of the few ministers with a decent approval rating, mainly because she has convinced the British public that she's someone who'd be fun at a party.

'Good to meet you, boys,' says Sharon. 'I've heard *all* about you, Hunter.'

I look at her in surprise. Hunter's efforts at the British Museum were successfully kept out of the press, but apparently even politicians of Sharon's standing are aware of it.

'How did you convince him?' Sharon asks Hunter in fascination.

Hunter shrugs. 'I told him the truth.'

'Fab,' says Sharon. 'We need more of that in government. And we certainly need more diversity among our ambassadors.'

So the woman is an ally. Even better.

We're interrupted by an impatient cough. I turn to see Quentin and Flora, who eagerly introduce themselves. Baroness Sharon looks blank. This is getting better and better. The Foreign Secretary may be hosting this part of the selection process, but I assumed she'd remain impartial. Instead, she's displaying what appears to be a significant bias in our favour.

Quentin mumbles at Flora, who digs into her bag.

'We brought you some cheese,' Quentin declares proudly. 'It's a Cornish Yarg.'

Flora produces an enormous wheel of cheese that appears to be wrapped in nettle leaves, which are doing a terrible job of containing its foul stench.

'Blimey,' says Sharon, holding her nose. 'Can you deal with that, Barry?'

Barry the Butler steps forward and takes the offending cheese. Quentin seems to think it's gone well, but Flora looks mortified.

'Barry will show you to your rooms,' says Baroness Sharon. She smiles at me and Hunter. 'I've given you boys the Royal Suite.'

'Lovely,' says Quentin enviously. 'Where are we?'

Sharon offers him a glacial smile. 'You're on the Servants' Corridor.'

Barry the Butler leads us up a grand wooden staircase with our bags. We pass what feels like a dozen doors before being deposited at ours. The room is vast, with a wide sash window overlooking the lawns and a lake beyond. Next to a marble fireplace sits an antique writing desk and armchair. The fabrics are all various shades of pink and coral, while the painting above the fireplace is of a nude woman reclining in some sort of Turkish bazaar. Centre stage is a four-poster bed with a dark mahogany frame decorated with carvings of ostrich feathers.

This isn't a bedroom. This is a boudoir.

I can't look at Hunter. Somehow, our week of sharing a bed at home has prepared us for nothing. After this morning, I don't know how I'm going to cope tonight.

'Are you OK?' Hunter asks.

I hesitate. Now is not the time to have a talk about what's going on between us.

'Yeah. Just, you know, nervous.'

Hunter takes my hands in his. 'Max, did you hear Baroness Sharon back there? She's on our side.'

'More yours than mine, let's be honest.'

'I'll play my part,' says Hunter. 'But this is your time to shine. You got this.'

A short while later, I head downstairs for the first assessment. I'm desperate to know what form it's going to take. They didn't provide any details in advance. As I arrive, it's clear that all the other candidates are equally in the dark. They're seated around a long mahogany table in the centre of the room, fidgeting and shuffling papers.

When Baroness Sharon enters, the whispers fade. She's accompanied by her Chief of Staff, a pompous former debate champion who is known for harbouring ambitions to be a politician. Alongside them is Ambassador Gibbons, who strides in with his sleeves rolled up, tie loosened, in conspicuous work mode. It doesn't suit him. He'd clearly rather be schmoozing in some black-tie setting.

'Thank you all for coming,' says Sharon.

'Yes,' says Wrettham. 'Thank you *very* much.'

Sharon grimaces. 'We're delighted the ambassador felt able to fly over for a second time this month.'

'Yes,' says Wrettham, 'and we're even more delighted that Baroness Dewsbury was able to squeeze us into her busy, busy schedule.'

Damn – they're both mad the other's here. I'd love to see the emails that led to this.

'As this trade deal is ongoing, we thought we'd involve you all in the action,' says Sharon. 'We've actually been in talks with one of the major Greek stakeholders, and he has come to visit us this weekend. He'll be joining us in a second.'

There's a buzz of excitement among the candidates. This is clever. We're not just being assessed – we're actually getting involved in the workings of government. It heightens the stakes and will weed out anyone who can't handle the pressure.

'Pavlos Papadopoulos,' says Wrettham. 'I'm sure you're all familiar with him. He's a spokesperson for the Hellenic Chamber of Shipping.'

Everyone makes noises of agreement, even though personally, I've been on this deal for a year, and I can't say his name rings a bell. Sharon invites us to open our information packs, which inform us that Papadopoulos is the scion of a long-established shipping family based in Piraeus who studied maritime policy at the London School of Economics and had a background in shipping law before his current role.

'Pavlos isn't entirely happy with certain aspects of the deal, as I'm sure he won't hesitate to tell you,' Sharon says. 'It will be your job to alleviate his concerns.'

There are more excited murmurs. This is even more thrilling. We're all applying for this job because we want to be close to the action, and now here we are, right at the heart of it. I notice Quentin already skimming his information pack and I race to do the same. I can't let him seize any kind of advantage. But it's too late – one of Sharon's aides enters, and behind them is Papadopoulos. The room falls quiet, and everyone rises to greet him.

When I get a look at him, my mouth falls open.

It's not Pavlos Papadopoulos.

It's failed Shakespearean actor Gerald Pope.

29

Hunter

I feel like I'm in a Jane Austen novel. I don't mean because of the house, though there is that. It's the fact that I'm here at all. My husband is downstairs doing something important and work-related, and I'm supposed to – what? There are hours until I'm needed at drinks this evening, and I don't want to spend the whole time thinking about my *Hamlet* audition. I wander downstairs and find my way to what's called the smoking lounge.

The first thing I see is a large number of very prominent No Smoking signs. You'd think either a name change or a policy change might be in order. But there's no point in attempting to apply logic in a setting like this. The walls are lined with books whose spines look like they haven't been cracked since 1879. There are sofas upholstered in expensive silks and green reading lamps next to every seat. In one corner stands a drinks table stocked with so many vintage bottles that it's an expenses scandal waiting to happen.

I jump as I realize I'm not alone. Flora is seated in an armchair by the window.

'Bloody ridiculous, isn't it?' she says.

'This place?'

'Well yeah, but I meant the fact that we're here.'

I smile ruefully. 'It's definitely a new one.'

'It happens,' says Flora. 'My dad was a boarding school headmaster, and my mum was the headmaster's wife. It was all very official. She got a little stipend and everything. Hosted events. But I mean, that was what she did. Whereas I . . .'

She trails off, unwilling to finish that thought, but I know what she's saying. She's the brilliant Flora Forbes, as Max likes to call her.

'I get it,' I say. 'Not that I'm complaining. There are worse places to spend a weekend.'

'True,' says Flora.

'Hey, do you want to go for a stroll?' I ask.

Flora looks out the window. 'We definitely could,' she says. 'Or we could just get drunk.'

Twenty minutes later, we're seated in the sunken garden surrounded by beds of tulips and daffodils and drinking a stolen bottle of Chablis. Flora is telling a story about how they had to remove all the door knobs in the dorm of the private school she attended because the girls wouldn't stop using them to masturbate. It's left me slightly speechless, but I'm not sure if it's the anecdote or the fact that Flora is happily telling it at 11 a.m. as we drink wine straight from the bottle. We did originally plan to bring glasses out with us, but somehow that felt even more criminal.

I've had almost half a bottle myself, so I counter with stories from my own youth – episodes I haven't thought about in years. The time the teacher had to call in my parents because she was so disturbed by a story I wrote about being the only living person in a town full of ghosts. When I was cast as Rolf in a college production of *The Sound of Music*, and a reviewer claimed I was so charismatic that it amounted to promoting fascism.

Flora and I both laugh so hard we cry. It's only when we return to the topic of what we're doing here that her mood sours.

'How do you think they're getting on?' I ask.

Flora lets out a derisive snort.

I frown. 'What does that mean?'

'I think it's about time my little laddie grew up and fended for himself.'

I can't believe what I'm hearing – or what she's implying. 'Now?' I ask. 'With the prize in sight?'

'Prize?' scoffs Flora. 'Hosting a party for the fourth night in a row while some foreign politician tries to feel me up as I offer him a canapé? Yeah, can't wait.'

I'm in shock that this version of the brilliant Flora Forbes exists, let alone is revealing herself to me so freely.

'I hate who I turn into at these events,' says Flora. 'You've seen me.'

I smile at her. 'Whose idea was the cheese?'

'Quentin's. Obviously. But I go along with it all. God knows why.'

My eyes widen. 'So you're not keen to move to Athens?'

'Is that really so surprising?'

'I mean . . . I just thought that was the plan.'

Flora shakes her head bitterly. 'Do you realise where I'd be as a lawyer if I'd really put in the work? If it was Quentin accompanying *me* to functions every week?'

I look at her in surprise. 'Have you not had that conversation with him?'

Flora sighs. 'I don't know if there's any point. It's not like being a lawyer was ever my dream.'

She turns to me, heartfelt. 'I envy you so much. I always loved musical theater, but my parents would never have let me pursue it.'

I'm taken aback by her candour. 'It's not too late.'

Flora smiles. 'I don't think that's my calling. Not as a performer, at least.'

She finishes the last of the wine. 'Did you always want to be an actor?'

'Yeah,' I say. 'Still do.'

Flora frowns in confusion. 'I haven't done any acting since I moved here,' I explain. 'It's so difficult to find work, let alone work that's actually meaningful.'

'Isn't that your agent's job?'

'Kind of. She does her best. But there are so many factors out of her control.'

'Isn't that part of the fun though?' says Flora. 'Being strategic. Trying to beat the odds. Sounds like fun to me.'

She looks wistful, the specific kind of wistful that is brought on by getting unexpectedly drunk in the middle of the day. That kind of drunk that makes you feel qualified to offer advice to people you barely know.

'You'll find your place,' I say. 'The way I see it, all the people in the world are billions of little cogs. And you shouldn't worry about what type of cog you are, because we need all sorts to make the world go round. It's just about finding where you fit.'

Flora thinks it over. 'But don't you feel like, if you fall back on the orthodontics, you'll have failed somehow?'

I look away to hide my guilt. We've really been bonding. She's revealed her whole self to me. And here she is, still thinking that I'm Edwin with my sensible back-up career. I pause to consider how I can answer as truthfully as possible.

'I think anyone who defines themselves by what they do for a living is making a mistake.'

'Then what are we doing with Max and Quentin? They're both completely work obsessed. When are they going to realize there's more to life?'

Again, I have to pause and think. Not because I'm not sure how to lie but because I'm not sure what the truth is. Yes, it's clear how much Max wants this job, but I don't think I've ever truly understood why. Maybe he doesn't either. But while Flora might feel stuck with Quentin, that's not how I feel about where Max is at.

I look at her sincerely.

'I can't speak for Quentin, but Max . . . he's still figuring himself out.'

30

Max

This is it. The moment when I land the plane. I'm about to get one step closer to everything I have ever wanted. I have to hand it to them – this role play is genius. I was surprised they were involving actual government business in a job assessment. Now it all makes sense.

I'd be fascinated to know how this came about. Maybe Doily pitched the idea to Mariam at our wedding. It's the perfect job for a failed Shakespearean actor like Gerald Pope. He's probably too snobby to do medical role plays, but could he resist an invitation to Chevening to share the stage with Baroness Sharon? Evidently not. I glance at the others. Surely none of them realise what's going on. I've got the upper hand. I need to use it.

But how? Wrettham briefed us on the situation, but it's clear that he and Baroness Sharon are holding back rather than getting involved. It's time to seize the initiative.

'Er, it's an honour to meet you, Mr Papadopoulos,' I say. 'My name is Max.'

He greets me coyly. I'm sensing he's nervous. I wonder what he's thinking. Is his head fully in the game like Hunter's would be, or is he distracted by other thoughts?

Does he find me attractive, annoying, anything I can work with?

'I understand that you have some concerns about the deal,' I say.

Gerald snaps into the scene.

'Absolutely,' he says with an accent straight out of *Borat*. 'It—' He checks his notes. 'It concedes far too much to UK logistics.'

It's already obvious to me why Gerald hasn't had more success as an actor. If he bothered to read the notes in advance, which I doubt, he evidently hasn't got a clue what they mean. Any minute now, some of the other candidates are going to realise he's an actor. I need to use my advantage. What would convince Gerald the actor to do something resembling good diplomacy? There's only one answer: flattery.

'Mr Papadopoulos,' I say. 'I really must commend you for your insight. We're glad to have your perspective, as it will ultimately strengthen the deal.'

'Then tell me what you're going to do!' he shouts.

I step back in shock. I guess flattery isn't the answer. I wasn't expecting that kind of response, but maybe Gerald has been instructed to be difficult. I'm trying to figure out a new strategy when Quentin comes forward and pushes me out of the way.

'I hear you, Mr Papadopoulos,' he says. 'And that is something we take *very* seriously.'

This bastard! Quentin didn't even give me a chance to respond, but his approach appears to be working better than mine. He's doing what we've been taught to do in diplomatic negotiations, which is to start by making sure the other person feels heard. Why didn't I do that? Quick, what's another principle of negotiation? Build options before making any offers.

'Indeed we do,' I say, 'and that's why we want to consider a range of options in terms of how we proceed.'

I glance at Baroness Sharon, hoping she approves of my approach. But Papadopoulos frowns.

'I don't want options!' he shouts. 'I want a solution.'

I step back, chastened. This is not going to be easy, and not only because Gerald's acting is barely meeting the standard of a village pantomime. The other candidates are following my and Quentin's example and trying to get involved. A couple of them know what they are talking about, suggesting we can work on making sure that maritime arbitration doesn't fall too broadly under British jurisdiction. But Gerald is unable to substantively respond to any of these points.

'Mr Papadopoulos,' says Quentin. 'Might I propose opening up bilateral talks with maritime stakeholders?'

Damn. That's a great suggestion. But Papadopoulos says no. He's saying no to everything. I survey the assessors. Wrettham appears to be enjoying the spectacle, but Baroness Sharon is tight-lipped, perhaps because she's doubting the wisdom of leaving a formal job assessment in the hands of a bargain bin actor. For all I know, the government only agreed to it because Doily offered to waive her commission.

But that can't be right. Surely Baroness Sharon wouldn't go along with a strategy that foolish? There must be an answer, some way to pass this test. I pause to think. What would Hunter do? I recall the way he handled Monty at the British Museum: calm, decisive, and devastating. He showed him every sympathy, but he didn't back away from the truth.

That's what this situation needs. Someone to cut through the bullshit.

I step forward, chest open. 'Mr Papadopoulos, let's put our cards on the table. This deal isn't perfect. You know it. I know it. Both sides feel they've drawn the short straw. That's always the way.'

Unsettled by my swerve away from diplomatic formalities, Gerald Pope is listening. So is everyone else. This is my moment to shine.

'You're right,' I continue. 'It's not good enough. But the deal has been signed. This is what we have to work with. So you're going to have to spin it to your people and I'm going to have to spin it to ours, because that's what we do here. That's diplomacy.'

I turn to take in everyone's reactions. The other candidates are staring at me open-mouthed. They can't believe I've had the balls to say what we all know to be true.

Except . . . is that really envy on their faces?

My gaze drifts to the assessors. Sharon's eyebrows are arched, Wrettham's lips are pursed. Their eyes meet, and something in that shared glance hits me like a cold wind. They're not impressed. Not even a little. My stomach twists, and my moment of victory crumbles. I've gone too far. Broken the code that defines our profession. The very skill they were testing.

I've blown it.

31

Max

What was I thinking? Why did I allow him to get in my head? Yes, Hunter came to my rescue that one time in the British Museum. But that doesn't mean his approach was the right one here. I don't know how I come back from this.

We break for lunch, and I walk out of the assessment, desperate for some fresh air. But as soon as I step into the corridor, I spot Hunter.

'Max!' he cries. 'Did I just see Gerald Pope?'

I ignore him, too upset to respond.

'What the hell is he doing here?' Hunter asks. 'How did it go?'

I say nothing, striding out towards the gardens.

'Where are you going?' Hunter asks.

I glare at him. 'I just need some air.'

Hunter is confused but follows me outside. I don't want to explain what just happened. It won't come out well.

'Hey, I have good news,' Hunter says.

I continue to ignore him.

'I've just been speaking to Flora,' Hunter says. 'There's trouble in paradise.'

I don't want to hear it. None of it matters any more.

'Max, what's going on?'

'Nothing,' I say, finally turning to him. 'Please, I need some space.'

I assume that's the end of it, but I hear his footsteps continuing to crunch along the gravel behind me. I turn round, infuriated.

'What are you doing? I just said—'

'Max, I'm giving you some space. I'm going to walk a step or two behind you. But you're in the middle of a job assessment and you're storming off into the countryside. You don't seem in a good place. I'm not going to lose sight of you.'

His comments hit me in a way I wasn't expecting. How can I stay mad at him when he's being this considerate? At the same time, I don't have it in me to vocalise any kind of gratitude. Now I'm annoyed at him for making me less annoyed at him, which is not the kind of sentiment I can share without sounding ridiculous. Still, I'm too mad to stay quiet.

'I don't need you, Hunter.'

Hunter remains calm. 'I didn't say you did.'

I turn and continue to walk. I can hear him following behind, but he's giving me space like he promised. Gradually, my annoyance at him fades. I want to let him help me, but I don't know how, so I just slow down until he's walking beside me.

'Come on,' Hunter says gently. 'Tell me what the matter is.'

I look around. We're far enough from the house that nobody can see or hear us. I turn to face him.

'Why did you encourage me to be honest?'

Hunter looks confused. 'What?'

'On the train here. You told me no more lies.'

'No I didn't. I mean, yes, but I was talking generally. What happened in the assessment?'

I let out a sigh. 'I tried to be like you. Like you were at the British Museum. But I completely misjudged the situation. It was a disaster.'

Hunter looks at me, thinking it over. 'So you're not mad at me. You're mad it didn't go well.'

'No!'

Hunter jolts in surprise.

'No,' I repeat more softly. 'Well, yes. But I don't think it's just that.'

Now that he's forcing me to articulate it, I'm not sure why I'm so mad. And mad at Hunter specifically. Maybe it's because I don't believe I could ever have a moment like he did. I don't have his conviction. I don't have that cut-throat edge. But is that what's upset me? I'm not sure I want to be like that. I like it when Hunter takes the lead for me. But no way am I ready to tell him that.

'Max, can I ask a question?' Hunter says eventually.

I tense, but I don't say no.

'Why does this job matter so much to you?'

The question surprises me. This has been a settled assumption for as long as I can remember. But I guess I've never explained it to Hunter.

'I want to see the world,' I say. 'I want to make a dif-ference.'

I repeat all the statements I made in my recent job application. But none of them ring true, or at least feel like enough. Hunter listens, but I sense he has the exact same feeling I do. That I'm not telling the whole truth.

'How long have you wanted this?' Hunter asks.

I don't have to pause to answer that one. It was the one-two punch of my mum dying, then receiving that letter from her. Until then, I'd been working in the Department of Education, but reading what my mum said about seeing the world and knowing the kind of conflict that resulted in her losing her life, I wanted to honour that. Build bridges in the way she tried to do.

I tell Hunter about the letter. I've only told a handful of people over the years. It's brought more than one person to tears, but when I finish, Hunter doesn't look touched. He looks angry.

'What?' I ask, confused.

Hunter chooses his words carefully.

'I'm sure your mum meant well.'

I'm flushed red hot with anger. 'What are you talking about?'

Hunter doesn't flinch. 'I just . . . I think that's a lot to put on anyone.'

'What do you mean?'

'Think about it, Max. Those were your mum's parting words. Don't you think you felt some pressure to live up to them?'

His words hit a nerve so raw, it's physically painful.

'You don't know what you're talking about! You haven't even read the letter.'

Hunter holds my gaze calmly. 'All I'm asking is if this is what you really want, or what you think she wanted for you?'

It's a reasonable question, but I can't take it. It's too much all at once, and it comes bubbling to the surface in the worst possible way.

'Fuck you, Hunter. I don't have to listen to this.'

I storm off ahead of him. We're a long way from the house, but I don't care. I thought I was upset because I screwed up the assessment, but now I feel like my whole world is falling apart. How can he talk about my mum like that? She wrote that letter with love.

But as I walk on through the fields, past ancient hedge-rows, Hunter's words nag at me. It's true that what my mum wrote in that letter has echoed through the years since. Not only the lines about seeing the world, but the ones about looking after my dad. How could they not, when that was all I had to cling to? I read and reread that letter until I had it memorised. I have no doubt the last thing my mum intended was to put pressure on me. But maybe it was unavoidable. I wonder what state she was in when she wrote it. She can't have truly believed she was going to die or she wouldn't have gone. She wouldn't have written it.

Then it hits me. It's right there in the letter. My dad made her write it. This all came out of his fears, not hers. I feel a flash of anger, but this time, it's not towards Hunter.

I turn round and see that he's still following at a safe distance. We've arrived at a copse of trees on the edge of a stretch of woodland. A vast oak tree is lying felled and covered in ivy and moss. I take a seat on the tree, and when Hunter catches up, he sits next to me. We're both quiet for a bit.

'Sorry for saying fuck you,' I say eventually.

Hunter smiles. 'I've heard worse.'

I let out a blunt laugh.

'I might be wrong, Max,' Hunter says. 'I haven't read the letter, I didn't know your mum. I'm just telling you how it comes across.'

I glance down and pick at a loose piece of bark.

'I know. I'm grateful, honestly. And you might be right. I definitely always felt like I was doing what would make my mum happy.'

Hunter smiles in sympathy. 'I'm pretty sure you being happy is what would make her happy. I doubt she felt like she was giving you instructions.'

I'm suddenly overwhelmed with sadness at the thought that Hunter and my mum will never meet. I'm not sure why. He's not even my real partner. But right now, he's exactly what I need. I tell him the source of my sadness.

'I'm sorry too, Max. She sounds like an amazing woman.'

'She was.'

I smile as I recall the two of us racing along a country lane in Norfolk on our bikes, her scarf flapping in the wind, as my dad cycled behind us and screamed that we were breaking the Highway Code.

'She just . . . loved being alive. You're right, she would never have given me instructions like that. I'm pretty sure the letter was my dad's idea.'

Hunter frowns. 'That makes sense.'

'What does?'

'That she was writing it for him, not you.'

I go quiet. It's unnerving to think that those words I have given so much weight came from a woman who was trying to calm down her husband, not someone who truly believed her son would ever read them. But in an unexpected way, it's also freeing.

Without either of us saying anything, Hunter and I get up and walk into the woods. I'm aware that I have to get back for the second part of the assessment and I can't keep running away indefinitely, but I feel like the deeper I go into the wilderness, the more I'll unearth.

'You're pretty good at this,' I say to Hunter. 'Better than my therapist managed in a year.'

'You've had therapy?' Hunter asks.

I shoot him an insulted look, only to see him grin mischievously.

'Sorry,' says Hunter. 'Couldn't resist.'

'No, you're right,' I say. 'She told me when I started that I would get as much out of it as I put in. So I was like cool, no need to put in anything.'

Hunter laughs out loud. 'At least you know.'

I frown in confusion.

'Oh come on, Max. From what I've witnessed, you're not great at being honest about how you're feeling.'

I walk on in silence, but in my mind, I go back to where this conversation started. Hunter is right. I didn't want to shout at him. I didn't want to have it out. I shut down. I wanted to get away from it all and sulk. I can't think of any feeling more familiar. Growing up, I knew there was no point in voicing sentiments like that. It's not that my dad would get annoyed. It was worse. He'd panic. Make it about him. I learned not to discuss my feelings at all, knowing that any negative emotions would get turned into my dad's problems. I don't know how to say any of this to Hunter, but I do my best to explain it.

'It's not too late,' says Hunter.

I furrow my brow.

'To have that conversation with your dad.'

The mere suggestion fills me with fear. My dad and I don't talk. Not like that.

'I don't think that would go well.'

'That's not a reason not to try. You didn't want to have this conversation.'

'You're not my dad.'

'Forget about how he's going to react. There are things you need to say to him.'

I'm overcome with gratitude that I embarked on this crazy adventure with Hunter. Even if nothing else comes out of it, even if I don't get the job, I needed this conversation. I needed someone to push me like only Hunter could. I look him in the eye.

'Hunter . . . thank you.'

Hunter looks surprised. 'For what?'

'For not letting me get away with anything.'

Hunter shrugs. 'I just say what I see.'

'Easier said than done.'

Hunter smiles. 'You've done pretty well today.'

I feel a surge of affection that almost knocks me off my feet. It's going to take me days to process everything that has happened in the last hour. But as I think back to the assessment, I realise I still want the job. Yes, I may be chasing a diplomatic career for sentimental reasons.

No, I may not be the ideal candidate. But admitting that hasn't diminished my desire to achieve it.

'Shit,' I say to Hunter. 'We'd better head back. We must be miles from the house.'

'Nope,' Hunter says with a smile.

I frown. 'But we've been walking further and further away from it.'

'We've done a big loop,' says Hunter. 'I made sure.'

Damn him. Just when I thought I couldn't appreciate him any more.

I look at him sincerely. 'Hunter, I still really want this job.'

Hunter smiles back at me. 'Then go get it.'

32

Hunter

Max makes it back in the nick of time, heading straight in for the afternoon assessment. I'm not sure doing it on an empty stomach is ideal, but he doesn't have a choice. At least the past hour has focused his thoughts.

I need a moment to catch my breath myself. That was an emotional rollercoaster, especially coming after the conversation Max and I had on the train. There, it was Max who held me. Here, the roles were reversed. I'm starting to think that my relationship with Max is the first time I have experienced true partnership. It's completely different than what I had with Rafferty. Max and I have bared our souls to each other, and I don't think it's going too far to say that it has changed how we see each other. We showed each other our deepest wounds, and for me at least, it hasn't made me want to back away. Quite the opposite.

But what are we supposed to do about it? This has gone way beyond a mutual crush. It's a friendship, for sure, but it's more than that. It feels like the start of something bright and blazing. Letting it burn freely could be irresponsible, but I don't know how to contain it. I want to fan the flames of our desires and see where it takes us.

What I really need is to speak to Zosia and Thiago about it, but Thiago is spending the afternoon dressed as Princess Peach and handing out cupcakes in Leicester Square, and Zosia is auditioning to play a manure farmer in Lena Dunham's feminist reimagining of *My Little Pony*. Instead, I head up to our room and lie on the bed in a state of paralysis until Max comes back from his assessment.

'How did it go?' I ask, scanning his face.

'Better,' he says.

He explains what they were tasked with, which thankfully didn't involve Gerald Pope this time. The candidates were asked to brainstorm and pitch soft power initiatives, and Max's idea of a touring art exhibition was chosen as the winner. Nothing too bold, nothing offensive, just good clean diplomacy. He's relieved it went well, but the day has left him exhausted. He declares that he needs a shower.

I hear the water splash over his body, and my imagination refuses to stay idle. I picture him covered in soap suds, his hand gliding between his butt cheeks then around to the front. The thought turns my blood to fire.

When Max emerges, he's wearing a crisp white bath robe, a single lock of hair falling over his eyes. He puts his hand on his neck and groans.

'What?' I ask.

'Nothing.'

'It's not nothing.'

Max hesitates. 'It's been a long day. My neck hurts.'

Now that I look at him, the tension is visible.

'Do you want me to give you a massage?'

All the air is sucked out of the room. We both know that a massage is dangerous territory, but I can see how much he needs it.

'Don't worry about it,' says Max.

'Max. I'm here for you.'

'You've done enough for me today.'

'Lie down.'

The command stops him short. He walks over to the bed, then hesitates. I realize it's because he's naked underneath his bath robe. I'd love nothing more than for him to lie there naked, but it's better for both of us if he doesn't. I tell him to lower the robe to his waist, then avert my eyes as he gets in place.

Still, when I turn towards him, the sight stops me in my tracks. The curve of his back glistens with droplets from the shower, and I can see the top of his butt peeking out of his robe. I need to shift it down just a little to allow my hands to move smoothly, so I check that he's OK with that before doing so. But now his butt feels like it's teasing me.

Damn. The things I want to do to this boy.

I sit on top of him and get to work. With the massage, I mean. As I knead his muscles, I feel how knotted and tense he is. But slowly, my hands do their job. In some ways, this feels just as useful as the conversation we had earlier, undoing him in a way that words never could. His body yields to my touch, and it's like he's surrendering to the feelings we discussed on our walk. It's a beautiful thought, which is why it's a shame about the situation between my legs.

I'm not sure what I expected. I can feel the threads of Max's bathrobe against my calves. I can't resist imagining what's underneath. It's not that I'm being suggestive with my movements. I'm being entirely professional. But that's making it worse. Each time my hands stop at the top of his butt, my urge to slide lower grows stronger, and my dick gets harder. I tuck it into my waistband so it doesn't flop against Max by mistake, but now it's straining to be set free. I'm doing everything I can to ignore it when Max lets out a moan.

'Too hard?' I ask.

'No, no! All good!' Max gasps.

Now my thoughts run wild. Is he turned on too? He must be. I could swear his breathing has got faster. Maybe his body is betraying him too. Maybe he's longing for me to take this in the direction we started on our wedding night. I can no longer resist the impulse. But it has to come from Max too. There's one very easy way to find out if he's up for it. Face to face, neither of us will be able to hide.

'Do you want me to do your front?' I ask.

A scene flashes before my eyes: Max rolling onto his back, us seeing the unmistakable evidence in each other's pants, reaching in and taking it from there.

Is that what he's hoping for?

If he is, surely he'll detect the note of mischief in my voice, but that's as far as I'm prepared to go. I've put the ball firmly in his court. If he wants to keep this platonic, that's his call. I hold my breath as I wait for him to respond.

'Thanks,' he says, 'but don't worry about it. We should get ready for dinner.'

33

Max

It pained me to say no. There was nothing I wanted more than to turn onto my front and let Hunter see how hard I was. That's why he asked, right? It has to be. He knows I'm less experienced than him. He saw how I hesitated the first time we slept together. He's so sensitive towards me that it's almost as if he's afraid of corrupting me.

But what if I want to be corrupted?

I guess that's what he needs to hear me say in so many words. Because I do want that. If he's really open to being intimate, then I'm ready. I know it will blow up everything, but I don't care. I need to taste those lips again, feel his skin against mine, get my hands on every part of him when we're not shuffling around in the dark.

But there's a time and a place for something I have no doubt is going to shake me to my foundations. Right now, I need to focus.

We get dressed for dinner without sharing the bathroom. We barely speak. As we head downstairs, I'm actively glad we stopped where we did. I can only imagine the state that would have left me in, and that's not what this weekend is about. My performance in this afternoon's assessment was better than this morning, but I still feel like I'm playing catch-up. I have to be on form at dinner.

The dining room at Chevening is grand enough to impress but still intimate. The polished wooden table is lined with candles that cast their glow onto silver cutlery and crystal glasses. The first person I see is Wrettham. He's getting a top-up of champagne while lecturing the waiter on what angle he should be pouring it at. *Bloody prat*, I hear my mum say. She was a master of the withering insult. I'm not sure what she would think about me working for a man like Wrettham, but I guess I'll never have to find out.

Hunter pulls me to one side as he notices a seating plan.

'Ooh,' he says.

'What?'

'You've got Baroness Sharon.'

Nice one. That puts me in the hot seat but in the most fun way possible.

'Who have you got?' I ask Hunter.

He looks at me, deadpan. 'I'm really going to be earning my dinner.'

I look where he's pointing. He's been seated next to Wrettham.

I can't help wondering who came up with this seating plan. Hunter and I have been placed next to the two most important people in this assessment. That can't be a bad thing. Maybe they feel like they know Quentin and Flora fairly well, whereas they want to get to know us better. Or maybe it's random, but I plan to make the most of this opportunity, and I assume Hunter will too.

Baroness Sharon arrives just as we're told to take our seats. She has changed into a tailored jumpsuit with a sequinned blazer. Compared to her usual outfits, this is positively demure.

I settle into my chair and get ready to make small talk. But Baroness Sharon is distracted. She's sending emails on her phone, which is not surprising for a politician at her level. But her demeanor has changed.

Gone is the spirited woman who greeted us on our arrival. She's possessed by an anxiety that, despite her best efforts, she's unable to conceal.

'Sorry about that, Max,' she says, putting her phone away. 'Where were we?'

As the meal is served, I'm surprised by how difficult it is to make conversation. I was expecting us to be hooting with laughter over my dating disasters and her political enemies. Instead, it's all very formal. She asks me about the town I grew up in, and we have a long conversation about the fact that nobody knows where eels breed, but Sharon keeps checking her phone and replying to more emails.

To make matters worse, I have a clear view of Hunter and Wrettham, who against all odds are having a blast, their laughter ringing out across the dining room. At least Hunter is doing what he came here to do. But it's all so awkward between me and Sharon that by the time we reach dessert, I feel like I have nothing to lose and can bring up the subject that has been on my mind all evening.

'I screwed up the exercise this morning, didn't I?'

Sharon frowns. 'I can't discuss that, I'm afraid.' She hesitates. 'But you're welcome to share how you found it.'

'I don't want to make it worse.'

'You won't.'

I sigh. 'I just felt like . . . no one was saying what we were all thinking.'

Sharon takes a sip of her wine. 'That's diplomacy. Don't mention the elephant in the room, because it could be used against you.'

I pause, deep in thought. 'How do you cope with that?'

Sharon smiles. 'Badly.'

I raise an eyebrow.

'It's true.' She glances around, then lowers her voice. 'Max, I've fucked up.'

My ears prick up.

'We've been finalising the long form of the trade deal. My finger slipped and the documents got shared with the wrong people. Now I'm being accused of leaking state secrets.'

Damn. That explains her mood.

'How are you responding?'

'I can't decide. Some of my team think we should claim it was a crowdsourcing initiative to get junior staff involved. Others think I should just admit to the fuck-up.'

I pause to consider. 'Honestly, I'm not sure either of those are going to work.'

Sharon tilts her head, intrigued.

'The first one is obvious bullshit. People can't stand it when politicians lie.'

Sharon nods in agreement.

'The second one is relatable, but it does risk you looking incompetent.'

'You're right,' says Sharon, biting her lip. 'So what do I do?'

'Find a middle ground. Honesty with a bit of spin. Say you sent it prematurely because you're so proud of this deal and so excited to share it with the world.'

Sharon smiles. 'Do you know what? That is by far the best option I've heard.'

She pulls out her phone and fires off an email.

'Thank you, Max.'

She switches off her phone and puts it in her handbag.

'Right. Party time!'

That felt good. Not only because I seem to have impressed Sharon, but because it came to me naturally, unlike the knots I was tying myself in during that first assessment trying to be someone I'm not.

After dessert, everyone is shown through to the smoking lounge, as those who didn't have prime seating spots seize their moment. Wrettham is approached by either Henry Herbert or Herbert Henry, while Priyanka Patel makes a beeline for Baroness Sharon. I race straight over to Hunter.

'How was Wrettham?' I ask.

'He didn't disappoint,' says Hunter. 'He's *convinced* I was attacked by a baboon. He was telling everyone. We spent most of the meal talking about homosexuality in Ancient Greece. He's thinking of recreating the first Olympics at the British Embassy, clothing optional. I can't tell if that makes him secretly gay or incredibly heterosexual.'

I fill Hunter in on how it went with Baroness Sharon. I can see that he's pleased, but I'm not sure how closely he's listening. Even as I talk, I can only focus on what's unsaid, the spark that reignites every time we look into each other's eyes. But I don't want to leave it unsaid this time. As I finish my update, I soften my gaze.

'I have to be honest ... I was missing you the whole time.'

Hunter is lost for words, stunned in the best way possible.

I waltz off towards the drinks table, grinning. It feels good to be a little reckless after how carefully Hunter and I have been tiptoeing around our mutual attraction.

Thankfully, the original plan of the brilliant Flora Forbes performing some selections from the Greek classics as after-dinner entertainment appears to have been dropped. Instead, as everyone gets their drinks, DJ Redacta sets up her decks on top of an antique bridge table. It is no revelation to any of us that DJ Redacta is Baroness Sharon's club kid persona, for the simple reason that when a Member of Parliament has a club kid persona, it's unlikely to be much of a secret. The press have dragged her to hell and back for her partying tendencies, but Sharon doesn't care. She pops on some oversized shades, and within minutes, we're all bopping along to 1990s club classics. You'd think that a group of civil service job applicants might make for an awkward collective, and you'd be right. They're not the smoothest set of movers and shakers I've ever seen.

But I only have eyes for Hunter. I know we're surrounded by people, but it feels like they are no more than a backdrop for a private dance between the two of us. We move close, brushing against each other, hands grazing waists, hips nudging. Hunter undoes a button and I catch a flash of pec before looking away. When I glance back, he's meeting my eyes and smiling just enough to make me wonder if he knows what he's doing. My chest tightens.

Now every brush, every glance, feels loaded with meaning. I try to lose myself in the music, but each time I open my eyes, there he is, swaying his hips in a way that makes me weak at the knees. If this lasts much longer, they'll have to carry me out on a stretcher.

After a while, Sharon leaves her decks and approaches us. She has a drink in her hand that one of her aides has kept topped up throughout the night.

'Tune!' Sharon yells.

We both enthusiastically agree, even though we're at least a decade too young to know what tune she's talking about.

'Boys, I don't care what happens with this job,' Sharon slurs. 'Promise me we'll stay friends.'

I smile. 'We promise.'

At that moment, the beat drops in the song that's playing, and DJ Redacta dances off, pumping her fist in the air and spilling her drink everywhere. Her Chief of Staff orders a waiter to mop it up and races after her, tutting.

Hunter and I share a grin.

'The selection committee are very invested in our relationship,' I say.

'Tell me about it,' says Hunter. 'It would be a shame to disappoint them.'

He gives me a knowing once-over, biting his lip with a devious glint in his eye.

My stomach lurches and my legs feel like jelly.

What the hell am I meant to say to that?

Flustered, I glance away and catch sight of Quentin and Flora. They're at the back of the room, locked in an argument. Flora is letting rip at him in that way you can only do when you're several drinks in, while Quentin looks shellshocked. Hunter notices I'm distracted, and turns to see what I'm looking at.

'Oh dear,' he says.

'It's all falling apart.'

'You never know,' says Hunter. 'Our argument earlier brought us closer.'

As he looks back at me, I see everything clearly for the first time. There's no mystery to how he feels about me. We're on the same page. And Hunter and I both know what we want to happen next.

'Hey,' I say. 'Let's get out of here.'

34

Hunter

That was the cue I was looking for. No more second guessing. We don't just want this – we need this. We need each other. These feelings have been growing in intensity ever since that first kiss. We can worry about the consequences tomorrow.

I thought Max would take me up to our room. Instead, he holds my hand and leads me along the corridor. The sound of the party fades behind us, and Max peers into one room, then another. I realize he doesn't have a destination in mind, he's just seeing where the mood takes him. Eventually, we reach the back of the house and step through an arched door.

I stop and gasp. We're in some sort of conservatory. Tall glass panes rise to a vaulted ceiling, brushed by the tops of orange trees planted in vast terracotta pots. The fruit gives off a heady citrus scent that hangs in the night air. Between the two rows of trees lies a spectacular indoor swimming pool, its aquamarine tiles shimmering beneath the moonlight. Max and I exchange a look, amazed at where we've found ourselves.

Max nods at the pool. 'Shall we?'

My heart starts to race. This is precisely the kind of situation I might have sought out in the past. There's no question that we're not meant to be here. Max's career is on the line. But that's not what has my heart racing. I'm just so excited to be doing this with him.

'Why not?' I say with a smile.

Max grins and reaches up to unbutton his shirt.

'Wait,' I say.

Max's eyes search mine. I hold his gaze until he understands. Our faces drift closer, a fraction at a time, until our lips meet in the faintest brush. I can hardly breathe. Knowing how hard we have tried to resist this only makes it more intense. Soon, my other senses take over. I can feel Max's breath, his tongue, his hands in my hair. He tastes of the wine we've been drinking all evening. The taste takes me back there, so the sense of exquisite and excruciating anticipation mingles with the blissful awareness that this is happening right now.

This feels like a first kiss. Yes, we kissed in front of our guests at our wedding, then again in the dark that night, but this is the first time we have stood together, just the two of us, and truly allowed ourselves to drink each other in.

I keep pulling back and opening my eyes to gaze at him in wonder. I'm not sure if it's out of disbelief or because I can't get enough of the sight of him.

As the kiss becomes deeper and more intense, Max's hands drift down my torso and grab at the bulge in my pants. Nothing turns me on more than the sight of his desire. I give him a nod, letting him know I'm up for whatever he wants to do.

He peels my shirt off, and I savour the warmth of his hands on my skin. He traces a line down my chest, pausing at every ridge and hollow, before he drifts lower. He kneels in front of me, nuzzling closer, feeling the swell of me beneath the fabric, then runs his finger along the inside of my waistband, unbuckles my belt and pulls down my pants.

My dick pings up as it's let loose. Max laughs.

'The response every man wants,' I say dryly.

Max looks up at me. 'I just . . . I've never seen one this big.'

He holds it in his hand, feeling its weight. I'm the last person to think that being hung is some kind of achievement, but I'm not going to pretend I don't enjoy it. What man wouldn't? There have been guys in the past who have made me feel like a piece of meat, but with Max it's pure delight and curiosity.

I give him a wicked smile. 'I bet you can make it bigger.'

Max exhales a hot breath of air, then starts to tease me with the tip of his tongue. I let out a gasp and feel it ripple through me. My breath quickens. Max explores every inch of me with his mouth, pausing occasionally to look up at me. Each time our eyes meet, it drives me wild. There's an awestruck look, but also a hunger. Seeing it ignites my own desires.

I pull Max to his feet and tug at his shirt. His clothes come off in a flurry, and before I know it, we're both naked. Our bodies press together, then we trip backwards and stumble into the pool with a splash.

We rise to the surface, laughing. I brush a strand of wet hair from his eyes, then we start kissing again. The kiss pulls us underwater, and I feel air pass from my lungs to his as if we're keeping each other alive. We surface again, our lips staying locked.

We splash around, gulping for air when we can, our hands running over each other's bodies with abandon. At one point, Max swallows some water and has a coughing fit, pulling us out of the moment. But it only sends us into fits of laughter and straight back to kissing.

I steer Max to one side of the pool, then hoist him up so he's perched there, leaning back on his hands. The way he settles, proud and unguarded, is incredibly hot. I stand in the water, hands tracing his hips as I lean in and start to suck him. I take my time, enjoying every shiver that runs through him. His chest rises and falls, eyes closed, soft gasps escaping him, each one making me harder.

Then a sudden shout cuts through the night. Max's eyes fly open. It's only a random sound from the party, but it brings us back to earth.

Max smiles. 'Let's finish this somewhere else.'

We pull on our clothes, even though we're dripping wet. Max leaves his shirt open, water droplets glistening on his chest hair.

We can't walk through the house like this, so we slip out into the garden.

The moon hangs bright and low, casting silver light across the lawn, illuminating the dew on the grass and making the trees cast shadows.

We find a small clearing in the woods and lie down beneath the stars. The air is cool against our damp skin. I can feel Max breathing against my chest, smell the pine trees in the air. When I gaze into Max's eyes, I see his emotions swell and overflow.

'Hunter,' Max says, looking at me innocently. 'I think I'm falling for you.'

The words knock me sideways, but I smile at him coolly. 'You reckon?'

Max nods and bites his lip. Damn, that's cute.

'How do you think I feel?' I ask.

Max shrugs earnestly. I can't take much more of this cuteness.

'Max, I started falling for you a while ago. You're the most adorable man on this planet.'

Max looks like he's been hit by a comet. He blinks in amazement.

As I say the words, I'm amazed it's taken us this long to admit it. I have tried to avoid it in every way possible, but there's no more denying it.

We've fallen for each other.

Max furrows his brow. 'What do we do about it?'

He looks overwhelmed, as if the strength of his own feeling scares him. I want to answer him, but the question feels too big for this moment, so I offer him another smile.

'Don't worry about that now. I've got one idea.'

Our lips meet again. Before, every touch surged with desire, but now that we've acknowledged our feelings, there's something deeper firing our passion.

We grasp and tug at each other, then Max bends down and teases my dick with his tongue. My whole body flares with heat. Max grips me firmly, tasting and kissing, copying tricks I used on him indoors. I want to pleasure him, feel him hard in my mouth, but I don't want him to stop. I spin around so I can return the favor while he continues.

Max lets out a chuckle as he realizes what we're doing. I'm not used to laughing during sex, but with him it feels like the most natural thing in the world and the only correct response to a 69.

Not that it isn't also hot beyond words. I lose myself in the blend of sensations. Beads of sweat and pool water cling to us and bind us. I can feel the cool tickle of the grass against my skin.

Max's hands hold my waist as he takes the full length of me. At the same time, I guide his hips to thrust deeper into my mouth, matching each other's movements, over and over. His moans vibrate through me. He's getting close, blood pulsing. I'm right there with him, curled in this endless loop of pleasure, each trusting the other to guide us to the finish.

Now here it comes, in one pure burst. Max fills my mouth, and moments later, I do the same, just as I'm savoring the taste of him.

As we catch our breath, I wipe my mouth and shift around so I can look Max in the eye. He licks his upper lip clean and smiles at me. Overcome by his pure, sweet beauty, I pull him into my arms. We lie there beneath the trees, the moonlight bathing our bodies in silver, feeling our hearts beat in tandem.

I have never felt more alive.

35

Max

I never used to understand people who freaked out after sex. Post-nut clarity, the walk of shame . . . these were concepts that made no sense to me. And there's really no good reason why I would be feeling them right now. Last night was pure bliss. It was everything I have been longing for. Afterwards, we tiptoed back inside and fell asleep in each other's arms.

I woke a few moments ago, Hunter in bed beside me, his face angelic as he slept. But rather than curling my arms around him, I find myself slipping out of bed without waking him.

Maybe I just need some air.

I pull on some clothes and head out for a walk. Admittedly, I'm calmer than when I came here yesterday, when I wanted to run off into the wilderness and never return. But I don't feel anything close to peace. As I walk in the bright morning light, the source of my angst emerges in the form of one question – the same question that didn't really get answered last night.

What now?

This isn't like the time Hunter and I fumbled around on our wedding night. Looking back, that was little more than a release of tension. We were swept up in the emotion of the occasion and needed to let off some steam. But I can't say the same about last night.

That was intentional. Inevitable. The culmination of weeks of unspoken desire. There's no use denying how I feel about Hunter, especially now I know that his feelings for me go at least a bit beyond the purely physical. But I don't want that Athens job any less. And Hunter has given no hint that he's interested in moving to Greece with me. So we're right back where we started, only with the yearning cranked up to eleven.

Oh god, don't think about the sex. That was a revelation. In the past, sex has always been about me reading the other person, working out what they wanted and giving it to them while hoping I hadn't made a fool of myself. If they walked away smiling, it was a success. But I see now it meant I never claimed much space for my own desires.

I recall the way that Hunter hoisted me onto the side in the swimming pool. He didn't ask if I wanted it, not because he didn't care but because he already knew I did, and he wasn't going to apologise for giving me pleasure. Man, that felt good. Hunter clearly knew what he was doing, but he didn't make me feel inferior. It felt like the start of an adventure, one that could lead me to places and feelings that I've never even imagined.

But no. Stop. I mustn't imagine them. It was just one night. It doesn't mean anything. We mustn't do it again – at least not until we've talked about it. Maybe it didn't mean as much to Hunter as it did to me. Either way, I need to know. We need to have a conversation. And I can totally do that. It'll be fine. Completely fine. I'm not freaking out. I'm calm. I'm collected. The definition of someone not spiralling about sex that definitely didn't change everything.

I don't want to scare Hunter and make him think I've gone missing again. I text him and say I'll see him at breakfast. A part of me believes that he'll have had second thoughts and that will be the end of it.

But when I see him in the dining hall, he walks straight over and kisses me on the lips. I feel a wave of guilt. That wasn't a performance. That came from the heart. He's all in on this. I thought he was supposed to be the one putting the brakes on. As we sit down to breakfast and we're drawn into a conversation with Henry Herbert or Herbert Henry about the historical evolution of cutlery, Hunter keeps catching my eye and smiling. Each time, it's a dagger to my heart. Why can't I just enjoy this? This isn't like me.

Needing a breather, I get up from the table and cross over to the coffee machine. Standing there is Baroness Sharon, making herself a triple espresso as her Chief of Staff observes judgementally. She's more hungover than any of us, but when she spots me, her eyes light up.

'Max!' she says. 'Have you seen the headlines?'

'What? No.'

She pulls out her phone and shows me. Admittedly, it's from a paper that is relatively friendly to the government, but it refers to her 'jumping the gun' on releasing details of the trade deal to the public. The article features her quote in the exact wording I suggested. I'm sure she'll still get blowback, but it could have been so much worse.

'Thank god I asked your advice,' says Sharon, casting a side-eye at her Chief of Staff.

'It's nothing,' I say.

Sharon scoffs. 'Don't be silly.'

She leans in so that her Chief of Staff can't hear. 'Good luck with the job, Max. They'd be lucky to have you.'

The train ride back is excruciating. The carriage is empty, but when Hunter grabs a bank of four seats, I sit diagonally opposite. I can't cope with two hours of gazing into his eyes. We hardly talk on the journey home. I look out of the window, he scrolls on his phone. I'm just not ready for what we might conclude if we talk about last night.

It's only as we get off at Waterloo and walk home to Kennington that we get some life back into us, focusing on a topic that doesn't involve us: what might have happened between Doily and my dad while we were gone.

I'm not expecting fireworks. This is my dad we're talking about. He's barely shown any interest in dating since my mum died, and in any case, I can't imagine him taking things quickly. But the fact that he's doing this project with Doily is evidence of his interest in her. There was a spark between them. Alone in the house together, who knows what might have gone down.

When we get home, there's no sign of my dad's car. Hunter and I share a look, then go in search of Doily. We find her in her office, which looks like the before and after of a home renovation melded into one. One side of the office is scrupulously organised, the other is messier than ever. That's the side that Doily is on. She's seated on the floor, sorting papers into two piles, one enormous and unwieldy, the other tiny.

Doily hears us enter but doesn't look up.

'I'm separating my regional theater programs into essential and non-essential.'

Hunter picks up a playbill from the larger pile.

'What's so essential about the Derby Playhouse's 2006 production of *Cinderella*?'

'Do you even have to ask?' tuts Doily. 'That was the one where the Fairy Godmother was played by Peppa Pig. Looking back, that was the beginning of the end.'

Hunter places the playbill gently back on the pile.

'Did my dad—' I begin.

Doily's face tightens. 'He had to leave.'

She continues sorting through the playbills, placing every single one on the essential pile with so much vigour that it's on the verge of falling over.

Hunter and I share another look.

'Is everything OK?' I ask.

Doily says nothing at first, but we wait.

'I do not understand this obsession some people have with putting everything in order,' Doily says eventually. She looks up at me. 'Are you the same?'

I frown. 'As what?'

'Your father.'

'Er, no, actually.'

Doily sniffs as if she doesn't believe me.

'What happened?' I ask.

Doily looks aggrieved. 'We were alphabetising my clients. Fair enough, you might think, but I wanted to keep a separate folder for the Geralds. Alan agreed to it, but when I got back from glazing my fruitcake, he'd included the Geralds in the F-to-H folder. After I'd specifically asked him not to. Can you believe that?'

I glance at Hunter. 'I . . . what did you say to him?'

'I asked him why he'd ignored my request. He told me—' Doily pauses to collect herself. 'He said there was no place for sentiment in filing systems, and if it wasn't logical, he couldn't put his name to it.'

Doily is flushed with anger as she recalls it. Sensing that I'm somehow giving her flashbacks to the cause of her misery, I leave Hunter to console her and head over to pick up Mr Peanut from the dog-sitter. On the way, I message my dad to get his perspective, but his replies are unrepentant, saying that he can't help someone who doesn't want to be helped.

I'm struck by how sad I feel. What was my dad thinking? Honesty was the last thing Doily needed in that moment. Whatever bond existed between Doily and my dad was built on a polite acceptance of the other's eccentricities. My dad crossed a line and shone a light on a side of Doily she had no interest in having illuminated.

It makes me fear that Hunter and I are too different to work as a couple. Sure, we have a lot of care and concern for each other, but it's a constant effort to meet each other in the middle. Maybe it would be easier if we each found someone who was more similar. Someone who wanted to live and work in the same country would be a good start.

When I arrive at the dog-sitter, Mr Peanut is delighted to see me. I'm not in any mood to hold back, so I kneel and let him lick my face as much as he likes, just like the old days. As we walk home, Mr Peanut immediately settles into our routine, showing as much interest in a discarded kebab wrapper as in the owner he's just been reunited with. A silly part of me is offended, but really I envy him this ability to live in the moment. He wasn't pining for me all weekend. He accepts what's in front of him and rolls with it.

I think about the conversation Hunter and I had on our walk at Chevening. It's hard not to see Mr Peanut as part of why I am the way I am. In many respects, I'm just like him, and that's not necessarily a good thing. Yes, there is something beautiful about being able to enjoy the present and not worry about what has happened and what's to come. But I can't live like that permanently. If I rush into something with Hunter without thinking about the consequences, I'll ruin it before it's had a chance.

Just like that, it's clear to me what I need to say to Hunter.

This isn't going to be easy.

When I get home, Hunter is standing in the garden drinking a coffee. The cherry tree has shed almost all its blossom, creating a carpet of petals.

'It's such a waste, don't you think?' I say.

'What?' Hunter asks.

'The cherry blossom. It lasts for such a short time, and then it just . . . dies.'

Hunter peers at me. 'What's up, Max?'

I hesitate. 'I think it might be a good idea to go back to separate beds.'

Hunter looks surprised, as if the suggestion doesn't match my mood. Then he takes in what I'm really saying, and his smile fractures. My heart breaks a little.

'Trust me,' I say, 'it's the last thing I want.'

It feels so hard to say this. There's nothing I'd like more than to jump into bed with Hunter every night. But it's not a good idea.

'Everything is so up in the air,' I explain. 'I don't know how my assessment went. You haven't heard back about your audition. But more than that . . .'

I pause, and swallow. 'Some stuff came up this weekend that I need to work through, before we can . . .'

I break off. Seeing Hunter's face sink into worry lines is devastating.

He nods and turns to leave, perhaps to spare us both any more agony. But I need to make sure there's no room for doubt.

'I want you, Hunter. I'm just not ready.'

36

Hunter

Maybe I notice the rain less when I'm happy. It's not like we don't get enough of it in London, and usually it blends into the background. But when it starts pouring shortly after my conversation with Max, I feel like someone has flipped a switch to match my mood.

Why did I let myself feel hope even for a fraction of a second? There's no good way for this to end. Max was only doing what I did a few weeks ago when I suggested not sleeping together.

In a weird way, I'm proud of him. He's learning to be honest with himself about how he's feeling and what's best for him. But that doesn't make this any easier.

I'm not one of those people who like to wander through the rain and get soaked to the skin. All I want to do is curl up in bed and watch a trashy movie. Unfortunately, I have plans. As one of her many wedding gifts, Doily arranged for me, Zosia and Thiago to go and hate-watch *Anna Karenina On Ice* at the Tower of London, a production that encapsulates everything that Doily despises about the modern theater industry.

The production doesn't disappoint, in that there's a lot to hate about it. It's unclear what the producers were thinking. Why did Tolstoy's most famous novel need to be adapted for the ice rink? Why not just stage a play? The cast is a mixture of professional ice skaters and celebrities who've appeared on *Dancing on Ice*. The acting ranges from mediocre to dreadful. There's barely a scene that isn't ruined by a random bout of ice skating, the worst example being a bizarre grouse-hunting expedition where the cast all start doing axels and triple toe loops for no apparent reason.

And yet I can't help but be drawn in. As Anna and Vronsky long for each other, I feel like I'm right there with them. I have never wanted anyone the way I want Max now. Being apart from him for just a few hours is physically painful. I want to gaze at him across a ballroom, run away with him to a remote country estate and make love all day, stand up in a crowded hall and declare my love for him.

But what shocks me, what rocks me to my core, is realizing what I want most of all. Until recently, seeing the tragedy play out between Anna and Vronsky would have confirmed for me that it was wrong to believe in love. So many times in the past when I've been down, art like this has reinforced my bleak view of the world. But as the play comes to its tragic and slightly ridiculous conclusion, I'm not comforted. Not even slightly.

What I long for more than anything is a happy ending.

As we file out of the theater, I get a text from Doily saying she's paid for a meal for us at Joe Allen, the restaurant beloved by London's theater community. There, as a West End stalwart stands by the piano and massacres 'Don't Cry For Me Argentina', we order cocktails and bitch about the show. But while Zosia and Thiago wet themselves laughing over the moment when Anna was skating to catch Vronsky's train and did what we all hope was an unintentional pratfall, I find I can't join them. Eventually, Zosia notices and frowns at me.

'Did you not enjoy that?'

'No, I did.'

Neither she nor Thiago believe me.

'I did! I actually got caught up in the romance.'

'OK,' says Zosia. 'What's going on, Hunter?'

I let out a sigh and tell them what happened at Chevening, how I finally felt like Max and I were going somewhere until he dropped that bombshell when we got home.

'Oh babe.' Thiago takes my hand. 'You've created a monster.'

I laugh bitterly. 'It's fine.'

'It's not fine,' says Thiago. 'It's bullshit.'

'It's not bullshit,' says Zosia firmly. 'It's just hard.'

I want to cry, but I can't do that or I might never stop.

'I'm not mad at Max,' I say. 'I'm mad because . . . I didn't think I would ever feel hope again. I honestly thought Rafferty had ruined me.'

It's a risk saying his name to these two because I immediately see their hackles go up. Zosia takes a swig of her cocktail and shakes her head.

'No,' she says. 'He never had that power.'

I give her a grateful smile. 'It's just so unfair that I finally get over him and then it's unclear if Max and I can be together.'

'There's so many ways you could be together,' says Thiago. 'If he doesn't get this job, he won't have to move to Greece.'

'But he wants to be a diplomat,' I say. 'He wants to travel abroad. I don't want to get in the way of that dream.'

'You won't,' says Zosia. 'You two would never do that to each other.'

'Yes, that's the problem!' I blurt out.

I can't bear it, I really can't. The prospect of a life without Max has fast become intolerable. But if I've gone to a dark place, my friends won't meet me there.

'Look,' says Zosia, 'Max is being mature. He's protecting his feelings. But don't tell me he's given up on you two. Don't tell me he's stopped dreaming.'

37

Max

I need to stop living with my head in the clouds. It's time to face reality. I'm on the train with Mr Peanut to go and see my dad. I hate to say it, but it feels good to get away from Hunter. I stand by my decision, but that doesn't make it any easier. You'd think that developing real feelings for each other would make it easier for us to pretend to be a couple, but now I can't bear the thought of it. If I get to the final stage of interviews in Athens, Hunter will be invited, but apart from that, most of the faking should be over.

Starting with today's mission.

I keep tabs on my dad with our daily phone calls, but I rarely visit him. It's hard to be in that house. As my train clatters out of London, I watch as five-storey townhouses gradually give way to run-down suburban terraces. After an hour, we arrive in Horsham, the town I grew up in. It's a perfectly pleasant place with some very nice parts, including a nature reserve and a museum. For my dad, however, its appeal was its proximity to the airport he worked at.

Arriving at our row of terraced houses with pebble-dash fronts, everything shrinks. You can only survive in a place like this by shrinking your horizons. This has to be the most relentlessly average street in the whole of England. Nothing exciting ever happens here. People mow their lawns, trade the same few phrases with their neighbours, buy the same products in their weekly Tesco shop. It only takes a few moments back here for me to be reminded of how desperately I longed to leave, make something more of my life, get precisely the kind of job I'm now in line for. I hate to admit it, given everything that's happened with Hunter, but as I walk up to my dad's front door and ring the bell, I've never wanted that Athens job more.

My dad opens the door and I throw my arms around him before he can escape me. He's not the type to initiate a hug, but I'm convinced he secretly likes it, and even if he doesn't, I really need one.

Some people I know love to surround themselves with photos of those they've lost. Not my dad. As I walk down the hallway, I pass the only photo he has on display. It's all three of us, taken on our last holiday together, my mum with her arms slung around both of us.

My mum and dad could never agree on where to go on holiday. My mum always longed for adventures, while my dad was keen to visit the same campsite each year where he knew the location of the emergency electricity supply and where to buy eggs on Sundays. But that year, we compromised on Amsterdam, and you can see from our smiling faces that everyone was happy.

My dad keeps the house spotless, but it still has that vaguely damp smell of a home that hasn't been redecorated in decades. He mumbles something about not knowing if I was staying for dinner, as if to excuse the meal he's prepared, which amounts to an incredible effort by his standards. He's bought a chicken pie and paired it with some sad-looking lettuce that's in bad need of Mariam's mythical salad tosser. I don't want to know what he eats on the nights it's just him.

We sit down to eat. Ordinarily, I would fill the first half hour of my visit with inane chatter, but my dad has barely taken a mouthful before he puts down his fork.

'I hope you aren't here to convince me to work with that woman.'

I pull an innocent expression. 'Am I not allowed to visit my own dad?'

He ignores me. 'I tried my best, Max! Offered her my help, no strings attached. The woman is impossible.'

I smile and shake my head. 'She's stuck in her ways. Remind you of anyone?'

My dad stiffens. 'My ways are logical.'

'To you maybe.'

My dad takes another bite and chews in silence. I press on.

'Maybe there's something beautiful about the way Doily sees the world. Let the Geralds have their own folder!'

My dad scoffs at the idea.

'You don't have to get it,' I continue. 'You don't even have to respect it. But that doesn't mean you can't let Doily be the way she wants to be.'

'Max, she can be who she wants. That's not the issue.' He examines his plate without lifting his fork. 'I just don't want to work together if feelings are going to get hurt.'

He keeps his eyes glued to his plate.

'Feelings?' I ask hopefully.

My dad looks up. 'She's a lovely woman. And perhaps . . . you know . . . she feels likewise. But it's not going to work. So let's leave it there.'

Now that he's admitted this, I'm not sure I can bear to leave it there. But I know my dad. He won't be persuaded of anything.

'Fine,' I say. 'That's actually not why I came here.'

My dad frowns in surprise. I take a deep breath. No going back now.

'Dad, I've been lying to you.'

No reaction.

'About me and Hunter.'

'Hunter?'

I feel sick. 'Yes, you know – Edwin's stage name. Except . . . it's his real name. It was all fake, Dad.'

'What was?'

'Me and Hunter. We didn't really fall in love. It was a marriage of convenience.'

I proceed to tell him everything. How I found Doily. How Hunter and I only met moments before walking into the British Museum. How we knew we were breaking the law but did it anyway. How gradually, the feelings we were faking became real – and how we've decided to put everything on pause until we know where our lives are taking us.

As I talk, I track my dad's reaction. He's doing his best not to reveal anything, but I can tell this is paining him. I feel awful, but I can't look away. It's not only my dad I'm being honest with. It's me.

Admitting all the feelings it has been too difficult or inconvenient to acknowledge, and the impossible situation it has left me in.

'I'm sorry, Dad.'

He's staring at the table. I wait for what feels like ages.

'I could tell something was up,' he says eventually.

He looks at me. 'Why do you think I insisted on the pre-nup?'

I'm momentarily speechless. 'Wait, you didn't believe it from the start?'

'It's not that. I just thought it would be sensible to have a back-up plan. But no, I believed it. At least I did once I'd met him.' He thinks back wistfully. 'Then at the wedding, when you said your vows . . . I was so happy, Max. I felt like I can't have failed that much as a parent, if I can raise a son who's capable of this.'

I thought I'd felt all the guilt I could at the wedding. I was wrong.

'Dad, I'm so sorry.'

He looks at me with a forlorn expression. 'I don't know how I raised such a liar.'

The word stops me in my tracks. I hold his gaze. 'I do.'

My dad blinks in confusion.

'I never felt like I could tell you the truth,' I say.

My dad's brow creases. 'About what?'

'How I was feeling. I didn't want to add to your worries.'

My dad sits forward. 'What didn't you tell me?'

'Anything. Everything. When I was sad or angry or scared. Eventually, I convinced myself I didn't feel that way. It was just easier.'

My dad picks at his salad as he digests this. I feel bad holding him to account so soon after apologising, but this is a conversation we should have had years ago.

'I'm sorry you didn't feel you could talk to me,' he says. 'But I hear you. You can tell me when you're sad. Are you sad right now?'

I pause, struck by the question. Why is this the one thing we never admit to each other?

'I guess so, yeah.'

My dad nods, thinking it over. 'You know, you and Hunter don't have to decide about your future right now. You shouldn't hold off based on what might or might not happen. Enjoy each other while you can.'

We both know he's thinking of his own marriage.

'I'm scared,' I say.

'Of what?'

'That it will hurt more if it doesn't work out.'

My dad looks at me wisely. 'It will hurt either way. Trust me on this, Max.'

As I catch the train back to London with Mr Peanut, my heart is lighter. My dad and I aren't going to make everything better with one conversation, but it feels like we've done the hard part and broken the ice. More than that, I think he's right about me and Hunter. Just because we're unsure of our future doesn't mean our present needs to be painful. I feel a rush of excitement at the thought of us sharing a bed tonight.

I let myself in quietly, and Hunter doesn't notice me at first. He's sitting at the kitchen table with a notepad and a pen. There's a half-drunk glass of milk on the table beside him, and remnants of white on his top lip. He's concentrating hard on what he's writing. After a moment, he looks up and sees me standing there.

'Hey,' I say. 'Can we talk?'

Hunter looks hesitant. 'I was going to ask you the same thing.'

'Oh. What's up?'

Hunter bursts into a smile. 'I got a callback.'

I'm stunned into silence.

'For *Hamlet,*' Hunter says. 'They loved my tape. The callback is in two days.'

'Oh my god, Hunter, that's amazing!'

I race forward and scoop him into a hug. I'm happy for him, genuinely happy, but I'm also keen to hide how much this news hurts. Hunter chatters about what they've asked him to do for his callback. He's so excited that it takes him a few minutes to recall how our conversation started.

'Wait, what did you want to talk about?' he asks eventually.

I could be honest with him, but this audition is everything to Hunter. He doesn't need any distractions.

I smile at him serenely. 'It can wait.'

38

Hunter

I mustn't get too excited. I don't have the role yet. But I'm going to be acting on stage at the Globe. Treading the boards, as they say. This is a moment I have dreamed about for as long as I can remember.

In this profession it's easy to feel that people like you more when you're failing. I know Zosia and Thiago are happy for me about my callback, but I'm worried they won't be able to avoid comparing it to what's going on in their own careers. This is not the kind of news it would be worth bothering my mom with. I thought about telling Ms Nelson, my high school English teacher, but she probably barely remembers me at this point.

There's only one person I can truly share this experience with, and ironically, it's the person who has the most to lose if I get the job.

I still struggle to believe that Max is being completely sincere when he says how much he wants this for me. But when I think back to the way he helped me with that first audition, I can't doubt him. He's not Rafferty. He's not built like that. He cares for me, and he wants me to succeed. It's no more complicated than that.

Any other time I've had a callback, I've gone into a hole to prepare. But I couldn't ask for anyone better to help me than Max. For starters, he's very perceptive. He sees details in the text that hadn't occurred to me. But he also keeps it light. He helps me find some surprising moments of levity in my performance.

I'm doubtful at first, as I don't want to look as though I've misunderstood the text. Let's not forget that I applied for this role with a song from a Disney musical. But when I see Max's reaction after I perform Hamlet's big soliloquy, I'm convinced that I've found the right balance. Who knows if this is the Hamlet they're looking for, but it's the Hamlet I'm born to be.

The night before the audition, I barely sleep. As soon as I get up, I'm frantic. I walk into the kitchen to find that Max has made me coffee and toast and placed a bunch of fresh flowers beside them. As I get dressed, Max gives me space, but I know he's there for me if I need him. Once I'm ready, he offers to walk me to the audition, and I can't think of anything I'd like more.

We stroll north, taking the scenic route through a garden square filled with crooked mulberry trees to the River Thames and the bustle of the South Bank. We pass teenage skaters zipping along the brutalist concrete underpasses, stalls selling secondhand books, and children chasing each other around the statue of Sir Laurence Olivier outside the National Theatre.

Eventually, we arrive at the Globe. I've been here many times before, but something about its tall exterior wall, more like a castle than a theater, feels more imposing than ever.

'Fuck,' I say.

'Listen,' says Max, 'you've done everything you possibly can.'

'I just . . . this is kind of a big deal.'

'I know,' says Max, resting his hand on my arm. 'But you've got this.'

A tide of tenderness surges through me. 'You really want this for me, don't you?'

'Yes,' Max says. At first, he doesn't understand my surprise, but then it hits him. 'I'm not your ex. I want you to aim high. Hell, I find it attractive.'

I shake my head in disbelief. 'The funny thing is, me starring on Broadway would only have benefitted him. It would have helped our reviews, his earnings, his career. And he still couldn't support me. Whereas you—'

I stop myself. We both know the part I'm not saying. That Max is helping me even though if I'm successful, it will place our lives on separate paths. I can see that it pains him as much as it pains me.

'Come on,' says Max. 'You mustn't be late.'

He starts to leave, then turns back. 'Just promise me one thing. Enjoy this.'

Inside, the foyer hums with the activity of a working theater. A group of schoolchildren in hi-vis jackets cluster by the entrance, their guide declaiming lines from *King Lear* as if he's mid-performance. A workman on a stepladder changes a light while humming a show tune.

A harried stage manager with a clipboard and a headset shows me into the auditorium.

As I enter, I feel like I've stepped back in time. The theater stretches out before me like a living model: the polished wooden stage, the wooden beams and thatched roof, sunlight spilling through the open windows.

I'm auditioning for three people today, seated in a line in the front row: a casting director who smiles far too easily, a stony-faced producer who won't stop taking notes, and the theater's artistic director, a woman who radiates quiet authority.

'Gender-flipped *Grease*, huh?' the artistic director says. 'How did that work?'

'Mixed,' I say. 'Some people felt the Pink Gentlemen were too queer-coded. But the all-female "Greased Lightning'" was awesome.'

They chuckle, and I look at them earnestly. 'I get where this industry's at. But I'm so excited to do some classical theater for once.'

'You've come to the right place,' says the director. 'That's what we do here at the Globe.' She gestures up to the stage. 'Whenever you're ready.'

My stomach plunges. This is it.

I step up onto the stage and hear the creak of the floorboards under my feet. I focus on a point in the middle distance. I've pictured this moment so many times, but it's hard to believe I'm actually here. All the way from my small town in Rhode Island to the boards that Shakespeare's actors trod, give or take a restoration or two. And now I have two minutes to show that I'm worthy.

My throat has gone dry. I'm struggling to remember my lines. Not the famous one. A toddler could remember that. But what comes before it? My mind is blank.

'Are you OK?' the director asks.

The fact that she has to ask is clear evidence that I'm not. There's too much riding on this. How do I pull myself out of it?

Then I notice a movement out of the corner of my eye. I glance upwards and my heart lurches. There he is. Max. How did he get in here? As soon as he sees that I've spotted him, he raises his hands and forms them into a heart.

It hits me like a physical blow. This isn't just a cute gesture. He believes in me. He wants me to succeed, not for show or out of obligation but because my happiness means that much to him. He's not Rafferty, scoffing at my ambitions. He's Max, my secret anchor, my silent cheerleader.

A rush of love floods through me and I'm unsteady on my feet. All my doubts vanish, replaced by the unshakeable certainty that I can do this. Not for myself, but for Max, for us. His belief has become my belief.

I look at the director and give her a thumbs-up. Then I close my eyes and find my way into the character. I take a deep breath, imagining the salty air and dusty tapestries of Elsinore. I hear the footsteps of castle guards. I think of my father, the king, with a pang of grief.

When I open my eyes, I'm no longer Hunter auditioning for the role of my life. I'm Hamlet. The people in the front row might as well not be there.

I allow the lines to emerge from within. When you've done this much work to prepare, the key is to switch off. If you're consciously reproducing each gesture and inflection, you're bound to come across as mannered. By now that I've gathered myself, my Hamlet shimmers to life. I'm not trying to control him, and I couldn't tell you if this constitutes a good or bad performance. I'm simply letting him exist.

It's only after I finish that I look down at the front row. A spell has fallen over them. They're rapt. After a moment, they snap to attention.

'Thank you,' says the director. 'That was really something.'

As I walk off the stage, they confer in low tones.

'Actually, Hunter,' says the director, 'before you go . . .'

She looks slightly bashful. 'This is a bit cheeky, but we've got a long day ahead of us. Would you mind giving us a spin of "I Just Can't Wait To Be King"?'

Max and I walk home in silence. We both know how well that went and what that might mean for our future. Neither of us can bring ourselves to say anything. When we arrive home, there in the driveway is a Skoda. Max notices it the same time as I do.

'Is that your dad's—'

'Yeah.'

We head inside without another word. The hallway is filled with the scent of garlic and herbs. We make our way to the kitchen, where Doily is standing over the Aga, Mr Peanut seated beside her and clearly assuming that this is his dinner she's cooking. Max's dad is at the kitchen table sorting random bolts and screws into about twelve different categories. He looks up as we enter, then immediately turns back to his screws.

'I'm making your father a cassoulet,' Doily announces. 'You hear that, Master Peanuts? It's not for you.'

Max looks at his dad. 'I thought you said you'd let me know next time you were coming.'

Max's dad shrugs. 'I'm not here for you.'

Max is about to take offence when he sees the way his dad is looking at Doily. She sees it too and blushes, then turns to Max.

'Your father apologised for his reaction. Well, perhaps not apologised, but he acknowledged it. More to the point, he changed his mind. The Geralds are going to have their own folder.'

Max's dad's shoulders tense. 'It's not how I'd do it. But this is Doily's business. And she has assured me we can do everything else my way.'

Max and I share a look.

'Everything else?' Max asks in surprise.

Max's dad scratches his chin and glances away. 'As with all my projects, I'm committed to seeing it through to delivery. Doily has kindly agreed to accommodate me for that period. Starting tonight.'

Oh my god. They're going to fuck. If they haven't already. They're going to digitise records all day and fuck all night.

Doily turns to me. 'The thing is, I'm not doing this for the tax man. I'm doing it because it's time to retire.'

I feel a jolt of shock. Doily, retiring? It's unimaginable. She's woven into the fabric of the London arts scene, and without a doubt its biggest vault of gossip.

'You're retiring?'

'Yes. I'll be sad to give up some of my clients, none more than you. But I wasn't lying when I said I'd received an offer I couldn't refuse on the house.'

I stare at her in shock. 'What? I thought you were loaded.'

'Asset rich, dear. I haven't been great at paying my bills over the years. Let's be honest – I've never been great at the business side of things.'

I'm still too surprised to really take this in, but Doily is philosophical. 'I knew this day would come. I've thought about it for years.'

She gazes lovingly at Max's dad. 'I was just waiting for a sign, I suppose. A reason to pack it in.'

I glance at Max. I wonder what he's thinking. Personally, I'm having that bittersweet feeling when someone you know finds love before you. I'm happy for them, more happy than I can say. If anyone deserves it, it's these two. But seeing their happiness reminds me of the position I'm in. And the selfish part of me can't help wondering – will that ever be me?

39

Max

Doily is one of those people who, once you've accepted their basic level of insanity, nothing they say or do surprises you. Even so, I can't say I saw her turning her back on showbiz for a retired air traffic controller from Horsham. She invites us to join them for dinner, but I want to leave them to their cassoulet and whatever else they've got planned. I should be feeling inspired. Doily and my dad are proof that romance is possible against the odds. But this is no longer a question of beating the odds. Hunter and I need the stars to align.

We both know he nailed his audition. I try to come up with various ways that he could get the role and we could stay together, but they all come back to the same caveat – I'd have to give up my dream of being a diplomat. There's just no way that both of us can pursue our ambitions and be in the same location. Living with him has taught me that's how I want to be in a relationship. I don't want our lives to be spread across two countries or cities, constantly trying to squeeze each other in. I want intimacy. Routine. The life I've had with Hunter for the past few weeks.

Impossible, in other words.

Of course, if I don't get this Athens job, it won't be an issue. But seeing Hunter so engaged and motivated only confirms how much I want that for myself. I'm surprised I still haven't heard back from the assessment weekend. Then, on my way to work the next morning, I log into my email and find one from the selection committee.

I've been invited to interview in Athens.

It's hard to know what I feel in that moment. My stomach does a flip, part exhilaration, part dread. For years I've pictured this moment, stepping into the big leagues, but instead of a rush of triumph, there's a weight pressing down on me. I should be elated, but it's clear why I'm not.

Athens means distance. Distance from Hunter.

Athens means no more us.

Not that making the final stage means I'm going to get the job. Whoever else has been chosen is bound to be a strong contender.

When I arrive at the office, the first person I see is Quentin. He looks like he's in a terrible mood. Damn. If he hasn't made the final cut for Athens, I'll almost feel bad for him. He wants this job just as much as I do.

I cross over to Mariam, since I can't resist gloating that I've made it to the final stage. She's at her desk staring at her computer, looking vaguely stunned.

'It's done,' she says without looking up.

'What is?'

'The trade deal. We've agreed the fine print. It's being published tomorrow.'

She looks bereft. No doubt she will be assigned a new project within the next few days or weeks, but until then, she has no idea what to do with herself.

'Did you see the final shortlist for the Athens job?' I ask.

'I did.'

I wait for her to congratulate me. Nothing.

I glance over at Quentin, who's continuing to sulk at his desk.

'I take it Quentin didn't make the cut.'

'No, he did,' says Mariam.

Huh. Now I'm even more confused.

'So it's between me and him?'

'Yes,' Mariam says pointedly. 'You were always the favourites.'

Is she seriously not going to congratulate me? A switch flips inside me.

'You know, I have never understood why you don't want me to get this promotion.'

Mariam is taken aback.

'You've never once encouraged me. You've always backed Quentin. I don't get it. What does he have that I don't?'

Mariam glances around, then lowers her voice. 'Wrong way round.'

I frown in confusion.

'It's not that I want him to get it. It's that I don't want to lose you.'

I'm momentarily speechless.

'Quentin has never brought much to this role when he's not being handheld by Flora. But you . . . on a good day, you're brilliant.'

I cannot believe this. 'I . . . no.'

'What do you mean, no?' says Mariam. 'It's a compliment!'

'Just because you think I'm good doesn't mean you get to keep me indefinitely. I have my own ambitions.'

I'm worried that I've pushed it too far, but Mariam doesn't look annoyed. If anything, she's impressed.

'I've always known you had your own ambitions,' she says. 'I just never thought I'd see you stand up for yourself.'

The conversation with Mariam leaves me rattled. She seemed to genuinely think I'd be flattered, but how can I be when she's effectively been rooting against me? She can't just hang onto me permanently because it makes her life easier. It's outrageous when you think about it. But this is not a country that values ambition.

Yet another thing that I love about Hunter.

I'm tempted to go and speak to Quentin, but I decide I'd better let him stew in whatever's bothering him for a little while longer. I cross over to my regular desk, barely glancing at the random woman sitting in Nessie's usual place. It's only after I sit down that I do a double take and realise that the random woman is—

'Nessie?'

Nessie looks up from her computer. She's had her hair straightened.

'Any better?' she asks bashfully.

That's putting it mildly.

'*So* much better.'

Nessie smiles in relief. 'Max, I can't tell you how grateful I am that you were honest with me. It really inspired me.'

'Yeah, you look great.'

'I'm not talking about that. I texted my friends, the ones I went on the hen party with. I came up with a reason why each of them was more boring than I am.'

Nessie gets out her phone and proudly reads me the reasons, which include the fact that one of them has only ever done missionary position with her boyfriend, one of them forced everyone to join an app to track their hormone levels, and one of them spent twenty minutes telling the group which hairdryer she decided to buy. It's the least Nessie thing I've ever heard, and I love her for it.

Suddenly it feels ridiculous that I've shared her whole journey but I haven't told her even a hint of what I've been going through myself.

'Hey,' I say impulsively. 'Do you want to grab lunch later?'

Nessie says yes like she's been waiting for me to ask for years. Honestly, I can't wait to spill the beans and get her perspective. I don't expect it all to be positive – I have lied to her, after all – but I can take it. Learning to be more honest is about what I share with others, but it's also about what I'm able to receive.

I wonder how differently things would have turned out if Nessie had been in on it from the start. If I'd gone for lunch with her the day after Buckingham Palace and told her what I was planning, would she have advised me against getting a fake boyfriend? And if I had, would I be in a better or worse position than I'm in now?

I've grown so much over the past few weeks that it's hard to have any regrets. But the dilemma I've ended up in is torture. At least I'm no longer the kind of person who keeps it all to himself. As the morning ticks to a close and I prepare to head out to lunch with Nessie, I look at my phone and see a message from Hunter:

You need to come home. Now.

<h1 style="text-align:center">40</h1>

<h2 style="text-align:center">Hunter</h2>

It's a sign of how much else has been going on that I completely forgot that our visa hadn't yet been approved. When the doorbell rings, I assume it's a delivery driver. I see the man and don't recognize him. Then I take in the woman, her stern haircut and impassive expression, and it all comes flooding back.

'Hello, Hunter,' says Janet. 'May we come in?'

I freeze, my heart in my mouth.

'Er, can I ask why?'

'We just have a few follow-up questions.'

My palms start to sweat. I keep them clamped to my sides. 'Am I allowed to say no?'

Janet is surprised. 'Legally, yes. But we may then be obliged to seek a warrant.'

Jesus Christ. Now I'm imagining a SWAT team busting in, bundling me into a van and shipping me back to America. Let's not make this any more difficult than it has to be.

'Please,' I say to them. 'Come in.'

'Is Max home?' asks Janet.

'No, he's at work.'

'Could you get him home?'

'I can ask.'

I show them into the living room and run to the bathroom. I fire off a text to Max, then splash my face with cold water. Wait, does that look guilty? Too late now. When I get back to the living room, Malcolm is flicking through a copy of *Acting for Dummies* with immense interest while Janet peruses the various oil paintings on the wall as if she's trying to spot a fake.

'Max should be here soon,' I inform them. 'Please, have a seat.'

We perch opposite each other, and Janet offers me an icy smile. 'Now then, tell us – how's orthodontist school going?'

For the next twenty minutes, I break all my rules. There's no way I'm sitting here and answering Janet's questions until Max gets home, so I start recounting every one of Doily's anecdotes that I can recall, from the time she got into an argument with Maggie Smith in Fortnum and Mason over the last remaining quince jelly, to the day that Bill Nighy rescued her Mulberry handbag from a motorbike thief by beating the guy with his umbrella. Janet isn't interested, but Malcolm laps it up. All that matters is preventing Janet from interrogating me. It's not that I don't think I can come up with answers – I just don't want to say anything that Max contradicts once he walks in.

Finally I hear the door open. 'Max!' I cry, leaping up and planting a kiss on his cheek.

Max takes in our guests. He looks like he prepared himself on the way.

'Lovely to see you again!' says Malcolm. 'This is my colleague, Janet.'

Janet peers at him. 'Hello, Max. This won't take long.'

Max stays standing. The air of forced conviviality over the past twenty minutes has given way to an unmistakable chill.

'Sorry,' says Max. 'What are you here for?'

'Standard procedure,' says Malcolm.

Janet purses her lips. 'It was Malcolm who initially collated your answers. After being reviewed, they were found to have a couple of discrepancies that Malcolm had thought fine to ignore.'

'Very minor discrepancies,' says Malcolm, flustered. 'Nothing that prompted any serious concern.'

'Still,' says Janet, 'it was felt that a home visit would tie up any loose ends.'

I shoot a look at Max. This is exactly what I was worried about. He promised me it would be fine, but look at us now. Although for some reason, Max doesn't seem anxious.

'No problem,' he says. 'Can I make you a cup of tea?'

Janet shares a look with Malcolm, then turns to Max. 'How about a bite to eat?'

'Oh,' says Max in surprise. 'Have you not had lunch?'

'Yes,' she says, 'but you told Malcolm you like to cook for Hunter. Something Hunter made no mention of.'

Damn. Damn, damn, damn.

'It must have slipped his mind,' says Max.

'Not very memorable, your cooking, is it?' asks Janet.

'It certainly is. Nobody forgets my pancakes.'

'Come on then,' she says. 'Let's see what you can do.'

My heart is pounding out of my chest. What the hell is Max going to do? This cannot be legal. They can't deny us a visa because he's a terrible cook. Can they? Or will they use it as evidence that he lied? Is this all they need to fail us?

As we head over to the kitchen, I'm terrified to witness Max in action, but he produces the ingredients, pulls out a whisk, sifts the flour, and cracks each egg one handed. He whisks as he drizzles in the milk, smooth as anything, chatting to Janet and Malcolm about how he prefers to use full fat to add that bit of extra depth. Janet is taken aback, and I have to say, I'm with her.

How the hell is he doing this?

Once the pan is hot, Max adds butter with a sizzle, then tilts it to coat the pan. He pours in a ladle of batter, spreads it paper-thin around the pan, then flips it. As I watch the pancake fly through the air, it feels like time slows down and our fate is hanging in the balance, but the pancake lands perfectly. Max slides it onto a plate. He prepares two more in quick succession, then places the pancakes on the table in front of us alongside some Nutella and maple syrup.

'Bon appetit,' Max says with a flourish.

Malcolm digs in, smacking his lips. Janet is too livid to say anything. I have no idea how Max has transformed himself from kitchen amateur to husband material star chef, but I'm in awe. I offer him a grateful smile, and he grins back at me.

'Scrummy,' says Malcolm. 'I think we can put a nice big tick in that box.'

'You do that,' says Janet, before turning to me. 'Now then,' she says, 'let's see some of this rare pottery that you and Max like to acquire.'

Just when I thought we were safe.

Why did I say that? Rare pottery?

My chest tightens as Malcolm's brow lifts expectantly. I glance at the mantelpiece. Elton John's gnome stares back at me like it knows the game is up. No way. Admitting to theft is not an option. My eyes dart frantically around the room, but this flat is practically minimalist compared to Doily's trinket museum. I curse myself for clearing out her bizarre ornaments.

'This way,' Max says, calm as anything.

What the fuck? How has he got this covered too? I frown at him, but he gives me the smallest nod. I don't know what he's thinking, but I follow. Right now, Max is all I've got. He leads us down the hall to the spare room and opens the door. Sitting on the windowsill, tucked in the corner, is a china figurine of a slightly cross-looking badger wearing a waistcoat and holding a teacup.

Janet's lip curls. 'What's that?'

Max doesn't hesitate. 'That,' he says, perfectly deadpan, 'is an original Giles Wibberley.' He leans in conspiratorially. '*The* Giles Wibberley.'

Something inside me sparks. Max isn't spouting lies randomly. He's *acting*. Calm, prepared, and in character. That's all the cue I need to slip into performance mode, and suddenly, we're off. Max and I spin a story about how we drove down to an auction house in Sturminster Marshall and bid seven times our budget.

As Max tells them we named the badger Percy, I speak in Percy's pompous tones, and Max scolds me for stealing his impression. We finish each other's sentences, laugh in the right places, back each other up like we've told this story a thousand times.

We're lying through our teeth, but it doesn't feel like lying. It feels like the kind of scene only the two of us could play: Max's rapid-fire invention paired with my flair for delivery.

We're a team. A real one. And Malcolm and Janet can't miss that.

Janet purses her mouth. 'Right, I think that's everything.'

She can't hide her disappointment. She hasn't been able to lay a glove on us. She and Malcolm head for the door. Relief floods through me. They're almost gone. We've done it. We've survived. Then the door to the main house creaks open.

Please don't let that be who I think it is. We really could do without Doily walking into this scene. But here she is, clutching a pile of books, and wearing tangerine sunglasses and an electric pink headscarf that causes Malcolm to subconsciously genuflect as if he's in the presence of a celebrity. Doily doesn't even notice him.

'There you are, boys,' she says. 'Sheila Hancock was clearing out her old books to make space for a loom. I found a couple you might like.'

She hands me a tattered copy of *Favourite Jams of Lower Lincolnshire* and Max a pristine edition of Julian Clary's memoir *A Young Man's Passage*.

'Thank you,' I say, attempting to usher Janet and Malcolm out of the room.

'I do beg your pardon,' says Doily. 'Do you have guests?'

'This is Janet and Malcolm,' I say. 'From the immigration office.'

Doily catches on immediately. 'Lovely.'

'So you're the landlord?' asks Janet.

'Precisely.'

'Do you have a copy of the tenancy agreement?'

Doily had to be more or less bullied into making my residence in her home official, but thankfully we convinced her it might be necessary, and it turns out we were right.

'I do,' says Doily. 'Follow me.'

Doily heads over to her office with Janet and Malcolm. As soon as they are out of earshot, I turn to Max.

'What the hell? How did you make those pancakes?'

Max smiles coyly. 'Didn't I tell you we'd be OK if they ever checked up on us?'

I nod, still in disbelief.

'I didn't think they ever would,' says Max, 'but I knew you were worried about it. So I planned for the worst-case scenario. The pottery was easy. The pancakes took longer. I've been doing YouTube tutorials every night I've been home alone.'

I stare at him. 'Wait, are you saying you learned to make pancakes in case you ever got tested?'

Max laughs. 'Not exactly. I was just . . . trying to make the truth catch up with the lies. I never thought

I'd be tested like that. But I thought it would be a nice surprise for you one day. Guess it was.'

My heart feels like it's going to burst. This is just about the most considerate thing anyone has ever done for me. Before I can say any more, Doily, Janet and Malcolm return. Janet is clutching a bunch of documents.

'Got the paperwork?' Max asks Janet.

'Yes,' she says tartly. 'That's everything.'

I have never seen a woman look so defeated. It's hard not to take it personally. To be fair to Janet, maybe she could tell when she met us that something was off. But a lot has happened since then. As we see them out and Doily heads back to her part of the house, I turn to Max with a gulp of relief.

We dissolve into an embrace, long and tender. I didn't realize until now how much I needed it. Eventually, we pull back.

'Hunter,' says Max. 'We need to talk.'

It's painful to even look each other in the eye, but we both know we can't avoid this any longer. I take a seat at the kitchen table. Max sits opposite me.

'You know what I'm like,' says Max. 'I talk around the subject. Find a way to spin it that will keep everyone happy. But in this situation, there's no way round it.'

Max holds my gaze determinedly. 'I have feelings for you. Serious ones.'

I can't help smiling. 'You're making it sound like a medical diagnosis. Maybe try spinning it a *bit*.'

Max blushes. 'Fine. How's this? There are times when you walk into the room and I think I'm going to faint at how beautiful you are.'

'That's better,' I say with a grin. 'Keep going.'

'It's not just about that,' Max says. 'I wish it was. This would be so much easier to handle if it was purely physical. You have a beautiful soul, Hunter. You see the world in a way no one else does, and you're brave enough to say what you see. You're honest with me like no one ever has been. You open my mind, challenge me, make me question myself. You make my whole world burn more brightly. And I think . . . I think I do the same for you. I keep you laughing, keep you from spiralling into your worst anxieties. We make each other better, Hunter. And I know for a fact you make Mr Peanut better. Look how attached he's become to you.'

I can't describe what hearing these words does to me. At first, my heart leaps, buoyed by the sheer, dizzying joy of how Max feels about me. But almost instantly, the joy twists into something sharper. My chest tightens as reality creeps in: we're caught in this impossible tangle of timing and distance.

Max looks at me. 'How was that?'

I frown. 'I wish you hadn't.'

Max's smile fades. 'Why?'

'Why do you think?'

His face is lined with worry. 'Because you don't feel the same way?'

'No, Max! Because I do.'

It's hard enough to be on the receiving end. But seeing him react to it is even worse. That brief burst of delight, followed by the immediate knowledge that we can't enjoy it.

'I want us to be together,' I say. 'I'm not saying I want to commit my life to you or do anything crazy like get married—'

Max can't resist letting out a laugh.

'But I want to give our story a chance to continue.'

Max nods soberly. He knows precisely how much this hurts.

'Right now,' I say, 'we're both on the verge of getting things we've always dreamed about. I want that for both of us. In some ways, I want it more for you than I do for me.'

'Same,' Max says despairingly.

'Damn you,' I say. 'Why can't you be a selfish asshole like my ex? It would make this so much easier.'

Max looks guilty. 'Sorry.'

My heart floods with affection. 'Max, you have nothing to be sorry for.'

I can't bear to see him so crushed. Not when he did such a beautiful job of helping me through my audition.

I take his hands in mine. 'When we get to Athens, I need you to go for it. I'll be mad if you don't. Give it everything, like you made sure I did. Once we have the results . . . then we'll figure out what to do.'

41

Max

I'm not sure I ever understood until now what it really means to feel two things at once. But as we head to the airport together, I feel like I have two separate lives. On the one hand, I'm living a dream I never thought possible, with my dream man right beside me. On the other hand, I'm bitterly sad knowing that for all its hope and potential, this situation is not going to work out in a way that is acceptable for either of us.

I'm shocked by how much it moves me to know that Hunter supports my dreams. When I backed him for his auditions, it felt like the natural thing to do. But now that I'm on the receiving end, I appreciate what a gift it is. It breaks my heart how much he's rooting for me to get the job that might permanently set my life on a different path from his. I keep waiting for the moment when I realise this isn't what I want, that I'd be happier staying in London with Hunter, but somewhat inconveniently, I appear to have given up lying to myself.

As we arrive at the airport, I notice that Hunter has gone quiet.

'Are you all right?' I ask.

He looks away. He clearly doesn't want to burden me with whatever it is, but I wait for him to open up.

'What if they quiz us at customs?' Hunter says fretfully. 'What if they find us out this time?'

'They won't.'

'They'll smell my fear a mile off. I always feel guilty passing through customs, even when I haven't done anything wrong.'

I'm filled with a wave of sympathy. 'That's how they want you to feel.'

I squeeze his hand. 'We'll be fine. No country cares about who's leaving it.'

'So what, they'll arrest us when we get home?'

'No. We convinced them. We're safe.'

It's not that I'm a hundred per cent confident. But I can see how much Hunter needs my reassurance. Thankfully, we make it through customs unscathed. As we arrive at the check-in gate with more than an hour to spare, there's Quentin, slumped in his seat and staring into space.

He looks even more crushed than the other day in the office. We approach tentatively, but when he notices us, he barely reacts.

'Where's Flora?' I ask cheerily.

Quentin's expression darkens. 'She's not coming.'

I share a look with Hunter. We take seats on either side of Quentin. He continues to stare directly ahead. 'She had an epiphany at Chevening. She's decided her future lies elsewhere. She wants to rediscover herself or some nonsense.'

I can't believe what I'm hearing. Quentin and Flora are an institution. But maybe it's not that surprising.

Hunter said that when he spoke to Flora that day, she sounded worn down. She must have been stewing over this for a long time.

'How are you doing?' I ask with sympathy.

'How do you think?' Quentin snaps.

He has a point. He's hardly trying to hide it.

'I'm so sorry,' I say. 'But look, you can do this. All you have to do in the next twenty-four hours is get through it.'

Unfortunately, that's not all Quentin has to do. He has to be at his best in a high stakes interview in a foreign country for an extremely competitive position. Early signs suggest that might be a challenge for him.

When our flight is announced, Quentin needs to be virtually lifted out of his seat and onto the plane. It was always evident how much he and Flora were glued together, how reliant he was on her, but for that reason I never stopped to picture what he would be like without her.

The answer, of course, is barely functional.

I feel so bad for him that it's only once we're in the air that it occurs to me what this means for my chances. It's a good thing, surely. Even if Quentin does manage to get himself into a positive state of mind, he's simply not capable of acting without Flora's guidance. He's not that good. I've got to be the favourite now – a status that gives me incredibly mixed feelings. To distract myself, I suggest that we watch *Mamma Mia* on the in-flight entertainment. I thought it would be the perfect escapism, but every time Pierce Brosnan opens his mouth to sing and Hunter mimes shooting himself in the head, it's a dagger to my heart.

I used to dream of having a boyfriend to travel with. It always felt like one of the most magical things you could do with your time on earth, to have someone by your side as you soared above the clouds and discovered new horizons. Now I've got that. I'm living that dream. And while I might not have imagined that the dream would involve laughing over the vocal flaws of Hollywood actors en route to a job interview in Athens, I know perfect happiness when I see it.

This is precisely the kind of moment my dad told me to enjoy while I had the chance. But I can't. I don't know how. For all that I treasure this time with Hunter, I just can't shake the thought that my dream job and my dream man don't go together, no matter how I spin it.

When we land, we get into a taxi with Quentin and hurtle through the urban sprawl of outer Athens and past the historical centre to the harbour. The Embassy has arranged for me and Quentin and our guests to have a boat trip to a nearby island. When I saw the schedule, I thought it might be a nice little trip for the four of us. But without Flora, this could be awkward.

The taxi drops us off near a small boat. The skipper is a weather-beaten man in his sixties called Angelo who reminds me of my dad if he had spent his life under the Mediterranean sun rather than the English clouds.

We board the boat and it sets sail, leaving behind the harbour's industrial cranes and clanking machinery in favour of the Aegean's shifting shades of turquoise and deep blue. Quentin and Hunter take a seat at the front, but I find myself drawn to Angelo, so sit at the back with him. He's happy to chat over the roar of the motor, but when I tell him about my job, he tenses.

'You're part of that trade deal?' he asks gruffly.

I hesitate, unnerved.

'I was involved, yeah.'

Angelo scowls and looks away.

'Are you not happy about it?' I ask.

Angelo laughs. 'Have you spoken to any of the ship workers?'

'Er, I haven't had the chance. But tell me.'

Angelo shakes his head angrily. 'It's nothing we haven't seen before from this government. They will make money from the deal. We will make less than we do now.'

I frown. This is the opposite of what I've been hearing for the past year.

'But . . . that wasn't the plan.'

'No.' He gives me a world-weary look. 'It never is.'

I do my best to persuade Angelo that there are plenty of upsides for the Greek shipbuilding industry. But he tells me that none of them will filter down to the workers. It's hard to argue with him. For all the stakeholder meetings and cross-cultural exchanges we've had over the past year, he's right – none of them involved any of the people on the ground.

I encourage him to make his views known to the government, and he claims that he will. But I'm relieved when our destination comes into view – a perfect dome of low green hills dense with pine trees rising from rocky shores. The sea calms as we enter a pristine cove, the water clear enough to see pink fish darting over white sand. The yacht nudges into its docking post.

'Welcome to paradise,' says Angelo.

As soon as he turns off the engine, I hear cicadas, distant birdsong, and the gentle slap of water on the boat's hull. Angelo heads off, promising to return in a couple of hours, and we walk along a rustic jetty that leads to a shack with an open bar and a barbecue where lamb chops are on the grill. I peer into the trees beyond the beach and notice deer resting in the shade and peacocks pecking at the dusty ground. I feel like we're interrupting their calm, but they strut towards us with curiosity.

Quentin announces that he's going to hike to the top of the island. I suggest that might not be the best idea in this heat, but he sets off before we can stop him.

As we pad down to the water's edge, Hunter rests a hand on my shoulder. 'Are you OK?'

I shrug. 'Bit of a weird conversation on the way over.'

'Yeah, I sensed that.'

'It's fine. But he wasn't a fan.'

Hunter frowns. 'Of what?'

'The trade deal.'

Hunter smiles. 'So you met the Greek version of a grumpy taxi driver. It's not your job to keep him happy.'

He's right, but that doesn't bring me any comfort.

'Seriously, Max, I love that you care. But forget about it just for a minute. Look where we are!'

I take in the scene and see how right he is. Not only our surroundings but the fact that we're here together.

We decide to go for a swim while a chef prepares our lunch. The water is warmer than any sea I've ever been in. Warmer than some baths I've had. Hunter floats on his back and closes his eyes as I bob beside him. Feeling the powdery sand between my toes and the sun on my face, looking at the beautiful man in front of me, I'm finally able to relax. My future with Hunter is as uncertain as it's ever been.

But right now, in this moment, I couldn't ask for more.

Eventually, my feet start to wrinkle, and Hunter and I come in from the water. We're wrapped in towels, devouring our lamb kebabs, when Quentin stumbles out of the woods. As I look up at him, I almost gasp. He's managed to burn himself so badly that he's turned the shade of beetroot. His lips are chapped and there's a glazed look in his eyes. He can barely stand upright.

'Damn, Quentin, have some water,' says Hunter, leaping up and pouring him a glass.

'I made it!' says Quentin. 'I made it to the top.'

He bends down to rub his knee, and I notice that it's badly scraped.

'What happened?' I ask.

'I'm fine,' says Quentin. 'Had a little run-in with a peacock, that's all.'

He offers us a deranged grin.

'See? I don't need Flora. I can totally do this.'

Neither Hunter nor I want to come out and say it, but the path in front of me is clearing. There is surely no way that Quentin can get this job now, if he even makes it to the interview in one piece. Back on land, a taxi trundles us over cobbled streets past bleached white buildings that make up the picture postcard side of Athens, and drops us at a charming little boutique hotel covered in honeysuckle in full blossom. Our room looks out on a quiet internal courtyard filled with pistachio trees. Hunter showers first, and when he emerges, he's wearing one of those crisp white hotel bath robes.

In an instant, I'm transported to our room at Chevening, where he wore a similar robe as he gave me a massage. In some ways, that massage was even hotter than what we did later that night. And given the current uncertainty around our status, I'm right back in that place of exquisite tension. I hurry into the shower in the hopes of cooling off. But getting naked hardly helps. Afterwards, I throw on a matching bath robe, then head back to the room and suggest the least erotic activity I can think of to pass the time: watching TV and ordering room service.

Since we're both in the mood to be decadent without filling ourselves up too much, we opt for profiteroles and champagne. Those are both basically just air, right? Once they arrive, we lounge on the bed and put on an episode of *Friends*. It's almost as blissful as swimming in the sea earlier. I alternate between asking myself how this is my life and knowing this is not my life, or at least there's no way this is how my life is set to continue. I try to put such thoughts out of my mind and focus on the episode. But that's hard when I've seen it several times before, and the man I adore is lying next to me on the bed in a white bath robe. At one point, we reach for a profiterole at the exact same moment. Hunter laughs, picks it up, and places it in my mouth. We share a lingering look that sets my heart alight. My heart, and other places.

I turn back to the TV, but now I'm fixated on the way Hunter's robe is falling across his legs, exposing the under part of his thigh. We've agreed to wait before deciding about our future, but we never said that meant a sex ban. Is he up for it?

I can't bring myself to ask, but I can test the waters. I rest my hand on the bed next to Hunter's leg and slowly shift until my hand is leaning against it. Hunter doesn't react. Then I notice a twitch under the cotton. He's turned on. That's my cue.

I slide my hand down until it's nesting between his legs. I can feel with the back of my wrist that even this modest action has got him hard, but still we keep up the pretence that we're watching the episode, its soundtrack of studio laughter so regular and familiar that you almost don't hear it.

I'm now very obviously pressing against Hunter's boner with my hand. I carefully manoeuvre my forearm until it's more or less running the length of it. I feel him twitch again.

I can't hold off any longer.

All it takes is a slight twist of my hand for his robe to slide open and me to have his dick in my grasp. Without letting go, I turn so I'm facing him, and we start to kiss. As my own robe falls open, I shrug it off my shoulders and let it slump into a pile with his.

Hunter naked is a vision I can't imagine ever getting bored of. I slow down and allow myself to savour it. The breadth of his shoulders tapering down to the sharp lines of his waist, the smooth definition of his stomach. Our day at the beach has enhanced his tan lines, pale against the warm gold of his skin.

I long to trace them with my fingers, or maybe my tongue.

My awe melts into something hungrier.

Hunter holds my gaze, willing me to give in to it. My breath becomes shallow, my pulse quickens. Desire crashes through me. I want him with a force that borders on vertigo.

I push him back onto the bed so that I can kiss every part of him. But how can I not be drawn to one part in particular? His dick lies hard on his stomach, reaching all the way to his belly button. I tease it with my tongue, delighting as even the slightest touch makes him shiver. Then I take him deep, making him moan. My grasp becomes firmer, my lips move faster. After one particularly loud moan, the silence draws attention to itself. I look up and realise that the episode of *Friends* has stopped playing.

'What do you want to do?' I ask.

Hunter smiles. 'Aren't we doing it?'

'You know what I mean.'

Hunter pauses, relishing the question. 'Tell me what you want, Max.'

I can hear my breathing becoming heavy. But I don't look away.

'I want you inside me.'

A look of raw lust flashes behind Hunter's eyes. I feel a rush of excitement from my head to my toes. We take a beat to make the necessary preparations, then Hunter flips me onto my front. My mind is spinning so hard that for a moment, I'm unsure where he is. Then I feel his breath on the curves of my butt, his tongue tracing along its edges.

He dives deeper and I gasp.

It starts as a flicker of warmth and wetness, disarming and shockingly intimate. Hunter's movements are delicate but assured – experienced, but still exploring, like he's figuring out which of his tricks make me quiver and shake.

Does he know no one's ever done this to me?

Can he tell from the way it ripples through my nerves and up my spine?

For a while, I'm torn between tensing and melting. Slowly, however, I give in to the sheer unadulterated delight. It feels like Hunter is unfastening something I didn't know was locked.

Before I know it, he's climbing up to kiss the back of my neck, then whispering in my ear.

'Are you ready?'

Ready? I could have kept doing that all night. I barely manage to whisper a response.

Hunter grins. 'Don't worry. I'll start slow.'

I'm expecting him to enter me from behind, but he turns me onto my back, hoists my legs up over his shoulders, then eases into me without breaking eye contact.

Oh. My. God.

The first push steals the air from my lungs. The line between pain and pleasure blurs for a heartbeat, but it's replaced by a heat so consuming it makes my vision swim. The physical sensation is almost unbearable in its intensity, but it's more than just my body reacting.

Because this isn't just anyone – it's Hunter.

Every thrust feels like it's binding us together, turning desire into something sacred. He leans in, kisses me, bites my neck. I cling to him, feeling the warmth of his lips.

Hunter pauses. 'You doing OK?'

I nod, barely able to speak.

Hunter smiles. 'Tell me how you want it.'

As I look into his eyes, only one word comes to mind. 'More.'

Hunter eases back in, and this time, everything feels easier. He gradually raises the tempo, but I can take it. I want to be undone by him, claimed by him, remade. The pleasure keeps climbing, impossibly high, rewiring me until I'm certain I won't survive the force. I can feel Hunter getting close, so I work myself until we're both ready to burst. Then we do, all at once, in one blinding, glorious explosion.

We collapse onto the bed and catch our breath.

After a second, I tilt my head to the side and glimpse the TV remote.

I want to reach out, press the pause button, and stay in this moment forever.

42

Hunter

I didn't know it could be like that. I didn't know that's how sex could feel. Sure, I've had sex that has blown my mind physically. But sex in the past, even within relationships, has been something different – a high, a thrill, proof that I was wanted. To burn so fast that by morning I was a pile of cinders. To leave feeling drained, even ashamed, like I traded a piece of myself away.

But that? That was different. Every kiss, every thrust, every sound was shot through with a tenderness that took my breath away. How could sex that hot be so loving? I thought passion had to be reckless, destructive, something you paid for later.

Yet here I am, wrecked in the best possible way, and instead of feeling hollowed out, I feel complete. Cherished, even. Being inside Max wasn't just a physical act, it was like being welcomed into the deepest part of him, a place he's kept safe for me alone.

It's a realization so overwhelming that I immediately get up to shower and dress. Thankfully, I have an excuse for my haste. As the sun starts to set, we put on our suits and head to the Acropolis. It's closed to the public for the day, but has been kept open especially for us this evening. We arrive at the ticket office at the base and hand over our invitations. The late evening sun has started to dip, and the sky is streaked with shades of coral and blood orange. From the moment we begin our ascent, the famous pillars of the Parthenon are visible on the top of the hill. We snake up a stone path that wraps around the mountain, and I imagine how awe-inspiring it must have been for some country peasant from ancient times to arrive in the city and witness this gleaming temple rising out of the landscape.

When we finally reach the Parthenon, it's far bigger up close than I was expecting. The pillars tower fifteen meters above us. It's not hard to see why this was once a sacred site. I feel freshly outraged that anyone could have seized sculptures from here and shipped them to England so they could sit in a museum. The Parthenon is a heritage site in a state of active restoration, but an area has been cordoned off for tonight's event.

The reception is a breeze. For starters, there's no sense that Max and I are faking anything. It's not only that our feelings for each other have become real. We trust each other. We know what we're here to do. I feel like a pro. I charm every person I meet. I sing Max's praises to all the right people, but it doesn't feel like strategy. It's what I really think of him. He has the patience, the curiosity, the sheer bloody-minded optimism you need in diplomacy. People open up to him because he listens, and they listen to him because he makes you believe in a better world. Max could be dropped into a roomful of strangers on the brink of war and somehow they'd leave believing in the possibility of peace.

The difficult part is when attention turns to me. More than once I'm asked about moving to Athens, how I'd feel about it, how it would affect my acting career. It's not that I mind lying. I'm past that. But it cements the truth in my mind, confirming that I would never want to do what I'm claiming I would. I really wouldn't be happy here.

Quentin arrives at the reception an hour late, having got lost on the way up. His sunburn has started to sweat, and it's an unfortunate metaphor for the state he's in. Max and I share a look. It's hard not to think that this is turning into a cakewalk for Max. Quentin sees us and wanders over. He raises his glass, clinking it against Max's.

'What's that for?' Max asks.

'Oh come on, Max. The job's yours.'

'We haven't done the interview yet.'

Quentin laughs. 'There's nothing I can say that's going to convince them. You've got this.'

Max continues to deny it, but it only enforces the fact that Quentin is right.

Eventually, Quentin is accosted by Topsy, who wants him to explain the junior county cricket system – whatever that is – to her friend. Max and I drift away from the gathering and stand looking out at the view of Athens by night.

'He's not wrong,' I say.

Max tries to shrug it off.

'Hey,' I say, 'you're meant to be the optimistic one.'

Max frowns. 'They're not just going to hand it to me. I still have to do a good job tomorrow.'

'You will. Do you want to run through your pitch?'

Anything to distract myself from the feelings that are swirling inside me. I make Max stand there and talk to me as if I'm on the interview panel. He speaks from the heart, explaining why he got into this line of work when he knew he could make twice as much money in the private sector. He tells me he tries not to think about the bleakness of what humanity is doing to the world because when he does, he feels helpless. By contrast, when he goes into work each day and helps implement the systems that keep our society running, he feels like he's making a difference.

Max's words hit me in the gut. I think a part of me thought he only wanted to do this because that's what his mom would have wanted. But he really cares. He wants to create a better world. And seeing that brings home the fact that I haven't just grown fond of him, I don't just long for him.

I love him.

I love Max. He's my guy. I want to spend the rest of my life with him. And now that I'm finally able to acknowledge that simple fact, I'm devastated. Because what prompted this was hearing how much he wants this job. The job that would take him away from me.

'Was that OK?' Max asks.

I snap back to attention.

'Yes. That was amazing. You really care about this.'

Max smiles bashfully. 'Yeah, hopefully I can convince them I do.'

'No, I mean you actually care. I can tell.'

Max looks almost guilty. 'Yeah. I guess I do.'

There's a lump in my throat, but that doesn't prevent me from returning his gaze sincerely. Even though it's the last thing I want, I have to give him the gift he gave me.

'I really hope you get this job, Max. You deserve it.'

43

Max

I wake up to the feeling of sunbeams on my face. I roll over and see that Hunter is already out of bed. I can hear him in the bathroom. Just for a moment, I'm pleased not to see him. Last night honestly felt like a break-up. I've tried so hard to push it aside, but it's finally hitting me what it would mean to come out here and live without Hunter. To try to be happy without him. I don't know if I could do it.

But I also don't know what it would do to me to turn away from a job that I desperately want. Look at Quentin and Flora. She put aside her own ambitions to support his career, and she couldn't go through with it. It destroyed them.

When Hunter emerges from the shower, he has a guilty expression.

'What's going on?' I ask.

Hunter pauses. 'The people at the Globe liked my audition. They want me to come back in and see them – today.'

My mouth drops open. 'Wait, why? Is this another audition?'

'No. They won't say. I have to sign an NDA.'

I feel a pang in my chest. 'This has to be good news.'

Hunter frowns. 'I have no idea.'

'It's not going to be bad news, Hunter. You have to go!'

This is killing me, but I can't let my own feelings colour this moment for him.

'I came here for you,' says Hunter. 'That was the deal. I can wait until after your interview. They can't just expect me to drop everything.'

'No,' I say. 'You did your part last night. I'll be flying home later today anyway.'

Hunter looks doubtful.

'Seriously,' I say. 'I'll be fine. Go.'

That's all the encouragement Hunter needs. He packs his bags, and before I know it, he's gone.

Honestly, I'm relieved. Being around him is becoming intolerable. Every moment together is soured with the unspoken knowledge that it might be our last. Every glance, every touch reminds me of what I might be about to lose. There's no way that him being summoned to London can be anything other than good news. If that's the situation we're going to be left in, I'd rather know. Because I'm now convinced that the worst-case scenario – by which I mean the best-case scenario – is what will come to pass. Hunter is going to get his job, I'm going to get mine, and the next time we see each other, we're going to break up.

An hour or so later, I get showered and dressed and make my way to the British Embassy. It stands on a broad, tree-lined boulevard, home to museums, several embassies, and neoclassical mansions, many of them hidden away behind iron fences and tall hedges. The embassy is a pale, sun-bleached structure set back from the road, framed by palms and cypresses. A security guard doesn't move his face a millimetre when I tell him what I'm here for, he simply raises a hand and gestures me in.

Inside, the building is invitingly cool and shady. You can hear the Athens traffic trundling past outside, but you get the feeling that nobody ever talks above a whisper. I'm shown along a marble corridor, hearing my footsteps ring out. As I take a seat on a leather stool, the portraits of past ambassadors and foreign secretaries on the wall opposite all feel like they are watching me.

It's strange, after the hijinks at Chevening, that all that's required of me today is an interview. I can't remember the last time I did one of these in person and with strangers. It must have been when I first joined the civil service. Ever since then, it's all been internal promotions overseen by colleagues. I think back to that naive twenty-one-year-old who sat in his ill-fitting suit in Westminster wondering what they were going to make of him. Would he be surprised to see me here now? Probably not, because he thought the sky was the limit. But he would have been shocked at what it's taken to get here.

Yet here I am, interviewing for a role in the field, in the birthplace of democracy. The last few days have been so intense that I haven't had a chance to sit and take it in. And yes, the only way I can do that is by not thinking of Hunter, but when I do succeed in blocking him out, I'm proud of how far I've come. Hunter is right – this is what I've always wanted and what I deserve. All I have to do is land the plane.

My interview is scheduled for 11 a.m. By 11.15, I'm wondering why I haven't yet been called. I notice various staff members hurrying about, talking to each other under their breath. What's going on? Please don't tell me something is getting in the way of my interview. Just when I think it's all about to fall apart, a woman comes along and invites me to follow her.

She leads me up a central staircase and into a long, narrow reception room. Tall windows flood the space with light, yet it still manages to feel gloomy. At one end of the room, there's a table with three people, a single plastic chair in front of them.

I take in the three panel members. The first two are fairly nondescript, but that's no surprise. Many of the roles in a place like this suit people who prefer to be part of the furniture. One is Greek and one is British, but they both have the same energy: formal, subdued, respectful of process. These feel like people who will do whatever they're told to do by their boss – the man sitting between them, Wrettham Gibbons.

'Thank you for coming all the way to Athens,' says Wrettham. 'Why don't you tell us a bit about yourself.'

The next ten minutes could have been scripted. I repeat the pitch I did for Hunter last night, but there's not a single thing I say or that the interviewers ask in response that doesn't feel totally predictable. It's not boring or underwhelming or fake or really anything. It just is what it is, and it's creeping towards its predictable end when I hear a commotion outside the window.

I'm not the only one. Everyone jumps at a series of loud shouts. I assume it's some sort of traffic-related argument, but then we hear loud, coordinated chanting. It must be a protest.

The interviewers lean in and confer with each other, unsettled by the interruption. It's not going away. If anything, it's getting louder. It occurs to me what the interview panellists have perhaps already realised: the protesters are not merely passing the embassy – they're targeting it.

Wrettham sighs. 'For god's sake.' He looks at me. 'It'll be the shipyard workers. They've been threatening something like this. Ignore them.'

Without warning, the chants rise in volume. We all share a look. It's immediately apparent what has happened, even if none of us can quite believe it. The protesters have entered the building.

My first thought is that this is another role play, but I rapidly conclude that this is wishful thinking. The reaction of the interviewers is far too real. The embassy wouldn't hire dozens of extras to make a scene at a random job interview, and in any case, the protesters sound too raw, too angry, too present.

Nobody seems to know what to do other than sit here and attempt to ignore it. But as I listen to the chants, I think back to my conversation yesterday on the boat with Angelo. Maybe he's among the protesters. I did tell him to make his views known. Either way, that's who's chanting – not an angry mob but dozens of Angelos, hard-working people who have reached their limit. If nothing else, I want them to be heard.

Without thinking, I get up from my seat and walk towards the noise. The rest of the embassy staff follow behind tentatively.

As I head down the stairs, my heart is pounding. I worry I'm making a mistake, walking into danger. But when I get closer, my fears fade. The protesters are passionate, but they're not here to cause damage. They're not fools. I think of my mum, who got heavily involved in various disputes over nurses' pay. I remember her telling me that no one advocates for their job better than the people who actually do it.

'What are they saying?' I ask Wrettham.

He rolls his eyes. 'More work for less money. We're taking away opportunities. Blah blah blah. Ungrateful sods. We've called the police, don't worry.'

His disregard takes my breath away. He has no intention of engaging with them himself. He conducts negotiations at a higher level, in backrooms and confidential memos. This is an intrusion into the world he occupies.

But someone has to talk to them.

I want to do it for Angelo. For my mum. For every one of these people who took a day off work to put themselves on the line.

'Do you mind if I speak to them?' I ask.

Wrettham looks surprised. 'Be my guest. You won't get anywhere.'

As I take a step down the stairs, a hush falls. Up close, I can see the anger in their eyes. They are ready to throw whatever I tell them right back in my face.

'Hi there,' I say. 'I'm with the embassy.'

The embassy staffers don't contradict me. They're all relieved that I'm prepared to take the lead.

'Sorry I don't speak Greek,' I say. 'I hope at least some of you can understand me.'

A young man, bearded and muscular, pushes to the front of the crowd. 'How can you justify this?' he shouts in perfect English. 'We're going to be worse off under this deal.'

Maybe it's the setting, but I immediately launch into diplomatic mode. Unlike yesterday with Angelo, I've got all the talking points locked down. But delivering them directly to the people affected feels different. They know this is spin. I don't have solutions to their problems. And they don't like it.

'This is bullshit,' the man says. 'It means nothing.'

I attempt a new tactic. I suggest that some of the terms are not locked down, that we might accept feedback on how they're implemented. It's not really true, but it has an effect. And now that I've started, I can't stop.

'I can promise you that we at the British Embassy are your biggest advocates. We know that a trade deal like this depends on the workers. And we won't proceed without your voices at the table.'

'Yes you will!' says the man mockingly. 'You're just telling us what we want to hear. You don't care.'

'I do care,' I say.

As he looks back at me, I feel like he can tell that I mean it. But it doesn't make it any better. Just because I care, doesn't mean I can do anything about it. His expression turns from contempt to something worse. Pity, or maybe lack of respect. Whatever it is, he can see that our discussion is going nowhere.

'Come on,' the man says to his comrades. 'I've heard enough.'

Though it takes a bit more jostling and arguing, the protesters begin to retreat. That interaction has left me feeling leaden and useless, but to my amazement, the embassy staff react as if I've saved the day. For Wrettham, the victory is getting rid of them. It doesn't really matter what was said. As far as he's concerned, I'm the hero of the hour.

Once everyone has recovered, one of the embassy staff asks me if I can step into a side room. I assume they want me to give a police statement or something, but only a few minutes pass before Wrettham comes to see me.

'Thank you for waiting, Max. Usually it takes us a little more time to discuss this but . . . we'd like to offer you the job.'

My mouth drops open. There it is. The words I have been waiting to hear for as long as I can remember. They want to make me an ambassador. This is really happening.

'Wow,' I say. 'Thank you.'

Wrettham looks expectant.

'Obviously I'll need to discuss it with my husband.'

'I'm sure he'll be thrilled,' says Wrettham.

I feel a pang in my chest at the thought of having that conversation with Hunter. I clock Wrettham frowning at me, and realise I must look morose.

'Yes,' I say, perking up. 'I'm sure he will be.'

'Splendid,' says Wrettham. 'Congratulations.'

I walk out of the embassy in a daze and blink in the sunlight. My chest feels impossibly heavy. This should be a moment of triumph. This has been my dream for so long.

But it's turned into a nightmare.

I want Hunter to hold me and reassure me, help me find a way to make this work. But nothing has changed. He doesn't want to move to Greece.

If I take this job, it's the end of me and him.

The thought is unimaginable. But right now, I'm not in a position to decide anything. I get out my phone to text Hunter the news, but I can't find the words. I write and rewrite the message as if there's some way to spin it that doesn't feel like a death knell for our relationship. But there's no way to escape it. In the end, I tell him the brilliant, awful truth.

I got the job.

44

Hunter

There's something nice about traveling alone. At least, that's what I used to think.

From the moment I leave Max, my mind is taken up by how much I miss him. It's not just a feeling. It's a weight in my chest. The plane feels smaller, the cabin air heavier. The thought that we might separate permanently feels unreal. But I need to get used to the idea. I've survived on my own for years. I can survive this.

I try to find a movie to distract myself. *Mamma Mia* is too painful. I settle on a selection of the most mindless romcoms known to man. You'd think it would be the last thing I'd want to see, but there's something comforting about watching a film where you know what the ending is going to be. No matter what third act complications they throw at the characters, true love will find a way. I'm happy for them. It's just a shame they are bound by the laws of genre, and I'm in real life. There are no guarantees for me.

It's only as we begin our approach to London that I allow myself a bit of excitement. Max is right – this meeting with the Globe has to be good news. They wouldn't fly me back urgently if it wasn't. This is the kind of thing every actor dreams of.

When we land, I turn on my phone and get a message from Max.

The words hit me in the gut.

He got the job.

I'm overcome by a crushing wave of sadness. I knew I would have mixed feelings, but this is beyond that. It's not even a selfish thought.

I'm sad for Max.

It's all there in what's unsaid in his message, right down to the lack of exclamation point. There's no way he's enjoying this. He must be wracked with guilt. Confusion. Fear.

But I'm sad for me too. Sad doesn't begin to cover it. This result isn't an accident. It's precisely what we wished for when we set out on this adventure. When I backed Max for this job, I really meant it. That unconditional support for each other has been the bedrock of this relationship.

And now we're facing the consequences.

I don't know what to reply. Congratulations feels like a sick joke. But I want Max to know how proud I am of him. I want to find some way to reassure him. I'm still trying to figure out how to phrase it as I pass through customs.

I glance at the officer on duty. He turns to his colleague and mutters something. The colleague nods. The first man steps forward.

'Hunter Moretti?'

'Er, yes.'

All the air leaves my lungs. A cold wave of panic runs through me.

'Heathrow Border Control. You are under arrest.'

My whole body goes numb. I knew this would happen one day. What did I tell Max? My worst fear has come true. The man makes me wait in a corridor for several minutes, then leads me to an interrogation room. For some reason that I'm convinced is deliberate, the room is boiling hot. The air is stifling, almost poisonous. Sweat drips down my back, soaking my shirt. Every nerve in me is raw.

My interrogators are waiting for me. There's a woman with a broad London accent, tall and chillingly friendly. Accompanying her is a younger guy, Scottish and really quite handsome if I was in a state to appreciate that kind of thing. They tell me their names, but I immediately forget them. We're kind of beyond that.

'Now,' says the woman, 'I'm sure you're aware that your application for a spousal visa was under assessment.'

I don't say anything. Didn't we wrap this up with Janet and Malcolm?

'Following your recent home visit,' the woman continues, 'your landlady was asked to provide a copy of your partner's tenancy agreement. Thankfully, she had recently digitised her filing system, which resulted in her handing over all documents bearing your partner's name. They included a transcript of this voicemail.'

She pushes a sheet of paper in front of me. My heart is racing, but I refuse to look at it. This can't be real.

The woman reads from it. 'Eleventh of June, 2.01 p.m. A civil servant by the name of Max Ashford calls your agent and tells her he's looking to hire a fake boyfriend.'

I feel sick. The records that Max's own dad digitised. We brought this on ourselves.

I hold the officer's gaze. 'I want to speak to a lawyer.'

'It won't make any difference, son. We know what you did. It's all here in black and white.'

I know better than to confirm, but denial feels useless. I broke the law. They've got the evidence in front of them.

I refuse to blink. 'I'm not saying anything until a lawyer gets here.'

The woman shares a look with her junior. I imagine there's a fair number of people who attempt to push this line and quickly break down, but they appear to have concluded that I'm not one of them. The woman shuffles her papers.

'Let's end it there then.'

What does that mean? Am I about to be thrown into a cell?

'What about Max?' I can't help asking.

'What about him?'

'Can I speak to him?'

'You'll be entitled to a phone call at some point.'

'Will he not be arrested?'

The woman looks at me as if I'm stupid. 'Not up to me, son. But I doubt they'll be seeking a custodial sentence. You're the one who breached the terms of your visa.'

I feel a rush of hope. 'Wait, so . . . will he be allowed to see me?'

The woman gives me a sickening smile. 'Well, son, that depends on how quickly you're deported.'

45

Max

Why hasn't he replied? I check his flight. It landed a while ago. I know my news must have been pretty hard to take, but I thought he'd at least say something. I call him, but he doesn't pick up. I send a follow-up message asking if everything's OK.

I've arrived at the airport in Athens far too early, but I still find myself rushing through security to get to the gate. Something about being there makes me feel closer to Hunter. Once I make it to the departure lounge, I settle into the seat closest to the check-in desk. I shut my eyes, trying to stay calm, willing a message from him to appear. Every notification that isn't from him makes my chest tighten.

As I board the plane to London, it occurs to me that I might soon be making this journey in reverse. When I next fly to Athens, I will be heading to my new home. It should excite me, not make my heart sink, but how can I even begin to contemplate the excitement of starting a new life when it would be a life without Hunter?

My mood doesn't improve once we take off. Seriously, why hasn't Hunter replied?

My one consolation is the thought that when I land, I can see him. However difficult the conversation, simply being in a room with him will be some comfort. All I need to do is wait for the time to pass.

Someone once told me you're more likely to cry at a film when you're up in the air. Something to do with the air pressure. After several bad experiences, I now only watch films I've already seen so that I never have to face the embarrassment of explaining to the woman in the seat next to me why the emotional backstory in *Kung Fu Panda 2* has me sobbing uncontrollably. For today's flight, I've downloaded a film I've watched dozens of times – *Miss Congeniality*. Its familiar rhythms are just what I need.

But today, it's hitting different.

In the film, Sandra Bullock is an FBI agent who goes undercover at a beauty pageant to stop a terrorist attack. But her journey ends up being much more personal. Through the friendships she makes, she realises that she has been drawn to her job as an undercover agent because she is so comfortable hiding her true self. By the end of the film, she has committed to a new, more honest approach to her work.

It's not hard to see the parallels. It's now clear to me why I didn't feel better after I got the job at the embassy. I lied to those protestors' faces. That's what the job is. When this trade deal hits bumps in the road, as it inevitably will, I won't be the one tasked with getting it moving. I'll be the one smoothing it over, insisting that everything is OK when everyone knows that it isn't.

And I don't think that's good for me. After the journey I've been on, I need to find a job that challenges me to be honest, not one that indulges my worst instincts. I'm not sure why I didn't see it sooner, but now I feel it deep in my gut.

This job isn't right for me.

It feels crazy to admit that after it's been my dream for so long. But even if it was my mum who originally inspired me, I'm certain she would agree with me now. She'd want me to be on the side of the protesters, not Wrettham.

I still believe in the work of government. I even still believe in the power of diplomacy. Someone's got to do that job. But I no longer believe that person should be me.

And if I'm not going to move to Athens . . .

I catch my breath as the truth hits me.

Hunter and I can be together.

The cloud that has been hanging over me for the last few weeks has finally lifted. All it took was Sandra Bullock at 30,000 feet.

I'm overcome with the need to tell Hunter the good news. In the absence of phone signal, I start to garble it to the poor woman sitting next to me, who clearly thinks I'm insane.

As I count down the minutes remaining of the flight, time slows to a crawl. Eventually, we begin our descent into London. I'm ecstatic at the thought of seeing Hunter. By the time the wheels hit the tarmac, I'm ready to leap off the plane and run all the way home to him.

But when I turn my phone on, there are still no mes-sages from him. I refresh it a few times. Nothing. His flight landed hours ago. And sure, maybe Hunter was focused on his meeting, but it's weird that he hasn't replied at all.

As I walk through passport control, I have a knot in my stomach and I can feel my pulse racing. But nobody stops me. When I get to the other side, my phone rings and I answer hurriedly.

'Max? It's Doily.'

My heart skips a beat.

'Hey, what's up?'

Doily inhales sharply. 'Turn right when you come out of Arrivals. I'm waiting for you.'

The tone of her voice makes me pick up my pace. When I turn the corner, I see Doily standing by a minibus with half a dozen youths. My dad is with them, and so is Mr Peanut.

But no Hunter.

I scan the group to double-check, but I can already tell from the look on Doily's face that something bad has happened. I race up to her and drop my bags.

'What's going on? Where's Hunter?'

46

Hunter

It pained me to use my one phone call on Doily rather than Max. But he was up in the air, and Doily was the only person I could rely on to be in touch with both Max and the *Hamlet* team. Not that the latter matters any more. Who cares if I can make the meeting when I'm going to be deported? Doily insisted she would get her lawyer on it, but the law is pretty clear. If the government wants to deport me, it will.

But I could cope with that. All I care about is Max. I asked Doily if she could go and meet him at the airport and make sure he's OK. She said yes, before revealing that she was in the middle of taking her calligraphy group to see the Lindisfarne Gospels. I'm not sure that what Max needs upon being told that I'm about to be deported is a minibus load of young people with a passion for calligraphy, but the call got cut off before we could get any further.

So that's it. I'm being held in a cell with no privileges and no information. I'm sure the people I love are doing everything they can to get me out of here. But will that be enough? I doubt it.

The light in this cell is broken, but I don't think anyone cares, myself included. I've completely lost track of time. I feel like I've been here for hours by now, but if someone told me it's only been forty minutes, I wouldn't argue with them. When I was locked up, I needed a moment to myself. Now, it's chewing at me, every second stretching out. I'm craving contact with anyone.

The absence of Max is unbearable. It pains me to think that, even if I get out of here, we could be forced to separate in weeks. Being here is really bringing home to me what it would mean to part ways. No more laughter, no more crazy optimism.

But worse than that, who will I be without him? I recall the Hunter I was in New York. That Hunter was miserable, skipping meals, hiding from the world in a fog of cynicism. Max changed that. He made me come alive again, capable of joy and hope. I can't go back to that other version of me. I don't know how I'd cope.

Without planning it, I pick up a pen and paper from the side. I don't have my phone. I don't have any photos of Max. Writing to him feels like the only way to draw him closer.

At first, it's painful to consider everything I love about him and might lose. But gradually, it brings me comfort, reminding me of what's good in the world. How much I have gained simply through knowing him.

By the time I'm done, I feel lighter. It's impossible to think of Max and feel complete despair. He wouldn't allow it. This situation might seem futile. I sure don't see any way to get out of it. But by entering Max's mindset, I've let myself feel a tiny ray of hope.

47

Max

As the words tumble out of Doily's mouth, the air is ripped from my lungs. My stomach twists into a knot so tight, I can barely breathe. I feel like someone has turned the world upside down and left me standing.

Hunter. Detained. The word strikes me over and over, as everything else blurs into a haze of panic and disbelief. I want to scream, run, charge into customs and break him out of whatever cell they've thrown him in.

And yet . . . some part of me, stubborn and ridiculous, refuses to accept it. I can't. I won't. My brain keeps insisting this is a horrible mistake. I clutch my phone like it's a lifeline, like if I keep it close enough, I can pull him back into my world. This is not like my mum dying. This is Hunter. My Hunter. And until I've seen a plane take off with him in it, no one can convince me he's out of reach.

In theory, I could follow him to America if he's deported. But I wouldn't bank on me being allowed in, not when I've been caught lying on a visa application. It might literally be impossible for us to live and work in the same country. But I cannot let that come to pass. I need to find a solution.

My first instinct is to stay at the airport, knowing that Hunter is being held nearby. I hate the thought of moving further away from him when all I want is to be with him. But hanging around Border Control is not going to help my case. I need to act fast. Sure, they might be planning to leave Hunter to rot while weeks and months of process unfold, but they might also attempt to remove him as fast as possible. Protocols go out of the window when it comes to deportations. In any case, neither option is tolerable.

'Any thoughts?' asks Doily.

Solutions? No. But I know one person who might be able to help.

'We need to speak to Baroness Sharon.'

I snap into action and track down the phone number of her Chief of Staff. When I reach him, he tells me that Baroness Sharon is far too busy for him to even mention my name to her. When I inform him that she'll be furious if he doesn't pass on my message, he mutters in irritation and hangs up. Two minutes later, he calls me back and sulkily tells me I'm to come in and see Sharon immediately. When I say I've got company, he goes off the line briefly, then tells me that Sharon is happy to grant clearance to whoever I'm with.

Which is how I end up heading into Westminster with Doily, my dad, Mr Peanut, and a minibus full of young people with a passion for calligraphy. One of the youths has tied a ribbon around his head, Samurai style, which is technically unhelpful but fully in the spirit of the occasion.

Baroness Sharon's office is inside the Palace of Westminster, but the security staff seem to have been prepared for our arrival, because we are all ushered in and directed up to the fifth floor.

When I enter Sharon's office, the first thing I see is the view – a spectacular panorama across the River Thames to the South Bank and the London Eye. The second thing I see is the new Prime Minister of Iceland. I know this because he's a famous figure, a twenty-two-year old tech genius who conducts all his meetings wearing a hoodie and is accompanied everywhere by a drone that live streams him.

'Come in,' says Sharon, nonplussed by the fact that there are almost a dozen of us. Some of the calligraphy youths gasp when they recognise Iceland's Prime Minister.

'Are we interrupting?' I ask.

'No no,' says Sharon. 'You don't mind, do you, Björn?'

Björn waves a hand to indicate he isn't bothered. He pauses his live stream.

'Oh Max,' says Sharon, throwing her arms around me. 'How did this happen?'

I give her as quick a summary as I can. Sharon's frown deepens.

'Is there anything you can do?' I say. 'I hate to ask, but—'

'No, you must.' Sharon fiddles with her bangles. 'But it is a bit complicated.'

'How come?'

'You did break the law, darling.'

When you put it like that.

'This is really the Home Secretary's realm,' Sharon continues.

'Can you ask her?'

'God no. She can't stand me, the snooty cow. Plus she's obsessed with deporting people.'

I don't know why I thought Sharon would be able to work miracles. No one is going to have any sympathy for two people who deliberately broke the rules.

'I'd help if I could,' says Sharon. 'You know what a fan I am of Hunter.'

Then it hits me. Sharon's not the only one who's grateful for how Hunter handled the situation at the British Museum. He saved the trade deal. This country owes him.

'We've kept quiet about Hunter's role until now,' I say to Sharon. 'But we don't have to stay quiet.'

Sharon raises an intrigued eyebrow.

'Britain has come out of this well,' I continue. 'So many people in the international community have praised the decision to give back the Elgin Marbles. What if it leaked that the person responsible for that was being deported?'

Sharon thinks it over. I can tell the idea appeals to her, even if she's not sure how she'd sell it.

'We could make a fuss,' I say, turning to Doily. 'Couldn't we?'

Doily smiles. 'Say the word and I can have the entire cast of the upcoming *Peloton* movie protesting at the BAFTAs.'

Sharon bites her lip. 'You do understand that the press could spin it another way if this all goes public? You'd get dragged through the mud.'

I have a brief vision of how horrendous that would be. Hunter would get denounced as the immigrant who's stealing British actors' roles. That's before they found out about Elton John's gnome. But it doesn't scare me.

'They wouldn't win,' I say to Sharon.

'Are you sure about that?' Sharon asks.

'Yes. First, we're on the right side of history. Second, this is a love story.'

48

Hunter

This doesn't feel real. I keep grabbing hold of the train seat to prove to myself it's not a dream. But no, I really am on the tube, on my way to see Max.

When they released me, nobody explained a thing. I'm not sure if they'd been kept in the dark or were mad they weren't going to get to deport me. They just dropped me in arrivals as if I'd stepped straight off a flight. I couldn't get out my phone and call Max fast enough.

He wanted to meet halfway so he could see me at the first possible moment. But I didn't want to meet at a random tube station. I want to get home. I need to be behind a locked door, before I can feel safe. Max agreed to wait for me there.

Even as I hurtle towards him, I'm convinced this isn't going to work out. Every time the train stops, I'm scared that officers are going to get on board and rearrest me. But station by station, we edge closer. Eventually, I arrive at Kennington.

I walk back from the station, passing my favorite pub and the house of the neighbor who keeps a golf cart in her front garden. She could be keeping a unicorn there today and I wouldn't notice.

All that matters is reaching Max.

I arrive home and put my key in the lock. I let myself in and close the door behind me. Even now, I'm half-expecting Janet and Malcolm to emerge from a cupboard.

I call out for Max.

No response.

I feel a jolt of panic. Then I look down and see a trail of cherry blossom leading along the hallway and out into the garden.

My heart starts to race.

I follow the trail outside.

The garden is more beautiful than ever, dipped in the long afternoon light and fragrant with honeysuckle. I see Mr Peanut first, lying outstretched on the grass. Then, seated on the bench under the pear tree, there he is.

It feels like a glitch, like my brain needs a few beats to catch up, to believe that it's really him getting up and stepping towards me.

But no, it's him.

It's Max.

Before I can say a word, he's in my arms, crashing against me so hard it knocks the air out of my lungs. Technically, you'd call it a hug. But it feels more like being stitched back together.

The unmistakable physical reality of Max. The scratch of his hair against my cheek, the heat of his chest pressed to mine, the weight of him, solid and unshakable. I want to cling to him forever, but I pull back to look at his face and prove to myself that it's really him. He looks the same – messy, exhausted, beautiful. But everything is different, because for a moment I was truly scared we'd been separated.

And now, impossibly, here we are.

'Was the blossom too much?' Max asks, blushing.

I smile. 'Glad you found a use for it.'

Max shrugs. 'Had to kill the time somehow.' He raises a hand and brushes my cheek. 'You're here. I can't believe it.'

But as he smiles at me, I feel a pang that causes me to pull back.

We're reunited, yes. But for how long?

'Hey,' I say. 'Congratulations on the job.'

'Thanks.'

Max holds my gaze. 'I turned it down.'

I can't have heard that right. 'Wait, what?'

'I don't want the job. It's not for me.'

He explains his reasoning. At first, I almost don't want to believe it, scared it's too good to be true. But the more he talks, the more sense he makes. He *has* changed. This job *isn't* right for him. Which means . . .

'You're staying in London?'

Max bursts into a grin. 'I am if you are.'

Me and Max. Max and me. Here. Together.

I thought I knew the depth of my feeling towards him, but now that I know there are no obstacles standing in our way, my heart is so full that it's impossible to keep it to myself.

'Max,' I say. 'There's something I need to tell you.'

I reach into my pocket.

'What's that?' Max asks, frowning.

'I wrote it when they detained me.'

Max smiles at me in amazement. 'You wrote me a letter from jail?'

I laugh. 'Kind of.'

I clear my throat.

'"Every day with you, I discover new layers. When we first met, I sensed a beautiful innocence that I wanted to protect. As I got to know you, I saw that it wasn't just innocence, but a willful naivety. You've looked darkness in the face, and chosen light."'

Max smiles, charmed but a little shy.

'"That day on the train, when you allowed me to relive my lowest moments, I knew you were something special. But even then, I couldn't see how we could be together. We made a deal, and we stuck to it. We never once tried to convince the other to switch sides."'

On hearing this, Max looks sweetly proud of us. If I keep looking at him, I might not be able to get to the end.

'"I once read that Joan Didion and her husband walked around Central Park every morning. They didn't always walk together, because they liked different routes, but they would always find their way back to each other by the end of the walk."'

I bite hard to hold in my tears, remembering the place I was in when I wrote this.

'"I don't know if we will find our way back to each other. But I'll always be grateful we gave each other that freedom."'

I drop the piece of paper and look up at him. 'Guess we found a way.'

Then we can't help ourselves, throwing our arms around each other tighter than we ever have and letting the tears flow. I could stay like this forever, but after a while I pull back and look into his eyes.

'I love you, Max.'

Max blinks in surprise, then his eyes lock on mine, intense and soft at once. 'Damn.'

'What?' I whisper.

'I wanted to be the first.'

'The first what?'

Max adopts that innocent smile that makes my heart do backflips. 'What do you think? Hunter . . . I love you too.'

The world tilts. I stumble a little. It feels magical and yet so simple.

He loves me. I love him. Somehow, we've found each other.

I stand soaking up this beautiful reality, still in disbelief. Then I feel my phone vibrate. It's a text from Doily, checking I've made it home.

'Oh my god,' I say, suddenly remembering. 'My meeting.'

With everything else that's been going on, I completely forgot what I was flying home for. But Max smiles.

'Don't worry,' he says. 'Doily spoke to the people at the Globe.'

I look at him in intrigue. 'And?'

Max pulls a mischievous grin.

'You might want to sit down.'

Epilogue

Six Months Later

Max

'Max!' says Baroness Sharon. 'Have we had any response from the Embassy?'

'Not yet.'

'Get them on the phone.'

'Shouldn't we wait for a written response?'

'Absolutely not. Don't give them a chance for any more bullshit.'

As Sharon strides off, I get my assistant to set up the call. It's been six months, and I'm still not used to having my own assistant, much less to working for Baroness Sharon.

A few days after securing Hunter's release, Sharon asked if I wanted to be her new Chief of Staff. She admitted that she'd been tired of her current guy for a while now, and after learning I wasn't heading to Athens, she wanted to bag me before anyone else did.

There really hasn't been a dull moment, from sprinting through Rio airport to avoid Baroness Sharon delivering the wrong speech at the G20 summit, to the time she had an emergency meeting and I had to take over her DJ set at Ministry of Sound and got the whole crowd jumping to my favourite Backstreet Boys tropical house remix. It's been the best of both worlds – the excitement of international travel while being based in London.

It hasn't all been easy. This job is a tightrope, and when it comes to dealing with the press, the skills I learned as a diplomat have come in handy more than once. But behind the scenes, I try to be as honest as possible. I don't always succeed, but that's why this is the perfect role for me. Every day, I have to push myself, and I like that challenge. At the same time, I don't let it consume me. I've surprised myself by becoming one of those people who is happy to log off at 5 p.m. I love my job, but in many ways, after work is when the fun begins. Tonight more than ever.

I get to the theater ridiculously early. I feel a rush of pride as I see the posters outside advertising tonight's performance: Hunter Moretti in *Hamlet: The Musical*.

Hunter couldn't believe it when he found out. Nor could any of us. Apparently, the Globe was eager to cast him but were worried about putting on a show with an unknown star in the current climate. Turning it into a musical gave it broader appeal as well as showcasing all of Hunter's talents.

Hunter took about two seconds to say yes. There was a part of him that was disappointed not to get to act in a traditional Shakespeare production, and I hope he can one day. But given that he has a tendency to take his work a bit too seriously, I think it's good for him that his first big role has a few song and dance numbers.

I meet my dad and Doily in the theater foyer. Knowing my dad, he made them get here hours ago. Doily throws her arms around me for a prolonged embrace. Once I extract myself, my dad and I share a hug. I've noticed he goes in for them more since he started doing so much travelling.

'How was Manila?' I ask them.

'It was lovely,' says Doily. 'Eventually.'

She casts a pointed look at my dad.

'It started out well,' my dad says. 'The rest was all right.'

'Can you believe what I have to deal with?' asks Doily. 'People said to me, "Oh Manila is beautiful once you make it out of that horrible airport."'

'Which is silly of them,' says my dad. 'The airport's the best part.'

Ever since Doily retired, she and my dad have been fulfilling his long-held desire to travel the world. My dad has been planning this voyage methodically for years. He wants to visit all the countries he controlled flights to and from over his career. But he specifically wants to visit their airports. He genuinely doesn't feel the need to leave the arrivals hall, given that he finds airports infinitely more fascinating and less risky than the typical tourist attractions. But since Doily is not of that opinion, they usually spend a day or two trapped in an airport hotel before Doily convinces my dad to go and see, say, the Sagrada Familia or the Sydney Harbour Bridge. They do nothing but complain about the other's approach, but can't hide the fact that they are having the time of their lives.

We make our way to the VIP bar, where Hunter's guests have been invited to gather for a pre-show drink. All the members of Doily's calligraphy group have been invited, naturally. I spot Zosia and Thiago talking to Baroness Sharon, and I can only imagine the kind of love-off they're having.

'Look!' says Doily. 'There's Hunter's agent.'

Once Doily announced her retirement and Hunter's casting in *Hamlet: The Musical* was made public, he was swamped with offers for representation. But he never seriously considered anyone other than the brilliant Flora Forbes. It's the perfect career change for her. She gets to flex her lawyer muscles in a creative arena while being her own woman, although she's recently started dating a very hot doctor.

Flora crosses over to us and greets us excitedly.

'The buzz is off the charts, Max. There are some producers from A24 in the house tonight. They want to make a movie version.'

'*Hamlet: The Musical: The Film*?'

Flora smiles proudly. 'See you at the Oscars.'

We head into the auditorium and take our seats. As the lights dim, I'm nervous on Hunter's behalf. But from the moment he steps onto the stage, he's in full command. This is the role he was born to play, even if he never imagined 'To be or not to be' as an eighties power ballad.

I spend the entire duration of the play grinning from ear to ear. That's my man up there. The only moments when my smile dips are when I'm hit with that familiar sadness that my mum never got to meet Hunter. She'd be loving this.

I reread her letter recently, and it struck me that I've spent the past five years focusing on completely the wrong parts.

Other people are the only thing that can bring you true happiness.

I don't know why it didn't hit me sooner. Maybe because it took Hunter to make me realise.

I think back to the first time I saw him perform at the Menier Chocolate Factory, when I was moved to go up on stage and propose.

Maybe I knew then, deep down. Maybe something was pulling me towards him beyond the dilemma I was facing. I saw that even though he was playing a role, he stood there and told me precisely who he was, just like he's doing now.

It sometimes amazes me that he and I weren't caught sooner, but then I remember that everyone is faking it. Couples especially. Look at Quentin and Flora. Look at me with every guy I dated until now.

Ironically, Hunter was the one person I couldn't fake it with. When the stakes of being exposed were so high, we were forced to build real respect. Real friendship. Real support.

In the process, we fell in love. The kind of love that can't be faked.

And even though our paths may lead us in separate directions from time to time, I don't think either of us will wander off for too long.

Not when we know what's waiting for us back home.

Dear Mum,

Sorry it's taken me a while to reply. It didn't feel particularly urgent, given that you're, you know, dead, but I think I also needed this long to know what to say.

Guess what? I got a job. Not the one I always dreamed of, but one that suits me ten times better. I'm getting to travel a bit while living in London around the people I love. I'm pretty sure you'd be proud of me.

Dad met someone. She's nuts, but I think you'd like her. She couldn't be more different from him, which I've come to learn can be a very good thing.

I met someone too. It breaks my heart that you'll never get to meet him, but I know you'd love him. He's spectacular – gorgeous, talented, kind, and funny. I can't tell you how much fun we have together. More than that, he's made me a better person. More honest, with myself and others. In fact, if I'd written to you any sooner, I'm not sure you could have trusted my reassurances, but thanks to Hunter, you can believe every word.

I've got this.

I love you,

Max

Acknowledgements

Thank you to my editor Claire Johnson-Creek, who made this book so much better while preserving its voice; to Laura Gerrard for a thoughtful copy edit, Chloe Quinn and Jake Cole for a stunning cover, Enisha Samra, Eleanor Stammeijer and everyone else at Bonnier for your vision in guiding this book into the hands of readers. Thank you to my agents Jess Molloy and Annabel White, as well as Georgie Mellor, Aoife MacIntyre and Cynthia Okoye at Curtis Brown, and Ariele Fredman, Laurie-Maude Chenard and Elsa Knoke at UTA, for engaging closely at every step with insight, care and humour.

Thank you to my friends and my family for sharing in the excitement of my writing journey and bringing so much joy and laughter to my life. Thank you to all my new friends in the writing community who are the best cheerleaders I could ask for, and in the dog park, who help me to start every morning with a smile. Thank you most of all to my partner Vincent, for being an endless fount of inspiration, support and honesty.

Finally, thank you to my readers. It's a thrill every time someone connects with my writing and falls in love with my characters. You inspire me to reach for new heights with every book. Becoming part of the romance community has been an absolute pleasure and I hope that Max and Hunter enter your hearts as they have mine.

Don't miss Zac Hammett's brilliant enemies to lovers rowing romance . . .

Available now. Read on for a sneak peek.

CHAPTER ONE

LUCAS

Don't look outside the boat. That's all I can think right now. Don't look outside the boat. It's a shame, since I must have the best view in the house. To the left of me, the Oxford crew are poised in menacing silence. Behind them, a small flotilla of boats containing the umpire, TV crew and various VIPs. On the banks of the Thames, a crowd of people ten or twelve deep. At least, I assume there is. I can't look, but I can hear them, chanting out rival slogans as they sip on their plastic pint glasses and shuffle impatiently in the crisp March air. It still feels crazy to me that a student rowing race can attract this much attention. But I mustn't start thinking like that. If I don't look, none of it's real. Don't look outside the boat. Don't look. Don't look. Don't look.

There's only one problem with not looking outside the boat. I'm the Cambridge cox, which means I sit in front of our eight rowers, shouting orders and steering with my rudder. Directly opposite me is George, our all-American boat club president, setting the pace in what's known as the stroke seat. I once read that if you look someone in the eye for four minutes straight, you risk falling in love with them. George and I have conclusively disproved that theory. It's mad to think how many hours the two of us have spent sitting opposite each other in the boat like this over the past year. I know every inch of George's face; the sweep of his neat blond side parting that melts mothers' hearts, the masculine brow and perfectly proportioned cheekbones that remain tanned year-round, the stoic expression behind his grey-blue eyes. He looks like a model – mainly because he is one. In his underpants no less, plastered on billboards around the world. You'd think that would make him arrogant beyond belief, but it's much worse: George is a people pleaser, desperate to be liked by everyone he meets.

'Starting positions,' booms the umpire over his megaphone.

Shit. George and the rest of the team slide forward on their seats and grip their oars. The crowd falls quiet. This is it. I look down the length of the boat to check that it's straight. The current is pulling us dangerously off course. I raise my hand.

'Waiting on Cambridge,' the umpire announces.

George glances up and checks our position.

'We're good,' he whispers.

What's his problem? Steering is my job. I look back down the line. 'No we're not.'

Every single person lining the course or watching on TV is waiting for me to get on with it. But we need to start perfectly straight or we'll risk crashing into Oxford.

'We're good,' George says again.

'Wait,' I insist.

I look down the boat one more time, but now I'm doubting myself. Are we straight or not? Why doesn't George trust me?

'When you're ready, Cambridge,' the umpire says pointedly.

'Trust me, we're good,' says George, giving the umpire a big goofy thumbs up.

I stare at him. 'What the hell are you doing?'

'Just letting him know we're all good.'

'But we're not! What's wrong with you?'

George glances fretfully back at the umpire. I don't believe it. He doesn't want to annoy him.

'He's not going to give us extra points for starting on time, George. He's not going to pat you on the back.'

'Lucas—'

'Let me get the boat straight.'

'It is straight.'

'No it's not.'

'Yes it is!' George flashes me a kilowatt smile. 'You got this.'

I'm going to explode if he doesn't shut up. Now is not the time for a pep talk. Before I know what I'm doing, I lower my hand. Just like that, the umpire sounds his starting klaxon. The rowers pull on their oars, the crowd cheers like mad, and commands come tumbling out of my mouth. What I'm saying, I have no idea. I'm having some kind of out-of-body experience.

'Back off, Cambridge!' the umpire screams.

I snap out of it and glance to my left. The boat is off-course. It's heading straight towards Oxford. I yank hard on my rudder.

'Fucking hell, George. I told you!'

George pulls on his oar and says nothing. Once the race gets going, the rowers are like pistons in a machine, sliding backwards and forwards with mechanical precision, not an ounce of energy to spare, let alone brain power. It's me who has to do the thinking. I glance over at Oxford. They're already half a boat length ahead. How is this happening? How is this the race we've prepared all year for? I have to act fast. The course is four miles long, but the advantage switches hands depending on who's closest to the fastest river current at any given point. I've memorised the course's fluctuations. If we aren't ahead by the halfway point at Hammersmith, we never will be. And Oxford's lead is increasing.

'We need to do a push,' I say to George. 'Ready?'

A push means cranking up the stroke rate so high that the rowers might not have anything left for the rest of the race. As George slides forwards on his seat, I can see the beads of sweat on his forehead, the capillaries bursting in the whites of his eyes.

'It's too early,' he splutters.

I stare back at him, rage pulsing through my veins. What's he worried about now? Upsetting our coach by deviating from the race plan? I'm not an idiot. Doing a push this early is a hell of a risk. But it's now or never.

'It's not too early,' I scream. 'Now push! Push! Push!'

I hear a ripple of excitement pass through the crowd as the boat speeds past Thames Rowing Club. A lot of the real fans gather here, on the first half of the course, not at the finish line, by which point the race has almost always been won or lost.

As I shout at the rowers to crank up the stroke rate, I feel the boat begin to glide through the water. We're edging closer to Oxford. Is this the moment the tables turn? I glance to my side. Oxford have hit back with a push of their own. They've re-established their lead without a struggle. If anything, it's bigger than before.

I can already feel our rowers tiring. I can see it on George's face. I bring the crew back down to their regular stroke rate and glance at the Oxford boat. There's clear water between us. My gamble failed. Worse, our spirit has been broken.

Nothing is more demotivating than a bad push.

I try to rally the team, knowing there are still nearly ten minutes left of this torture. But I can see the Hammersmith Bridge approaching, the point at which we conclusively lose our advantage.

The race is over, and everyone knows it.

I close my eyes and feel the water hit me. The shower is too hot, painfully hot, but that suits my mood. I've been warned many times how bad it feels to lose the Boat Race, but it's done nothing to prepare me for the sheer sense of waste. All that training, all that anticipation, for nothing. At the end of the race, the rowers were physically spent to the point of collapse. I felt equally depleted, but I knew it was my job to get the team away from the cameras and back into the boathouse. I couldn't bear to look George in the eye as we rowed over to the shore. Neither of us said a word. Arriving at the boathouse, we received a pitying round of applause from our friends and family, which only made the humiliation worse. Compared to that, this shower is heaven, and I feel like everything will be all right if I can just stay underneath it forever.

'Guys,' says George, 'gather round.'

I open my eyes and scowl. George is standing in the middle of the changing room, a towel around his waist. We move towards him in various states of undress. When I first started rowing, I was self-conscious about all the casual nudity. But now I know these guys so well that I barely notice who's fully dressed and who's butt naked.

'Before we do the press conference,' says George, 'we need a team talk.'

Everyone trades glances. Waiting for us upstairs is an annoyingly large number of journalists. Evidently, George wants to get our story straight before anyone goes off message.

'Firstly,' he says, 'A for effort.'

The rest of the team ignore him. We're all still too raw for a positive take.

'Listen, we gave everything, and you can't ask for more. At the end of the day, there can only be one winner. It's as simple as that.'

The crew nod vaguely. Wait, don't start agreeing with him. I might be the one who shouts orders, but George is the president, and people tend to follow his lead. I can feel the anger brewing inside me. Are we really not going to talk about what went wrong out there?

'So don't be too hard on yourselves,' says George. 'In fact, give yourselves a pat on the back. Next year, we can come back stronger—'

'Let's hope not,' I snap.

Sometimes I just can't help myself. Everyone turns in my direction.

'What's that?' says George, his genial expression buckling.

'Let's hope we're not all back next year. Not if you're planning to fuck up the start again.'

George blinks as if he literally can't comprehend that someone's criticising him.

'You told me we were straight when we weren't,' I insist.

'Come on, Lucas,' says Johannes, 'what's done is done.'

Johannes is a six foot seven Swiss guy who does his country proud by remaining steadfastly neutral whenever there's a conflict.

'I gave my opinion,' George says calmly. 'That's all.'

'I'm the cox. It's my call.'

'You were freaking out! I was trying to help.'

'No you weren't. You were desperate to start because the umpire was getting impatient, and nothing is worse to you than the idea of pissing someone off.'

George is momentarily winded.

'He's right,' says a glacially posh voice.

I look over at Tristan Barnes, who has turned from his usual pasty white to a bright shade of red. Tristan is a politician's son with a thick neck and beady eyes who inspires no love in any of the crew, but he's the only one who shares my dislike of our president.

'You don't question the cox, George. Not at the start of a race.'

George can't handle being attacked from two sides.

'Look, Tristan, you're entitled to your opinion—'

Without warning, Tristan flings a shoe across the room and lets out a grunt of rage. We're all familiar with Tristan's mood swings, but George looks concerned to see that his strategy isn't working. I need to go in for the kill.

'Maybe your judgement was off,' I say. 'You got in pretty late last night.'

George is wrong-footed but recovers quickly. 'There were a lot of people at that dinner. I have responsibilities as president.'

'Do they include that girl you left with?'

The rest of the crew breathe in sharply. Now the gloves are really off. But George remains calm.

'She asked me to walk her home.'

'And shag her when you got there?'

'She'd had a long day.'

'Oh, so now your shags are a charitable service?'

George glances down at the contents of his towel then smiles at me breezily. 'Don't knock it till you've tried it.'

The rest of the crew ooh in delight. George has them in the palm of his hand.

I look him in the eye without flinching. 'I'd rather kill myself.'

I'm not sure that's strictly true. The first time I ever saw George, I had the same thoughts most people do when they meet him. I'm only human. But then we started working together, and believe me, those thoughts are in the past.

'Seriously,' says George, 'what's the big deal? If you were getting some, I'd be congratulating you.'

That's a low blow and he knows it. My love life is a barren desert. As I glare back at him, I feel a surge of humiliation. Only now we're not in the middle of a race. Now there are no cameras. I look at George, take a deep breath, and charge straight at him.